# Freedom's JUST ANOTHER Word

**A Novel**

## Dakota HAMILTON

HarperCollins*PublishersLtd*

http://www.harpercollins.com/canada

First edition

*Me And Bobby McGee words and music by Kris Kristofferson
and Fred Foster © 1969 TEMI COMBINE INC.
All rights controlled by COMBINE MUSIC CORP. and administered by
EMI BLACKWOOD MUSIC INC. All rights reserved.
International copyright secured. Used by permission.*

*"Uncertain Admissions" by Frances Katasse from the book* I am an Indian
*edited by Kent Gooderham. Used by permission.
ISBN 0-46-0-92551-0. Published by J.M. Dent 1969.*

Canadian Cataloguing in Publication Data

Hamilton, Dakota, 1947-
Freedom's just another word

ISBN 0-00-224572-8

I. Title.

PS8565.A5352F73 1998     C813'.54     C97-932328-2
PR9199.3.H35F73

98 99 00 ❖ HC 10 9 8 7 6 5 4 3 2 1

Printed and bound in the United States

to the gals in Maximum Security and O.L.U. (Open Living Unit)
at the Burnaby Correctional Centre for Women

# ACKNOWLEDGEMENTS

Heartfelt thanks to

— the Canada Council for its generous support (with special thanks to CHRIS MONDOR for his encouragement and help).

— my MOM and DAD, who never completely gave up hope that their daughter was actually doing something with her spare time.

— VILSON CHALISSERY and STEPHEN BAGNELL for saving my butt innumerable times in the scary world (for me) of computers.

— my neighbors, STEVE and GEORGE, who were such great support to me while writing this novel.

— KEITH MAILLARD, a great teacher, who taught me the importance of cutting scenes until my fingers bled.

— LESLIE ALEXANDER and KIM WATT, who read those first disastrous drafts all the way through, and who gave me great suggestions for improvement.

— COLUMBIA COLLEGE, who encouraged me to go back to U.B.C. where I learned how to write, and who gave me a day job that paid the bills while I wrote this novel.

# PART ONE

# INSIDE

ONE DAY MY HUSBAND, MONGREL, WALKS UPSTAIRS FROM THE BASE-MENT into the kitchen, where I'm making brownies. He points a gun at my head and tells me to sit down at the table. So, I do. Then he tells me that everything's a total fuck-up and we might as well both be dead.

I'm not arguing, that's for sure, especially not with a gun pointing right at me. I mean, he's a great shot and everything, but what if he misses and I end up with brain damage or something? I'm a vegetable for the rest of my life. I ask him if he wants a brownie.

"Mags, are you seriously asking me if I want a brownie?" he says.

"Well, they're right out of the oven, the way you like them," I say.

"I'm pointing a gun at your head and all you can think about are brownies?" he says, shaking his head. "I gotta wonder sometimes how we ever lasted as long as we did."

"You're just having a bad day, Mongrel," I say.

"No, Mags, I'm having a bad life," he says. Then he turns the gun around, points it at his chest, and pulls the trigger.

◆     ◆     ◆

I don't like stains. Grease stains, rust stains, blood stains. Before we got the dryer, I always hung things on the line. If something had a stain on it, I wouldn't hang it out. Didn't like the idea of someone seeing it. It took forever to get the blood stains out of that shirt. But

I did. Partly because I soaked it right away in cold water and partly because I used a lot of bleach.

◆     ◆     ◆

Before I got picked up for murder one, I sent my recipe for chocolate pecan hash brownies to *High Times*. It was the only magazine we had a subscription to. Here's the recipe:

## BET-YOU-CAN'T-SAY-NO CHOCOLATE PECAN HASH BROWNIES

4 1-ounce squares unsweetened chocolate

3/4 cup butter

4 eggs

2 cups sugar

1/4 teaspoon salt

1/4 teaspoon mace

1 teaspoon vanilla extract

1 cup sifted all-purpose flour

1 cup pecan pieces

4–5 grams of Moroccan High-Beam hash

Melt chocolate over hot water. Add butter. Beat eggs until light and fluffy. Gradually add sugar, salt, and mace. Stir in vanilla. Beat until light. Stir in chocolate mixture, then flour, beating until smooth. Add nuts and mix well.

*Important:* Take one third of the brownie mixture and

mix in the 4 or 5 grams of hash (warmed up until it almost becomes a powder).

In a greased and floured pan (10" x 15" x 1"), pour one of the thirds with no hash, then the one third *with* hash, then the final third with no hash. This way, most of the hash ends up in the middle of the brownies. Bake at 350° for 30 minutes. When cool, cut into squares. Makes around 24 nice moist brownies.

◆     ◆     ◆

One of the good things about jail is that you got plenty of time to think. I never seemed to have enough time when I was with Mongrel. It's not like I didn't have the time to think, but I was always so pissed off at him that all I could think about was how pissed off I was.

Mongrel was a biker. He thought a woman's place—and trust me, he never used the word woman—was in the house unless her old man was laid up with an injury. In his case—that was often enough, because even though he'd been riding Harleys for I don't know how long, he had this thing about accidents. He kept smacking into cars or trucks or lampposts or just about anything he could smash into that would land him in hospital for a few weeks.

I didn't really mind, though. I'd just go get a job cooking in some biker joint while he had one of his legs up in traction. Mostly I worked at Lou's, which was named after this biker chick who must have weighed close to three hundred pounds. Her old man had to do something extra to the suspension just to keep her riding on the back. But she sure could cook. And she always hired me on and paid under the table. So, it worked out for everyone. I learned how to cook and I got out of the house for a while.

And I also got to watch whatever I wanted to on TV. It wasn't like I was into those afternoon soaps or anything. Not that I didn't see the attraction, especially if you're sitting around at home, doing the ironing. You either listen to music, fume, or watch television. I was into fuming. When Mongrel was home, it was wall-to-wall sports.

Anyways, Big Dee likes my kind of TV. She's also dynamite on nails, those ones that get bonded on with acrylic. It stinks, but at the price you pay in here compared to what you pay on the outside, it's a bargain. She gives me a manicure every week—sometimes just a touch-up. My hands never looked this good on the outside.

◆　　　◆　　　◆

There's these two women who have a cell next to ours—Sam and Darlene. They're lesbians, or at least Sam is and Darlene is bi. When I first met them, Darlene said they were Lebanese, and when I told Big Dee that Darlene sure didn't look like she was from some Arab country, Big Dee almost died laughing.

Mongrel would shit a brick if he knew I was friends with them. He had a real problem with same-sex sex. For him, life was simple—meat and potatoes, beer and baseball, and men screwing women from on top, mostly. End of story.

Darlene is pretty. Red hair—natural. Big tits—implants. She spends a lot of time on her face and making sure that everything matches—like her earrings have to match her shoes and her nail polish.

Sam is the butch one. She has more tattoos than most guys I've seen and I've seen a lot of guys with tattoos. Mongrel had almost half his upper body done in all these pictures of skulls and snakes and daggers. But it was really good artwork—maybe a bit heavy for some people.

There's this one other woman on our unit. She's an Indian. She has a whole cell to herself. As far as I can tell, she's got this giant chip on her shoulder. She's really something to look at, though. Real tall. Hair down to her waist. Black jeans and T-shirt—her smokes rolled up at the shoulder where you can see this tattoo of an eagle flying, with its wings stretched out. It's good work. You can see every feather. Mongrel would've liked it—well, if it was on a guy. Her name's Stella.

Anyways, when Stella walks past you, she looks right through you. She gives off a vibe like she'd cut your throat with the lid of a tin can if you pissed her off.

Big Dee asks me about Mongrel. I tell her I met him when I was young, carhopping at the A & W. He was a regular. Used to roar in on his Harley, eat a couple of burgers and some fries, let rip a burp, then peel out. Always left a big tip. We went out a few times, me holding on hard to him on the back of his hog, him barely missing cars.

One night he drives in, eats three teen burgers, I think. Drinks about two quarts of root beer, and then, when I go to get the money, he chucks this ring at me—a gold snake with a ruby eye. He tells me he wants to get married. I ask him when, and he says in the morning, but he can't stick around afterward 'cause he's going to a show 'n shine in the afternoon, so he has to have the bike all polished.

Sometimes I try to tell myself that I don't know why I did it. It was like the right thing to do at the time. I wasn't really in love with him, but then I knew I wasn't exactly a movie star. I also knew he'd take good care of me.

Big Dee listens. The whole time she kind of stares at me and nods her head. When I finish, she just says uh-huh.

◆　　　◆　　　◆

The days go by. Sam tells me the best way to do hard time is not to look too far down the road.

"Maggie," she says. Everyone calls me that now. "Maggie, if you look too far down the road, it'll just fuck you up. It's like walking. You take one step at a time. And doing time is just doing one day at a time."

I guess that's so. But it's not like that when you're still waiting trial. You wonder if maybe you'll get off—like if there really are miracles. Or, if you don't, you wonder what's the worst it could be. Or the best. I seem to spend most of my time thinking about the worst.

If they get a conviction on me, it's twenty-five years. Except you don't end up doing the full twenty-five. More like ten, and I've already served one. But even so, I break it down into years and months and weeks and days, and some days I just don't think I can do it. I just lie on my bunk and cry. Big Dee says it's normal. She says I'll get over it.

◆　　　◆　　　◆

The other day, I'm talking to Big Dee. We're bitching about one of the guards. Then, I don't know, it just comes out of my mouth.

"Does anyone ever think about escaping?" I say.

Big Dee looks at me like she just got hit on the forehead with an axe. Then she looks over her shoulder.

"There's nobody around," I say.

"You crazy?" she says.

"No, I'm not crazy," I say. "It just seems to me that life isn't worth living if you don't have some kind of goal. Goals and plans give you a feeling of hope. I mean, I've been thinking about it ever since I got in here."

"You know what happen to you if some guard hears you mouthin' off 'bout anything to do with escaping? You find your little white ass doin' extra time all by you own self in seg."

Segregation is where they put you if you act up or get in a fight or whatever.

I'm not going to say it when there's a guard around," I say. "What do you think I am—stupid?"

"Yeah, well," says Big Dee.

◆　　　◆　　　◆

Once I get an idea, though, it's pretty hard for me to let it go. Mongrel used to say I was like a pit bull with a baby. I just thought it was the best way to get things done—to stay focused on one thing.

So, a few days later I'm talking to Darlene, and I ask her if she ever thought about it. She looks over her shoulder.

"Darlene," I say, "there's no one here."

Darlene looks relieved. She lights up a cigarette. She smokes rollies so she's always picking tobacco off her tongue.

"You got a plan?" she says.

"Of course not," I say. "I just got the idea so far. I needed something to think about besides recipes and how much time I might get."

"Well, we can't talk about it. It's too dangerous. We'll lose our good behavior time or something. I'll talk to Sam."

◆　　　◆　　　◆

It was Sam who came up with the idea.

"Okay, so the problem is we need to find a place to meet and talk that won't look suspicious. If we talk together too much the guards will know we're up to something."

"But we're always talking together," I say.

"Yeah, but it's different when you start talking about escaping. You're always looking over your shoulder in case someone's listening in."

"I noticed," I say.

"Why don't we talk to Tony?" says Darlene. "I bet he could get us a space."

"No way," says Sam.

"Why not?" says Darlene.

"'Cause he's a drug counselor. He'll just try to get us all into AA or NA. He's already tried to put his hooks into me. No thanks."

"Tony's all right," says Darlene. "He's been there and back."

"Where?" says Sam.

"He's in recovery."

"Oh well, that makes him special," I say.

"Look, who else we got to talk to?" says Darlene. "Tony's got pull in here. He might be able to swing a room. We'll just say we want to start our own group."

"Hey sure," says Big Dee, "call it MA—Menopause Anonymous. 'Cause we're all giving men a pause. Ha, ha."

"I ain't anywheres near the menopause," says Darlene.

"Well, you won't escape it forever," I say.

"Did I hear the word exscape?"

We all turn our heads at the same time. There's Stella, standing with a smoke in her mouth, looking straight at us. I think it's the first time I ever heard her speak. I look over at Sam.

Sam runs her hand through her hair and gives Stella a hard look.

"Look, Stella, if you walk smack into the middle of a conversation, you're sure as shit to get the wrong idea. But if we ever decide to plan an escape, you'll be the first to fucking know."

◆　　　◆　　　◆

I get voted to go talk to Tony. Sam's against it, just because Tony's a guy. I'm kind of 60–40. When I get to his office, he thinks I'm there for counseling. I set him straight right from the get-go that, first of all, I'm not an alcoholic and, second, I'm not an addict. He asks me if I'm sure. There's something about the way he asks that makes my jaw tighten up. I tell him that not everybody who drinks and drugs has a problem—just the ones who are too weak to handle it. He doesn't even go for the bait.

"So, Margaret, if you're not here about drugs or alcohol, what are you here for?" Big smile.

"We got this idea to start our own group." I smile right back.

He asks us which group we want to be a part of. We tell him we don't really want to join any of the other groups, because we want to work together, and most of the others are sort of burned out on the usual programs. So, we want to start a kind of program for everyone and it would be FA—Freedom Anonymous.

"Well, you know," says Tony, "I don't think there actually is any group by that name, but there *is* a twelve-step group called Feelings Anonymous. I'm sure they'd be happy to send you some books."

"Feelings Anonymous?" I say. "Whaddya gotta be addicted to—crying?"

Tony gets this cute look on his face whenever he thinks he's being made fun of.

"Just a suggestion." He smiles.

"We need a space," I say.

"I could probably arrange that," he says.

"Really?"

"Yeah, really. Is that all, Margaret?"

"I guess so, Tony."

"I'll get back to you," he says.

"Cool."

◆   ◆   ◆

It's amazing, but Tony's so into us doing this program that by the end of the week he got us an hour and a half booked every Wednesday night in the chapel. Not everyone's happy with the location.

"Shit, we're planning an escape from a bloody church?" says Sam.

"It's just a room," I say.

"Kind of gives me the creeps," says Big Dee.

"It's a space," I say. "It's private, which is all we need."

We hold our first meeting at the beginning of August. On the table there's five brand-new Feelings Anonymous books, some pamphlets, and a meeting format. Sam has been to a lot of AA meetings so she knows the routine.

She's the chairman, only she makes it real clear, right away, that she doesn't want to be called anything but the chairperson. Otherwise, it's sexist. She's really hard-line about that kind of stuff.

"So, I'm your chairperson for this evening, and I'd like to welcome the founding members of Feelings, a.k.a. Freedom, Anonymous," she says.

The words are barely out of her mouth when the door opens and these two women from another unit walk in. We never even thought about someone outside of ourselves coming to one of our meetings. Sam looks at Darlene. Darlene shrugs her shoulders. Big Dee stares hard at the two women who sit down.

Sam grabs the meeting format and starts the meeting. She gets Big Dee to read the twelve steps. It's not hard to tell that Big Dee hasn't spent a lot of time in school. She reads really slow and makes a lot of mistakes. I almost fall asleep. My mind starts to wander. I look around the room.

There's something about the whole situation that's just so weird. If I was still on the outside, I sure as hell wouldn't be doing this. I'd never be sitting in a room full of women. Too much female energy. Way too intense.

Sam says that, as chairperson, she has decided we'll talk about Step One, which goes like this:

## STEP ONE
## WE ADMITTED WE WERE POWERLESS OVER OUR FEELINGS AND THAT OUR LIVES HAD BECOME UNMANAGEABLE.

"Anyone who wants to speak, can."

Nobody says a word. There's just this dead silence around the table and a few glares aimed at the women from the other unit. If they had any brains at all, they'd pick up on the vibe and leave. But they just sit there looking down at the table. Finally, Darlene says:

"Well, I don't know, but it seems to me, you know, that when I was on the outside, and I got into relationships, you know, with guys, well, I always got really crazy. Maybe it was just the kind of guys I always went for, you know, but anyways, I kinda felt powerless. I think that's why I drank so much when I went out. At least then I had an excuse for being so crazy, 'cause I was drunk, you know, and when you're drunk, it's okay to act like a basket case. You know what I mean?"

A couple of people nod their heads. Sam looks really pissed off. I think Sam hates hearing about Darlene's old boyfriends.

"Next," says Sam.

"I don't never feel powerless," says Big Dee.

I can believe that, just looking at her. She's big as a house. I don't think anyone would mess with her. Big and strong—it's a scary combination. God, if I was that big, I probably wouldn't ever feel powerless either.

"I guess I always felt powerless," I say, "especially in my marriage. Maybe it was because Mongrel, that's my old man—well, he was until he shot himself. I suppose the best way to describe him is that he was oversized and undereducated."

I can't help but notice Big Dee giving me a dirty look.

"Anyways, as long as he was doing his thing and not in traction in some hospital, I pretty much stayed at home and cooked and took care of the kids. We had two kids. And then the dogs. Anyways, after Mongrel shot himself, I thought I'd feel even more powerless, but, you know, I felt more in charge. Well, I had to be. He wasn't there to tell me what to do. So, I had to figure out what to do all by myself."

I'm thinking maybe it was something I said because next thing you know Darlene's got her head down, making this whimpering noise. I stop talking. Everyone's looking at her. She slumps down almost on the table and now she's crying. But it's not like ordinary crying. It's like a baby crying. It sounds awful. To be honest, it gives me the creeps.

I look over at Big Dee. She shrugs. She doesn't know what's going on either. Next thing, Darlene's rocking so hard she practically falls out of her chair. Then she does. Right onto the floor, just like that. Boom. And she starts pounding her fists and stamping her feet.

"I'll never get out of here alive," she screams. I swear there's bubbles at the corner of her mouth.

"Get a grip, Dar," say Big Dee.

"Leave her alone," says Sam.

"Fuck you," says Big Dee, "she's making too much noise."

"Look, Big Dee. You don't interrupt when someone's talking, all right?"

"She ain't talking. She's foaming at the mouth, for chrissake. I ain't listening to this crap, and that's for sure," says Big Dee, getting up from the table.

"Give her a minute," I say.

Big Dee flops back down.

Darlene's still on the floor.

Sam lights up a smoke and just watches Darlene as if this is perfectly normal behavior. Big Dee drums her fingers on the table, rolling her eyes up in their sockets. I don't know what to do.

The two girls from the other unit look at each other. They don't look at any of us or even say goodbye. They both just get up and head for the door.

As soon as the door closes. Darlene gets up off the floor as though nothing happened.

"You gotta do what you gotta do," she says, shrugging her shoulders and sitting back down in her chair.

"Shit, Darlene, I thought that was for real. It was incredible. You shoulda been on stage," I say.

"Okay," says Sam, "after that prize performance, I lost track. What the hell were we talkin' about?"

◆     ◆     ◆

## Freedom Anonymous

### STEP ONE
## WE ADMITTED THAT WE WERE POWERLESS OVER OUR INCARCERATION AND THAT OUR LIVES HAD BECOME UNMANAGEABLE.

"All right," says Sam, "the first part is real true. We are fucking powerless in this joint. Aside from the guards, the shitty food, and the crummy attitude, do you know how many doors we gotta get through before we're on the outside?"

"Two?" asks Darlene.

"No, honey," says Sam. I think she's still pissed at Darlene for talking about men. "No, there's four because I counted them on my way in. Let's go backward. There's the door just outside the canteen, that's one, and it's electronic—well, they all are and every door has a monitor at Gestapo headquarters. So that's one, right?

"Then there's the one down the hall in the middle of nowhere, also electronic, on monitor. Then there's the one just beside the central control with the big glass window, so they can see you as well as hear you. Then you got to cross the waiting room in full view of the guards working in the control room.

"And you're still not out because you got the door at the entrance, which also has a buzzer and is in full view of the guards, and then there's the outside-outside door, which ain't locked. So that's five doors, four locked, and I say that makes us pretty powerless."

"C'mon, Sam," says Big Dee. "They's guys broke out of jails that they say no one can. You just ain't never heard of no women doin' it."

"How come?" I say.

"'Cause women don't think like guys," says Sam.

"So we gotta think like guys. I mean, this sure as hell ain't Sing Sing or Attila or nothin'."

"Attica," I say.

"Attica, Attila, who gives a fuck? You know what I's talkin' about."

◆     ◆     ◆

I trim Big Dee's hair today. It's tricky. Like a million springs. One minute she looks like she's got no hair. Then she puts this comb through it and it comes out way longer. It's hard to shape. I've been cutting quite a few ladies' hair in here. The word's getting around that I was a hairdresser on the outside. It's not exactly the truth, but close enough. It gives me something to do.

I like cutting hair. Actually, it's not the cutting that I like so much, it's looking at someone and just knowing how to make her look better. A lot of people don't know how to look their best. They choose some hairdo out of a magazine because some chick in the magazine looks hot. But anyone could look foxy if they were made up by the best make-up artists in the world. I mean, you see those models off work—they're dogs. It took a few months and a shitload of paperwork to get clearance to let me have a pair of hair-cutting scissors. I had to go through Johanna, the guard, to try to get them.

Johanna is one of those women who look so nice and talk like butter wouldn't melt in their mouth, but, in fact, she is one of the worst bitches in the universe.

"You want to order *scissors*, Margaret?" she says, like I just asked for a semi-automatic.

"Yeah, I cut hair," I say.

"Oh," she says, looking up at my own hair with this pukey look.

"I don't cut my own," I say.

"You don't have to be so defensive, Margaret," she says.

"I'm not being defensive, Johanna," I say, even more defensive.

"Let me see," says Johanna. "Maybe you could refresh my memory. What exactly are you in prison for, Margaret?"

"Well, Johanna, I'm in prison for allegedly murdering my husband," I say.

"That's right," says Johanna, this tight little smile on her face. "You murdered your husband."

"*Allegedly*," I say.

"Allegedly or not, Margaret," says Johanna, "I think it would be a high risk for us to put, in the hands of someone who *allegedly* murdered her husband, a pair of scissors, which could be used to murder someone else."

"I didn't murder my husband with a pair of scissors," I say.

"Really?" says Johanna. "What did you murder him with?"

"Nice try, Johanna," I snap.

"Request denied."

◆　　◆　　◆

"Maybe she thinks I'll get up in the middle of the night and stab you in the back of the head for doing my fingernails the wrong color," I say.

Big Dee throws her head back and lets out a big guffaw of a laugh.

"What's so funny, next door?" calls Sam.

We're in lock-up. It's the daily count-the-prisoners time. Happens every day at the same time—when there's a shift change. We call it the changing of the guard.

"I just told Big Dee I was going to murder her for putting hot pink on my nails," I say.

"Did you say murder?" calls Stella.

I look over at Dee and whisper, "Man, we gotta be real careful of that one. She got ears like a snake."

"Snake don't have no ears," says Big Dee, "'cept maybe that one," tipping her head at Johanna.

"See you ladies tomorrow," says Johanna, on her way out the door. "Unless you've got plans to go somewhere."

◆　　◆　　◆

Darlene tells me if I want to get scissors I better go see Tony. I'm tired of using the ones from the flower shop. They're too clumsy. Plus they're never sharp enough. I go to his office.

"Got a minute?" I ask. I'm leaning on the door frame.

"I think I could find one or two," he says.

"I need some help."

"I'm glad you came," he says.

"Look, Tony, it's not that kind of help, all right?"

"Hey, Margaret, you can let down the guard. I'm not going to say or do anything without your permission, okay? That's the way I work. You say you don't have a problem—fine by me—you don't have a problem. But you don't have to be an alcoholic to talk to me—or an addict."

"But it helps, right?" I say.

"Well, it gives me a place to start from," he says.

"Let's start with a pair of scissors instead," I say.

"Scissors?"

"Yeah, I cut hair. I need haircutting scissors."

"All right. What else?"

"That's all."

"Why don't you get them through the committee?"

"Because Johanna won't okay them. She thinks I'm going to stab someone with them."

"Really?"

"I never stabbed anyone in my life."

"Johanna likes to be careful."

"Johanna likes to be a bitch."

"So, you need scissors."

"Haircutting scissors," I say.

"I'll do what I can," he says.

◆　　　◆　　　◆

"We gotta have names," says Big Dee from her bunk.

"What?" I say. Big Dee has this way of starting a conversation as though you already know what she's been thinking for the past five minutes.

"I say we gotta have names—y'know, like the gangsters. Slim or Fat Eddie or One-Eyed Jack."

"What for?" I say.

"I dunno. Makes you feel different. Gives ya power or somethin'. I never like my real name. I was call Daphne. You imagine—me, Daphne?"

"No, I can't," I say.

"Daphne sounds like some skinny little white thing, like you, runnin' through a field of some kind of little flowers, like nastystershums."

"Nasturtiums."

"I know that."

"So, what do you want to be called—Slim?"

"Ha, ha." Big Dee slaps her knee and bellows out a laugh. She sits there saying the name over and over and laughing. It makes me smile. I never thought I was funny until I met her. She's always laughing at something I say.

"Slim, ha, ha. Nope, I don' think so. I already got my name. Big Dee. Gotta be big. 'Cause I's big. And black. And proud of both of 'em."

"Uh-huh," I say.

"You proud to be white?" she asks, looking over at me.

"I never gave it much thought," I say. And it's true. I never really thought much at all about my color. I thought about other peoples' color, but never my own.

"I guess'd you don't need to when you white," she says.

◆     ◆     ◆

It's macaroni and cheese day. Big Dee's in heaven, walking back to the table with her plate heaped and a big smile all over her face.

"Ooh," she says, her eyes like saucers, "I loves that macaroni and cheese," and plops down on a chair. You can almost hear the wood splitting.

"Shit," she says, looking down at the chair. "They don't make stuff worth shit around here. Make it for scrawny trash like Maggie here."

"I'm not trash," I say.

"Touchy," says Big Dee, looking over at Sam who just shrugs and shoves another mouthful into her face.

Darlene's picking at her food. She's scared to death she might gain a pound. "What's wrong?" she says to me.

"Nothing," I say.

"Well, if there was something wrong, what would it be?" she says.

I don't know what's wrong. I'm just feeling shitty. I was looking through the fence out on the track today. All the trees are turning color and I can't get near them or go for a walk in them. Or maybe it's because I haven't seen my kid for a while. Or maybe it's that I haven't had a period for a few months.'

"You pregnant?" says Sam.

"How the hell could I get pregnant?" I say.

"Maybe it's the change," says Big Dee.

"Menopause and prison in the same year? I'd stop believing in God."

"Might as well," says Big Dee, her mouth full. "He don't visit here."

◆　　◆　　◆

My mom—her name was Lillian, but everyone called her Lil—made the best macaroni and cheese. I think it was great because she didn't fuss around with it or add anything special to it. It tasted comfortable, like an old blanket you wrap around yourself. It made me feel happy, her macaroni and cheese. Mongrel wouldn't eat it, because it was my mom's recipe. He hated my mom. She felt the same about him. It's a long story.

## LIL'S REAL GOOD AND SIMPLE MACARONI AND CHEESE

Put 4 cups of water and 1 teaspoon salt in a saucepan. Bring to a boil. Add 1 cup of elbow macaroni. Stir occasionally to stop the macaroni from sticking together.

In another saucepan, place 2 tablespoons butter. Melt at low heat, then remove from heat.

Stir in 1/4 cup of flour. Mix to a creamy consistency.

Add 1 to 1-1/2 cups milk—mix well.

Return to heat, stirring constantly until you have a thick white sauce. Add salt and pepper to taste.

Grate 1 cup of cheese (English Red Leicester is best) and add to white sauce.

Drain macaroni and add to sauce mixture. Place in a greased casserole. Grate more cheese and sprinkle over the top.

Bake at 325° for 30 minutes.

◆　　　◆　　　◆

Sam has pictures of Harley-Davidsons all over the walls of her cell, at least on her side. She worries more about her Harley than anything else.

"I shouldn't a left it at Fred's place," she says, running her finger over a photograph beside the bunk. "I shoulda took it out to the country somewheres. Maybe even packed it in a crate. Paid some farmer to store it in his barn for a few years."

"I'm sure it'll be fine," I say.

"What the hell would you know about bikes, Maggie? That bike's worth a fortune. Ship it across the border. Take off the serial number. Give it a new paint job, and sayonara. It's a Duo-Glide, for chrissake."

"I know about bikes, Sam. I lived with a biker for over twenty years," I say.

"No shit?" says Sam. She's still staring at the photograph. She's like some teenager looking at the picture of her first boyfriend. It's like how little girls look at a photo of their favorite movie star when they're about twelve. She stares and shakes her head.

"You know, Maggie, there ain't many bikes that are prettier than this one. I took it to a show 'n shine in Point Roberts and they stood around her three deep. I had every bit of chrome polished. The paint job alone cost me close to two grand. See, look here, that's Marilyn Monroe airbrushed on the tank. Now that cost a few bucks, I'll tell you. And the rest of the bike's lipstick red. They was three deep, cranin' their necks to get a look at her. God, I was so proud."

"Mongrel was like that," I say. "He could spend a whole day just polishing the chrome on his bike."

"That's the problem here, you know," says Sam.

"What is?" I say.

"There's nothing in here to be proud of."

◆　　　◆　　　◆

I've got a job now, working part-time in the prison library. It's pretty small and needs a lot more books. It was a toss-up between working here or taking training for institutional cooking. I don't know, I figured I'd done enough cooking. I could get a job anytime I got out. Go back to Lou's. Some of my recipes were famous there.

Besides, by the time I get out of here, the whole world might just be eating pills and there won't be any food at all. But I don't even want to think about that.

Another thing that made me think twice about taking the chef's training was that you only learn how to cook for big groups of people. I didn't mind putting on the odd big spread for Mongrel's buddies. We'd have up to twenty ride in for Thanksgiving, hauling in kegs of beer and tequila and a shitload of drugs.

The best one ever, though, was the year Mongrel just about got killed. He was in really serious condition. He lost control of the bike and slid under this semi. Nobody knows to this day how he came out of that one alive.

I ended up working at Lou's. I took the kids. Chrissie, my daughter, was a real help. Max mostly just hung around and made the bikers laugh. She'd decided that we should put on a special Thanksgiving for the boys who didn't have old ladies. The word got down the line and, the next thing you know, we're up to our asses in turkeys and bikers.

We didn't have enough room in the oven so some of the guys dug a pit and we roasted the birds and the potatoes and yams in the ground. There must have been close to a hundred guys there, sitting around in the field back of Lou's, knocking back tequila shooters and cramming turkey down their throats.

By the time they'd eaten the pumpkin pie, they started falling over like dead horses. It looked like a battlefield—the losers' side. Bodies all over the place. Lou and I took a picture of them all laid out. Lou got it enlarged and framed and it still hangs in the restaurant to this day. She called it the Thanksgiving Day Massacre.

I had this recipe for pumpkin pie that put tears in the eyes of the toughest biker. I probably baked twenty pies that day. Mongrel used to call it The Best Goddam Pumpkin Pie in the Known Universe.

## THE BEST GODDAM PUMPKIN PIE
## IN THE KNOWN UNIVERSE
(from Grandma Gammon, Saskatchewan, circa 1950)

3 large eggs

1-1/3 cups sugar (half white, half brown)

2 cups mashed pumpkin

1 teaspoon ginger

1 teaspoon cinnamon

1/2 teaspoon cloves (powdered)

1-1/2 cups milk

1 tablespoon melted butter

Separate eggs into two bowls. Beat whites until stiff.

To the yolks add sugar, pumpkin, and spices. Beat thoroughly and add milk. Mix well.

Fold in egg whites to above mixture.

Pour into deep-dish pastry shell. Bake at 350° for 30 to 45 minutes.

(I jiggle the pie and if it doesn't jiggle, it's done. Let it sit in the oven with the heat turned off until oven and pie are cool. Refrigerate overnight before serving.)

◆　　◆　　◆

Tony dropped by the unit to see how we were doing and how our first meeting went.

"It was just fine," says Big Dee, looking over at Sam, who's rubbing her jaw like a guy trying to see if he needs to shave a second time today. "Yup," says Big Dee, "we almost all feelinged out, 'specially Darlene."

"Hey," says Sam, "it's not called Feelings Anonymous for nothin'. It's supposed to be anonymous, which means you shut the fuck up about what happened to someone else.'

"Whoa, chill," says Big Dee.

"Well, it's true," says Sam. "You look in the book, somewheres you'll see that it says, 'We respect anoninity . . .'"

"Anonymity," I say.

"That's what I said," says Sam.

◆　　　◆　　　◆

The second FA meeting gets off to a better start. The word has gotten out that our group is too heavy, so no one from any of the other units comes. Big Dee chairs.

"Welcome to the second meeting of the Last Resort chapter of Freedom Anonymous," says Big Dee. "First of all, I'd like to thank Maggie here for comin' up with a name for us."

Everyone claps.

"Okay. We got no unwelcome guests tonight, so I guess we get right to the plan. Who wants to share?"

"I'll share," I say. "You all know I'm working at the library now. So, the main entrance is off the central area of the prison, but there's a second door off the hall that leads to the guards' control area—where all the monitors are. The other day I was putting on some lipstick and I realized I could see into the control without them seeing me."

"I don' get it," says Big Dee.

"Me neither," says Sam.

"Well, think about it. The inside door of the library is already past the first electronically locked main door. At the end of the hallway, I can see the control window with the guards inside."

"Yeah, so what's your point?" says Sam.

"If I can see the guards, then there ain't four sets of doors, just three."

"No way," says Sam.

"Yeah, there is," I say. "I think you miscounted the doors."

"No way," says Sam.

"All right, count them. There's the one by the canteen. You pass through that one and I can see you from the library window. Next one is by the control area window. Then there's the waiting room, which leads to the outside doors, and only one of them is locked. So that's three."

"I think Maggie's right," says Darlene.

"Maggie the Cat, you pretty smart," says Big Dee.

"Four or three, I don't really see what's the diff," says Sam. "It's still all in view of central control. We ain't got a chance in hell of getting past them."

"Just a thought," I say.

"Anyone else?" says Sam.

"Well, I don't know if this is important or not . . ." says Darlene. "All right, I'm working half days in the flower shop, you know. Now, a couple a years ago I came in to visit this friend who was doing some time. She and I worked the same street, you know. Anyways, she invites me to this open house that they have every year at the same time, a few weeks before Christmas."

"What's this got to do with escaping?" says Sam.

"Let me finish," says Darlene.

"Yeah, let her finish," says Big Dee.

"All right, so all the visitors came in through a side door, you know. We never went through no visitor's area at all. We never even seen the control room. So, you know, if I remember right, we came through a gate from the parking lot. There was a guard there and a lot of people hanging around. Then the visitors came up some stairs and then through a door and down a hall and then we were at the open house. It's all happening near the flower shop, and down the hall was the sewing shop. I don't remember any electronic doors at all. Nothing."

"Really?" says Sam.

"Yeah," says Darlene. "So, yesterday I'm looking at those big double doors off the flower shop. And I'm thinking to myself that that's where they load the supplies. Only they never load them when we're working there. And those double doors go right to the outside, you know."

"Yeah?" says Sam. "Right into the yard?"

"Nope," says Big Dee. "They face east."

"How do you know?" says Sam.

"Old Indian trick," says Big Dee.

"Sure thing," says Sam.

◆　　◆　　◆

## IX: HERMIT

I thought it was pretty funny that the first card I pull in prison is the Hermit. I don't know, it just struck me. Here I am in prison, and the first tarot card I pull is that one. I think what really struck me this time was the way the two hands in the corner are holding each other. On the outside, I would have seen them as just two old hands, relaxed. But in here I see them as one hand holding the other hand so it can't get away—not letting it be free.

◆　◆　◆

## STEP TWO
## WE CAME TO BELIEVE THAT A POWER GREATER THAN OURSELVES COULD RESTORE US TO FREEDOM.

"I don't believe in that shit," says Sam. She's shaking her head. "I don't believe in it now. I didn't believe in it before. And I'm not about to start believing in it tomorrow neither. It's a fucking waste of time, as far as I'm concerned."

"I don't know," I say. "I figure we haven't got anything to lose. I mean, look here, Sam, what's your stubbornness got you so far? You just end up doing more time. We're trying to figure out how to get out of here. Maybe the answer's not just in some plan, like knowing which door's open when. Maybe we got to hook up to some greater power, if there is such a thing."

"Maggie's got a point, Sam," says Big Dee. "It don't necessarily mean you weak 'cause you bow your head once in a while and ask for a little help. I used to watch football games with my old man and you could see the guy who was going to do a field goal attempt—he was praying."

"That's right," I say. "And you listen to the other players being interviewed after some big game, they're always talking about how they prayed to make a touchdown. These are big guys we're talking about, Sam. Huge. And they ask for help. Like I said, we got absolutely nothing to lose. If there is a God, or whatever, then if we ask him for a little help and he gives it, all the better. If he doesn't exist, then we just wasted a little time talking to the air."

"I don't know," says Sam.

"What about you, Darlene?" says Big Dee.

"I think Maggie's got a point," she says. "Matter of fact, I know she does."

"How so?" says Sam.

"Well," says Darlene. "I know that if I hadn't come to believe in something greater than me, I'd probably be dead in some back alley somewheres."

Everyone looks over at Darlene.

"See, when I was shooting up, I used to see God every day, or the devil. I used to tell my friend, Carley—you know, she's the one I came to see here that time before Christmas. Well, you know, I used to tell her that you do cocaine for too long, you see the devil, but you do some heroin, you see God. You do too much of either of them, you get a personal visit, you know what I mean?"

"So?" says Sam.

"So, anyways, I went through this real bad spell once, when I was really wired. All I could think about was the next high. I didn't care about nothing else, you know, not even my kid. I don't even know how it happened 'cause I was always real careful about how much I did, even when I was really out of it. I knew when to stop, you know. I mean, I saw a few ODs and they weren't pretty. I didn't want to go that way.

"But sometimes when I was really high, I wanted to go. Just leave right then because there wasn't no more pain and life felt so good. I didn't care about nothing."

"What's this got to do with a higher power?" says Big Dee.

"Let me finish. So, this one time I'm shooting up, I can't even remember who I'm with, you know, but I start to feel weird, like I'm revving too fast or something. And I know I've gone too far. I know I'm in trouble. And just before I pass out, you know, I say this prayer.

"You gotta realize, I never prayed. I got raised Catholic and I swore I'd never set foot in a church, or anything close, as long as I drew breath. But just before the lights go out in my head, I see this woman. Well, it's like a picture I had on my wall when I was a little girl, you know, a picture of Mary, and she had this look on her face that was so soft and so full of love that I just melted. And so I tell her that I don't want to die, you know, not just yet, and I've made a real bad mistake, and I'm sorry, and I pray for her to help me. And, you know, she reaches right over and she puts her hand on my heart, which is stopped, I think, by that time. And then she just picks me up like I'm a little girl and she carries me.

"When I wake up, I'm in emergency. They tell me I was a DOA but some miracle brought me back. I know what it was. It was her. I stopped drugging after that—cold turkey. Only fell off a few times. But I pray now, you know. I pray to her."

The room is completely silent. I don't know who said it, but someone said that when a room goes quiet like that, it's because an angel's passing.

Then the door opens and Tony sticks his head in.

"How's it going, ladies?" he says.

"It's going," says Big Dee.

"Looks as if it's not a good time," he says. "Margaret, I just wanted to let you know that your scissors came in. You'll have to leave them in the salon. You can't take them to your room. But at least they're here."

"Praise the Lord," I say.

◆　　　◆　　　◆

Big Dee is doing my nails. We're in after dinner lock-up. She's picked this real bright color, a kind of fuchsia. I'm not too sure that it's me.

"I don't know if this color's me, Big Dee," I say.

"It you all right," she says, ignoring me.

"You don't think it's a little bright?" I say.

"Ma-a-aggie!" The way she says it, drawn out, it just reminds me of how Chrissie said it sometimes. We'd be sitting on the couch watching TV. I'd see some girl wearing a dress that was too short or too tight.

"That's disgusting," I'd say.

"It is not, Mom," she'd say.

"That dress is too tight, Chrissie. She looks cheap."

"Mo-o-om!"

I look over at Big Dee.

"God, you sounded just like my daughter."

"Hmmm" Big Dee smiles. "I guess you miss her."

"Yeah."

"Sometimes I'm kinda glad I didn't have any kids. Especially 'cause I spent so much time on the inside. It's hard on the kids. I seen it happen here lots."

"I know. I guess it's not so bad with Chrissie. At least I see her every once in a while, and we talk on the phone. But I don't know what to do about Max. He lost his dad. He won't talk to me. He and Chrissie never got along that well. He's too young to be without a family."

Big Dee bites her tongue in concentration. I'm looking at her, wondering what's going on inside her head.

"What you starin' at?" she says.

"Just thinking," I say.

"'Bout what?"

"I don't know. I was thinking about how you never feel powerless and I wondered if maybe being big helped."

"Maybe."

"So, you really never feel powerless?"

"Hell, Maggie, of course I does. And I had my share of feelin' powerless on the outside."

"You did?"

"Sure. See, you got no idea what it mean to be black. And a woman. And then never go to school on top of all that. They's nothin' I can do, really. I got no training. That's why I keep comin' back to jail. I can do things here. I get some respect," she says.

"That's for sure," I say.

"You know, Maggie, when I was married, the third time, I married me one real bad nigger. I still got scars to show for that mistake. Uh-huh. And my size didn't make no difference at all. I mean, I's a big woman, but compare to a big man, I's nothin'. He beat me and I took it.

"So, one day he come home all cranked up on some shit and he hits me acrossed the face and I ask him, Why, why you doin' this to me? I ain't done nothin', and he just hits me again and I see this blood fall right down on my clean white shirt. I look at that blood and then somethin' snap inside me.

"I grab that hot iron and I crack him acrossed his face and he falls back and hits his head on the wall. I don't know what come over me, but I see him lying there, not moving, and I take that hot iron and I lays it right on his face and burns him real bad. He scarred for life now. He never come near me again. 'Course, I did some hard time for it. Uh-huh. But it was worth it. Ha, ha. It sure was worth it."

Big Dee finishes the last nail. She's got a steady hand. She does a good job. She puts the lid back on the bottle and then she looks right at me.

"Yep, it was sure worth it," she says. "Now, Maggie the Cat, this here color look real nice on you."

◆ ◆ ◆

It's funny what you think about when something real bad happens. I remember when Mongrel shot himself, the first thing I thought about was how I was going to get all that blood out of his shirt. And how I didn't want it to drip on the floor.

◆ ◆ ◆

It's hard to explain your first time arriving at prison, especially the ride there. I guess if you've been in and out a few times it wouldn't be so bad, but even those women who've been in and out must have felt awful that first time.

If you murder someone, like they think I did, then you'll more than likely be in shackles. It's one thing to see them in a movie, but it's another thing to have to wear them. And handcuffs, too. I get to wear both. The leg irons make it so you can only take steps about a foot long. Nobody walks with steps that small unless they're wearing a skin-tight full-length ball gown.

I get into the van and I'm locked into this separate cage. All I know is that I feel sick to my stomach. I don't know where I'm going. I only know that wherever it is, I'm going to be there for a long time. The only pictures I have in my head come from movies I've seen, and those pictures aren't good.

When we get to this open field with no trees on it, I know we're getting close. Then the buildings come into sight. Off in the distance, they look spooky. It's like some architect took an old prison design and made it look all modern. But the newness doesn't hide what's going on inside. I feel like throwing up.

The van pulls into a loading bay and the sound of the security gate sliding shut is almost like the sound of my garage door at home. Well, not really, but close enough. And then I suddenly get it—that I don't have a home anymore. This is home.

◆　　◆　　◆

I get a message at the library that my daughter, Chrissie, is coming for a visit this Tuesday. I'm so excited I can hardly think straight. I haven't seen her for over two months. She lives out of town. It's hard for her to get here.

Johanna brings the message. She's been really pissy ever since I got the scissors, like it's grinding her. She hates not having control.

"I see you got your scissors, Margaret."

"Yeah. Tony got them for me."

"It's not really his job to do that, you know."

"Well, I guess he just did it as a favor."

"There are lines of authority here, you understand." She's not even trying to hide the threat in her voice.

"I do my best," I say.

"Things can get messed up."

"I don't know what you mean."

"I don't like being fucked with," she says, coming up real close to my face.

"That wasn't my intention, Johanna," I say.

"You think you're real smart, don't you? You think the rules don't apply to you."

"I do my best to follow all the rules, Johanna," I say.

On the outside, I would have told her to go fuck herself—have Mongrel ride by her place a few times at three in the morning, sit outside, go a little heavy on the throttle. But that's not how the game's played in here. At this point, you either lose it and end up in seg, or you go belly up and pay the price for that. Either way, it's a no-win situation. I go quiet.

"We'll see how you like the rules, Margaret—when they don't work the way you want them to," she says. She walks away.

After she's out of sight, I feel the sweat running down the inside of my blouse and my knees are shaking.

◆     ◆     ◆

"She's out to get me," I say to Sam.

"Ah, fuck her, she just ain't been laid in a long time. Makes her uptight. I could volunteer my services, but on second thought I think I'd rather hang myself in my cell," says Sam.

"She could fuck things around for me," I say.

"She can't do squat," says Sam. "You're taking her way too serious. She's a guard. A pea-brain in a uniform. And, in her case, a pea-brain with an attitude. Most of the guards are all right. But the ones like Johanna, they get a uniform on and they think they're cops, you know? They got big problems themselves but they ain't ever gonna deal with them, so they take them out on someone who's weaker. It's all about power. The ones that got it don't fuck with it, the ones that don't, like Johanna, do."

"She could screw up our escape," I say.

"That's if we don't do it first."

"What do you mean?"

"You don't really think we're going to do it, do you?"

"Of course I do. Why not?"

"I don't know. It just seems like a joke or something. I can't take it all that serious. Besides, we don't make it, we end up doing even more time."

"Look, Sam—there's always a snag."

◆     ◆     ◆

By Tuesday afternoon, I'm having a hard time sitting still. I'm finding it tough to concentrate at the library. I keep looking at the clock.

The time just crawls. I got this sweater on that Chrissie likes. Darlene did my hair this morning. Put a few streaks in it. She says streaks make you look younger. Hides the gray. Big Dee touched up my nails. Sam whistled when I walked past her cell.

"If I didn't already have Darlene, I might go for you," she says.

"In your dreams," I say.

After dinner, we're in lock-up until six. Visiting is at six-fifteen.

"Jeez," says Big Dee, "you gonna make me dizzy, way you walkin' up and down this cell. Sit down and chill. Don't never make time pass faster by tryin to outrun it."

"I'm just excited," I say. "I can't wait to see her face."

"Probably about the same as it was before," says Big Dee.

"You know what I mean," I say.

"Of course I do. How old is she now?" she says.

"She was twenty last month. A Leo. Loves to be the center of attention." I look at my watch. "How come the door's not open? It's after six."

"Barely," says Big Dee.

By five past I'm banging on the door. The night guard comes over. It's Jim tonight.

"Hey, Maggie," he says.

"What's going on, Jim? It's past six. I got a visitor."

"Gosh, kiddo, that's too bad. We got word there was some trouble in Unit C, so it's lock-up till after seven or at least till it's all sorted out."

"But my daughter's here." I'm feeling a hard knot in my throat. "I haven't seen her for over two months."

"Gee, Maggie, I'm sorry. You know if I could do something for you I would. You know that. But it's the afternoon shift that set this one up and we just got to abide by it. All the meetings and activities have been canceled."

"But that's not fair." I can feel my lip starting to tremble.

"Aw, honey, this is really bad luck," says Jim. "Look, I'll make sure your daughter gets the word all right. We'll see if we can't reschedule or something."

"I can't reschedule. You know that, Jim. You did this intentionally."

"Now, Maggie, you know that's not true," says Jim.

I wheel around to Big Dee.

"See? I told you. I told you that fucking bitch was out to get me. She set this up. There was no trouble in C. I was over there this afternoon. No one was even looking funny at anyone."

"You probably right," says Big Dee.

"That low-life, scumbag bitch."

Big Dee's just nodding her head.

I kick the bunk and start to pace.

"I knew she was up to something. I told you, didn't I? Fuck."

I want to throw myself against the wall. I want to hurt myself to stop the rage I'm feeling inside. It comes to me, right at that moment. I couldn't figure out why so many women in here cut themselves. Big scars. All up and down their arms. Old ones. New ones. I couldn't understand why someone would do that to herself. And then I could feel it. I was so pissed off and there was no way to send it out there, so I wanted to do something in here. To myself. Just to stop the rage.

Big Dee sits there nodding her head and saying uh-huh.

"I got to get out of here, Big Dee. I couldn't take being messed around like this for ten years. I mean, I didn't murder Mongrel and that's a fact, no matter what some court of law says. But I tell you, I could murder now. All the times I ever thought I couldn't kill someone, now I know it just ain't true. I could. You put a gun in my hand right now, I could do it. I can feel it. I don't feel afraid. You know what I'm talking about?" I say.

"Uh-huh," says Big Dee, "I sure do."

◆　　　◆　　　◆

I shuffle the cards. I have to chill out. I have to sit down and put my energy into the cards. Pull something. See if it makes any sense of the situation. I need something to take me away from this feeling inside myself. I need to let go of the hate I'm feeling. To back off. It's like how you have to remember to distance yourself from the shadow so that the situation can be seen different. Like with a different light on it.

Sometimes it means not getting caught up in things that seem to be true, that you believe to be true because they aren't necessarily true. Of course, that's easy to say. Really hard to do. I can't get there right now. And I know that where I'm at is blinding me. It's messing up my thinking.

I read somewhere that you should think of hate as a poisonous snake. I was reading this book the other day in the library. About Indian stuff—spirituality. Anyway, it talked about dangerous feelings and how you had to learn to look at yourself from the center of this thing called the medicine wheel. Because if you see yourself from that point, you see that even though you're small, you are still a sacred part of some greater whole. I try to remember these things, but sometimes I just can't.

◆    ◆    ◆

When I finally fall asleep I find myself with some man who I don't know in a place I have never been. I don't hear any music and yet we move into a slow dance. Every movement works as we glide in perfect sync. My body feels amazing and light. Our dance is almost sexual yet seems to have nothing to do with sex at all. Just the perfect movement of two bodies, flowing together. I never knew I could move this way. It's almost like flying. Weightless. My mind and body feel no pain.

I wake up suddenly and my mind kicks in, running on and on, bright violent pictures. Loud, harsh words. Over and over, I go over all the things that have happened between me and Johanna. I get her. She gets me back. I get her again. All that back-and-forth stuff. Her need to control. My stubbornness. But the ground isn't level. No matter what happens, she gets to beat me. She wins. She finds my weak spot, the place where I'm most vulnerable. She waits until she has me down and then she does me. And there's nothing I can do. Absolutely fucking nothing.

"Maggie?" Big Dee talking, in the dark.

"Yeah, Big Dee."

"You gotta let it go, honey," she says.

"I can't, Big Dee. I can't let it go. I can't get it out of my head."

"You gotta let it go or it fuck you up for sure," she says.

"She shouldn't have done it, Big Dee." I'm crying.

"No, she shouldn't of, but she did, and she be some mean bitch, but that how she operate. There always someone like her in these places. How you think she feels about herself to do somethin' like that? Hmmm? What do you think? You want to be like that?"

"I don't know anymore, Big Dee. I don't know what I want to be like. I'm changing in here. I'm getting more pissed off all the time."

"It won't get you nowheres, Maggie," she says.

"I can't stay here," I say.

"It's not forever, child," she says.

"It sure feels like it."

"Uh-huh, sometimes it sure do."

"How do you do it, Big Dee?"

"How do I do what?"

"Take it."

"I don't rightly know sometimes. I just take it a day at a time. Stay in the present. Don't think too much about what might have been. But mostly I don't never give them my dignity. They can take everything else, but they don't get my dignity."

◆　　　◆　　　◆

I wanted to get married in a church, wearing a white dress with a lace veil, the whole bit, but Mongrel wouldn't have anything to do with it. He didn't want my family there either. He'd already decided he didn't like them. And he knew they wouldn't like him. He was right.

My father took one look at his tattoos and that was the end of their relationship. My mother didn't say anything but she reminded Mongrel that his own mother had left him with a foster family when he was only three and had never come back. He wasn't about to get hurt again—not that he ever admitted that it hurt him. Fuck family was his attitude, and because he didn't have his own to throw his revenge at, he took it out on mine.

He kept saying it wasn't about the money, but he didn't feel like throwing good cash away on a dress that I'd only wear once, plus some priest who didn't give a rat's ass about either of us, plus all the food and booze that would just get snorted up by the bros.

"Hell, with that kind of money, we could buy us a bigger Harley."

"You already have a Harley," I say.

"Yeah, but this would be an investment, Mags," he says, "for both of us."

I couldn't see how that would work out for me, but Mongrel told me not to worry my fuzzy little head about these sorts of things that men had a better grasp on. I asked him how come men had a better grasp, and he said just because and stop asking fucking questions.

So, we got married at the city hall. I had on my favorite summer dress, even though it was pouring rain. My best friend, Josie, and her boyfriend were witnesses. Josie worked at the A & W with me. She and I had been best friends since the night I dumped a pair of banana milkshakes down the front of this guy.

I started out working in the kitchen. The pay was the shits and I went home every night with my hands stinking of onions and bleach. You were always handling onions to make the burgers and you had to use bleach for the clean-up. I've hated both those smells ever since. I kept bugging the boss to let me be a carhop.

Anyways, I finally graduate from the kitchen to carhopping, and my first night out a guy pulls up in his brand-new car. He was really laying it on thick. I'm not sure which he was more proud of—the car or the blonde beside him. Anyways, I took his order. He didn't even look at me.

"Gimme a double papa burger, a mama, two fries, and two banana shakes," he snaps.

"That's a double papa, a mama, two fries, and two banana shakes," I repeat.

"Is there an echo around here?" he smirks. His girlfriend giggles in the seat beside him.

I go get the order and carry it out to his car. Now, you can always tell a carhop who's experienced by the way she carries her tray. If she holds it high with one hand, then she knows what she's doing. But it's my first night and I'm carrying the tray with both hands and I'm being real careful. Even so, I can see that I'm shaking because the milkshakes are jiggling. I get up to the guy's car and he opens his window half-way down.

Now, maybe it's the way the window curved in, but as I try to hook the tray on the window, I tilt it too much and, well, everything, including the milkshakes, drops right into his lap. And this was before they had those plastic lids. Milkshakes are bad, and banana milkshakes are the worst. So he ends up wearing two milkshakes and calling me every name he can think of. I'm standing there, completely paralyzed, not knowing what to do. I think the last word I hear him say is 'cunt' as he peels out of the drive-in. Josie comes running up to me, takes the tray out of my hands, and throws her arms around me.

"That was fantastic!" she whoops.

"Huh?" I'm standing there, shocked.

"That asshole has been treating us carhops like dirt for I don't know how long. You were great. What's your name? Mine's Josie."

"I'm Margaret," I say.

I guess that's how we got to be friends.

◆　　◆　　◆

"My first pay job was deliverin' drugs for my older brutha," says Big Dee. "He gimme five bucks a time, and that's way more than most girls is making for any kinda work. 'Course, he's making a killing and I's taking all the risk, but I don't know no better so I just kep' on doing it till I gets busted. That little shit wouldn't even bail my black ass out of jail." Big Dee laughs.

◆　　◆　　◆

It takes everything inside me to go to Johanna.

"But Margaret, you applied for Tuesday," says Johanna.

"I know that. But the units were locked up past visiting hours last night, so I couldn't see my daughter."

"I'm sorry, Margaret, but we can't change the rules for one person or everyone would be asking for special exceptions."

"I haven't seen my daughter for over two months," I say.

"Some of the prisoners don't ever have visitors," says Johanna.

"She's come a long way, Johanna. She can't just go back. It cost her a lot to come down here."

"What are you saying, Margaret?"

"I guess I'm saying that it's not fair."

"It's not about fair, Margaret, as I have to keep reminding you. There was trouble on the unit and we have to make sure that everything has settled down before we let anyone out. We have to think about the security of the girls in here. This is a correctional facility, not a country club. We'll do our best the next time she comes to visit."

"This is about the scissors, isn't it?" I say.

"I don't know what you're talking about," says Johanna.

◆　　◆　　◆

News gets around really fast in a prison. I can feel the other women looking at me. Sometimes they just nod. They understand. But there's nothing to be done except to endure. Even Stella comes up to me.

"Sorry about your kid, eh," she says.

"Yeah," I say.

"By the way, I owe you from the other day," she says.

"Forget it," I say, but I know what she's talking about. She'd taken a swing at one of the inmates, a real mouthy bitch, in the library a couple of days back. I could have had her put in seg but I kept my mouth shut. Besides, I figured the other woman deserved it.

"I don't forget my debts," she says.

"You don't owe me anything, Stella."

"Yeah, I do. Alls I can tell you right now is you got to exercise your will," she says. "You got to hold onto your feelings just like a wild horse."

"Thanks, Stella, I'll be all right."

"Okay, but don't let that anger inside you get too big."

"Yeah, I'm working on it."

"I've got some sage over in my cell. I can burn some, you know, like cleansing. Maybe it would help. Come to my cell, eh?"

I figure, what the heck. I got nothing to lose.

Stella digs into a bag under her bed, pulls out this small sack full of dried leaves and stuff. She puts some in her ashtray and lights it. She comes over to me and starts moving the smoke with her hands from my feet, up my body, and then in front of my face. Then she moves behind me and does the same.

"Maybe you feel better tonight," she says.

◆　　◆　　◆

## STELLA'S SAGE CLEANSING
(for anger and other negative emotions)

This is best done by a native healer or shaman. In an emergency, if you can't find one, try the following.

> Dried wild sage
> Pan or ashtray
> Matches
> 1 good friend

Get some good dried sage (wild). It's now sold in some health stores and specialty stores.

Put a few sprigs of the sage in a fireproof pan or ashtray.

Light the sage. It will flare up at first but let it smolder.

It gives off a nice aromatic smoke.

Have a good friend brush the smoke up, starting at your ankles, then moving the smoke up past your knees, hips, stomach, chest, face. Then have your friend go around to your back and move the smoke, starting at your ankles, up to the back of your knees, past your butt, up your back, and past the back of your head.

The person who is brushing the smoke should keep the pan about four inches from your body, always brushing the smoke in an upward circular motion—pushing the smoke toward your body.

Have your friend do both sides of your body a few times.

◆     ◆     ◆

"Hey, what you guys smoking?" yells Sam.

Stella shakes her head and gives a quiet laugh.

"That Sam pretty funny sometime," she says.

Jim comes to the cell door.

"Hey, Maggie," he says. "Hey, Stella. Jeez, that some new kind of tobacco you gals smoking?" He laughs. "I'm real sorry about what happened last night. You know I wouldn't have done that to you."

"I know that, Jim."

"Anyways, uh, Tony said you wanted counseling, or something, tonight, before your meeting."

"I didn't make any arrangements with Tony," I say.

"Well, he told me to come and get you. Maybe he figures you need to talk to someone after what happened last night."

"It's all right, Jim. I don't need to. I think I'm just about all talked out about it."

"Maggie, I'm telling you that I'm here to escort you to Tony's office. He didn't say anything about you having a choice. So, let's go. If I'm wrong, I'll apologize."

I get off Stella's bunk. She looks at me and shrugs. I just shake my head. Jim unlocks the door. We walk down the hall and down the stairs to Tony's office. Just as we get to the door, Jim turns to me.

"Now, Maggie, I'm gonna ask you one favor, all right?"

"All right," I say.

"You're to keep your voice down when you get in there."

I'm looking at Jim. I can't figure out what the heck is going on until he opens the door and I see Chrissie, my daughter, standing there. Tony's inside, sitting at his desk. He puts his finger to his lips. I look at Jim, who winks and pushes me into the room. I'm so stunned, I just stand there, and like an idiot I'm crying all over the place. Chrissie runs over and throws her arms around me.

"Mom, I didn't think they were going to let me see you," she says.

Tony gets up and moves toward the door.

"I can only give you twenty minutes, Margaret," he says. "Now, I'm going to leave so that you can have some privacy. Try to keep your voices down as best you can."

"Tony," I say.

"Yes, Margaret," he says.

"You got no idea what this means to me," I say.

Tony puts his hand on my shoulder.

"Twenty minutes," he says.

◆　　◆　　◆

The only time I ever felt the presence of a higher power was when I was out in nature. Mongrel would be sitting in front of the TV watching baseball or something, a beer in one hand, a joint in the other. At that point, it was like I wasn't even there, so I'd go for a walk.

I used to love to walk in the forest, especially on a rainy day. I'd be by myself. Everything was quiet except for the sound of the rain falling on the branches and my boots squishing the wet earth.

Sometimes it took a while before the feeling came. I'd be standing there, looking up at the trees, feeling the rain fall on my face, hearing the sound of my breathing, sometimes even able to feel my heart pounding inside my chest. And then this feeling of deep quiet would fill me up and I'd know that there was something, some power, out there.

I miss my freedom.

◆　　◆　　◆

"He didn't," says Darlene.

"He did," I say.

"How'd he pull it off ?" says Sam.

"I don't know how he did it," I say. "I just know that I got to Tony's office and there she was. He did it somehow—him and Jim. You could have knocked me over with a feather. Jim must have told him last night.

"It was so great to see her. It was like Christmas Day and all the best days of my life all rolled into one. Tony let her stay at his place last night and sneaked her in. God only knows how he swung it. But I'm not supposed to tell anyone, so keep it quiet, all right?"

"I ain't tellin' no one," says Darlene.

"We all real glad for you," says Big Dee.

"All right," says Sam. "Let's look at the next step and see where we go from here."

## STEP THREE
## MADE A DECISION TO TURN OUR WILL AND OUR ESCAPE PLAN OVER TO THE CARE OF GOD AS WE UNDERSTOOD HIM.

"Okay," says Sam. "I got something to say, right off. I got a problem with this thing about God being a him. Who says we always got to have a him? Why can't it be a her?"

"Don't be ridiculous," says Darlene. "Who ever heard of God being a her?"

"I don't ever think of whoever it is as one thing or the other," says Big Dee. "Not that I believe, but if I did, I'd see maybe just a big light and that don't need to be no him or no her neither. Maybe just some spirit floatin' round. But I ain't turnin' my life over to no one else. I can run my own business my own self. Don't need no help from no God. He ain't helped me so far. Why he start now?"

"You never know," I say. "Maybe we could take a risk and see what happens. We turn the escape over to him or her, who knows, maybe we'll come up with something really original—like a tunnel."

"That's original?" says Sam.

"We have some fine old time diggin' a tunnel when we up on the second floor," says Big Dee.

◆　　◆　　◆

Making a decision had become something that was difficult for me, mostly because I didn't have to make them very often. Mongrel made the decisions and I went along with them. After a while, it's like a muscle that doesn't get any exercise and it loses its strength.

After Mongrel killed himself, I had to make a lot of decisions. At first, I could only lay in bed and sleep, I was so afraid. I thought my whole world would fall apart without him. I'd wake up with this feeling that something terrible was going to happen to me. What if I didn't do the right thing? I guess I didn't, judging by where I am now.

◆　　◆　　◆

The prosecution made a lot about me washing that shirt. I guess from the outside it did look like a suspicious thing to do. They said I was tampering with evidence. But, see, at the time it wasn't evidence, at least not to me. It was just Mongrel's shirt. My favorite. And it had blood all over it.

◆　　◆　　◆

We all have assignments now. Because I work in the library, it's my job to watch and see how the guards move around—to see what kind of pattern there is to their movements. I also keep notes inside my head on what's going on in the control room—who's in at what time and when the fewest guards are on duty. It's exciting. It makes the days pass way faster. Plus I'm learning quite a lot, working in the library.

Darlene's doing the flower shop area. She's trying to find out when the deliveries are made. She's also getting all the plans for the Christmas open house—what time the visitors arrive and when it's all over.

Sam's trying to make contacts on the outside so that if we do actually make it, we'll have someplace to go.

"I mean, there's no sense makin' it all the way out and then getting caught 'cause you ain't got nowheres to go," says Sam.

"I could go to my girlfriend Josie's," I say.

"Now, there's a plan," says Sam. "Maggie, that's how come people get caught. That's the most obvious place you could go. What do you think cops are—stupid?"

"Mostly," says Big Dee.

"Not *that* stupid," says Sam. "We need someone good on the outside. This can't work just from here. We got to get a contact person who's cool."

"What about Carley?" says Darlene.

"She's done time here," says Sam.

"So?" says Darlene. "Just because you done time don't mean you can't come back for an open house, or as a visitor. Besides, she knows the prison. That could be helpful, you know."

"And some guard recognizes her and we disappear and the guard puts two and two together and we're back in doing extra hard time, pronto," says Sam.

"Maybe she come in some disguise," says Big Dee.

"It's Christmas, not Hallowe'en," says Sam.

◆　　◆　　◆

Ever since the day Stella did the smudging with sage, she's been coming around fairly regularly. She's trying to teach me some stuff about native spirituality. She talks a lot about the medicine wheel. I don't really understand it yet, but I like to listen to what she says.

"See," says Stella, "just like there's four directions on the medicine wheel, there's four races too. Whiteman, that's you. And black is Big Dee. And red—that's me. Not many yellow people in prison. You notice that? Lots of red ones, though. Too many Indians in jail. How come? You ever think about that?"

"No, I never have," I say.

"I do. I think about it lots. If we are all supposed to be brothers and sisters, like all colors, how come there just too many Indians in here?"

"I don't know," I say.

"Medicine wheel breaks down into many sets of four. Four directions. Four races. Four winds. Everything in fours. Earth, air, fire, and water. Medicine wheel is about ideas. You study it for many lifetimes, you still never understand it all."

"The tarot cards are like that, too," I say.

"I guess so," says Stella.

"At first, I just liked the pictures. They made my thinking come alive when I looked at them. I could feel the meanings even before I studied about them."

I take my deck and spread it out on the bed.

"You like them?" I say.

"Yeah," she says. "Nice."

"Choose one," I say, fanning the cards.

"I don't want to pull a bad one," she says.

"No bad ones. Only lessons. Even Death's a good card. Don't be fooled by the names."

I like the feel of the cards. It's like holding all the questions and answers in the universe in my hands. Like all the possibilities. That's how I see the tarot. A lot of times I pull a card, just one. I know it's the right one because there's a space. I always choose the one that has the biggest space between it and the next card. I don't know why I decided to do it that way. It just happened, I guess. And I breathe into them. I breathe the question into them and ask them for an answer. Sometimes I don't like the answer I get. But it's usually right on the money.

## ACE OF WANDS: ILLUMINATION

That's the card Stella pulls. It's about letting go or even burning up your old ways. Like moving on to new things.

"See, Stella, you got this gift. It's like you can see the truth. That's not so easy because this world is full of assholes who won't say what's really happening for them."

"Like most white people," says Stella.

"I don't know about that," I say.

"Don't mean you," she says.

"Anyways, I think you might have special power in your hands. Maybe you're a healer."

"Shaman," she says.

"What's that?"

"Medicine woman."

◆     ◆     ◆

Someone died last night. From another unit. A drug overdose. It happens often enough. There's a bad feeling in the air. Nobody's talking. Everyone's closed in on herself—trying to understand.

It's harder for Stella because she knew her. Stella tells us that the woman had been cutting herself a lot—slashing her arms, hurting herself. She'd been taking some kind of pills for depression, but they'd been giving her these side effects. She couldn't sleep.

So, I guess a few days passed and she was getting more and more desperate. She stopped taking the pills, but she didn't tell anyone, thinking that would fix everything. Instead she went way down fast, out of control, into this really bad depression. All she wanted was to get away from her own head—escape from her mind. I guess she had some heroin stashed somewhere. So, she waited until everyone was asleep.

Freedom.

"Big Dee?" I say.

"Uh-huh," she says.

"That girl didn't have to die," I say.

"That's right," she says.

"I don't get it."

"Some people ain't built to endure," she says.

I think about that for a few minutes. Was that what this was all about? Some kind of test to see if we could endure? And how much?

"I sometimes wonder about me," I say.

"What about you?"

" Am I built to endure?"

"I can't tell you that. No one able to do that for you. Only you know. And sometimes you not be too sure, especially when you feel so alone. It happens in here. It always painful. She leave a hole—an empty space for them who got close to her, like Stella. Bad for those ones left to think about it."

"What can we do?" I ask.

"Well," says Big Dee, "we can pray. That's 'bout all. Then let it go, 'cause there ain't no point in holdin' on. She gone."

◆　　　◆　　　◆

Chrissie was born in the summer. I had sat on the back of a chopper right up to two weeks before she came. Mongrel rode all night to get back from some R & B festival somewhere across the line. He just about didn't make it. I was down to a minute between contractions when he comes busting through the delivery room door, covered in road dirt and oil from the bike.

"Don't come anywhere near her," says the doctor, as Chrissie's head pops out.

Mongrel takes one look at her head and the blood and me cursing him with every ounce of energy that's left in me, and the next thing you know he's flat out on the delivery room floor. When he comes to,

I'm holding our daughter. He looks down into her little pinched-up face and his tears make two rivers down through the dust on his face.

◆　　　◆　　　◆

"I got a daughter, somewheres, you know," says Darlene. "She's in a foster home. I had to let her go when I got so messed up on drugs. I couldn't take care of her, you know. I never knew who the father was. Some john. Must have been a looker, though, 'cause she turned out real cute. I got a picture of her. You want to see it?"

◆　　　◆　　　◆

Tony thinks the Feelings Anonymous meetings are doing us all a lot of good. He says we all seem to be a lot more focused. I tell him that we're working the program really hard and that the whole idea behind it is to gain some sense of serenity. Maybe that's what he's seeing in us.

Of course, what he's really seeing is four women with a plan. And all of us are a lot more focused now that we have the beginnings of the plan in mind. I'm always thinking through all the angles inside my head. It's like any kind of major operation. You got to work out as many bugs as you can think of beforehand. How can we get the four of us out of here, and then, how do we manage to stay out? It takes a lot of figuring. I see the other gals sitting on their beds, kind of lost in the clouds. I know exactly what they're thinking about.

I've been thinking a lot more about my higher power since we got into planning the escape. And what I'm starting to see is that I always saw my higher power as some old man, sitting way up above me, looking down on me, judging me, and making me feel like I'm a piece of dirt. No wonder I don't like to pray. So, I started thinking. Maybe I could make my higher power the way I most wanted him or her to be.

I remembered my Grade Four teacher, Mrs. Netterfield. She was really old, even then. Her hair was white and she had it done in a knot in the back of her head. One day, she came into the girls' washroom and she took the pins out and let her hair down while she brushed it. And it fell all the way down her back—pure white.

She never raised her voice to anyone, and she never had to because everyone loved her. I think she was the kindest person I ever met.

That's how I want my higher power to be—like Mrs. Netterfield.

◆　　　◆　　　◆

"I already told you, I don't believe in no higher power," says Big Dee. "You like this color?" she says, waving her hand in my direction.

"It's all right," I say.

"How come you keep askin' about that higher power stuff, anyhow?"

"I don't know. I'm just obsessing on it. It's what I do. I was thinking about how I used to see my higher power before, and how I'm going to make some changes, because the old way doesn't work anymore. Did you ever have anyone who really made a big difference in your life? Someone who made you feel special—and without that person, you maybe would have been a lot more unhappy. You know what I mean?"

"Hmmm," says Big Dee. "I don't think so."

"Nobody?"

"Well, maybe. I remember this old man, used to play a blues harp, sit on the stairs. I used to stand and watch him for hours. He'd wink at me and ask me how I was today. He always had somethin' like a candy that he stuck in my pocket. Or he said some nice thing when my face was too long. He could make everything seem like it was gonna be fine, just the way he talk. I wonder what ever happen to that ol' man. I ain't never thought about him for— Gawd, Maggie, you get me thinkin' on the damnedest stuff! How we get on this, anyways?"

"I was asking you about your higher power," I say.

"That's right," says Big Dee.

"Okay, so what if your higher power was like that old man?"

"You crazy," says Big Dee.

"No, why not?" I say.

Big Dee looks at me. She stops doing her nails. She shakes her head and lets out a laugh.

"You one crazy white woman," she says.

◆　　　◆　　　◆

"See," says Stella, "we're all one family. You look on the medicine wheel, you see that the four peoples are there. Black, white, red, and yellow. All one family. Not separate. Not fighting. And so we see the hands all different colors, open, trusting."

"That'll be the day," I say.

"Maybe you got some prejudice."

"I'm not prejudiced," I say.

"Hmmm," says Stella.

But it's not true. I am and I know it. It pretty much came with the territory, living with Mongrel. As far as he was concerned, Indians were still one step away from wild and given half a chance they'd still be taking scalps. But mostly he just saw them as a bunch of hopeless drunks who had no pride.

"They want to go back to the land?" he'd say. "Fine, take away their fuckin' satellite dishes."

Mongrel figured that anyone who wasn't white should be sent back to their own country. When I told him that meant we'd have to leave because the Indians were here first, he got really pissed and took off on his bike and didn't come home for a couple of days. It's hard work getting prejudice out of your blood.

"Actually, I am prejudiced," I say.

"Me, too," says Stella.

◆　　◆　　◆

The dream went like this. I'm standing in the kitchen, making short-bread cookies, when Mongrel walks into the room with a gun. He's smiling. I'm afraid because I haven't put enough butter in them, and I'm sure he'll notice. He points the gun at my head and demands one of the cookies. I tell him they aren't cooked yet, but he says he doesn't care—he wants one, now. I peel one of the raw cookies off the sheet and give it to him. He eats it.

When he's finished, he sits down at the kitchen table and, with the gun still pointing at me, he asks me what is most important in my life. I tell him he is, but he says I'm lying. He tells me that freedom is more important to me than anything else and that he is going to take it away from me. I think it's because I make such terrible cookies. He turns the gun around and shoots himself in the head. I wake up in my cell.

"God, I had a strange dream," I tell Big Dee.

"Uh-huh," she says.

"I dreamt about Mongrel last night," I say.

"Uh-huh," she says.

"He shot himself on purpose. Because he wanted to take away my freedom," I say.

"No shit?" she says.

"Well, that's what he said in the dream. He ate a raw dough shortbread cookie and then he shot himself in the head."

"He dumb enough to eat a raw cookie, no wonder he shoot hisself." Big Dee laughs.

I laugh.

"How come he do that, Maggie, really? Why'd he shoot hisself?"

"He fucked up his leg in the last accident. He couldn't ride a bike anymore."

"That all?" she asks.

"It was his life, riding. His bike was everything. He lived and breathed for that damn Harley."

"You believe that?" she says.

"I just know he didn't want to live anymore when he couldn't ride the way he wanted to. He didn't see any way out. He was too stubborn to make the change. I think it was too scary for him. He took the easy way out."

"Shootin' hisself ain't that easy, I don't think," says Big Dee.

"You had to know him," I say.

## A DEAD SIMPLE RECIPE FOR
## SHORTBREAD COOKIES

1 cup butter

1/2 cup icing sugar

1-1/2 cups white flour

1 teaspoon vanilla

Add all ingredients in a large mixing bowl and beat 10 minutes with electric beater.

Drop from spoon onto greased cookie sheets.

Bake at 350° until *very* light brown.

◆　　◆　　◆

It's been eight months now that I've been here, waiting trial for murder. Everything moves slow. At first, I couldn't believe that I would end up in a prison. And then I thought I'd kill myself when I got here. But it's like anything else—you get used to it. I've made some friends on the inside. I know it sounds weird, but in some ways they're closer than my friends ever were on the outside.

I hate the waiting—not knowing for sure how it's going to turn out. It's hard to believe that you can spend so much time in prison just waiting to go to trial. That's not the way they show it on television. Everything goes so fast on TV. They have to get the story told in an hour or maybe a half hour. People start to think that jail time goes that fast—that you get arrested, then you go to trial the next day, and then you either go free or you do your time. Quick, like that.

And people on the outside think that prison sentences are just numbers—like when you hear about a plane crash. Two hundred dead. It's just a number. You can't really imagine it unless you're picking up body parts on the mop-up crew.

So, maybe you hear about a prisoner doing time—five years, ten years, life. It's just numbers. But when you're serving it, every year has three hundred and sixty-five days and every one of those days has twenty-four hours. And those hours in prison aren't like hours on the outside. They're long hours. And they're made even longer by the fact that you're either bored or scared or feeling helpless.

And the worst part is, if you get proved innocent, then you don't get anything for the year or more you spent eating bad food and listening to those doors crashing shut all the time. And it's not like you just lose that year. Some people lose everything because of all the crap that goes on where they live—the gossip and everything.

Some of Mongrel's buddies thought I did it, and wouldn't have anything to do with me afterward. And that meant their old ladies had to stay away from me, too. Even my son, Max, thinks I did it. He won't come and see me in here. It's a long story.

I try to do what Sam tells me—live it a day at a time. Hold onto the good memories and don't spend too much time being pissed off.

"You can't afford to feel pissed off for too long," she says. "You just end up listening to your stomach eating itself."

I've had a lot of time to think about my life in here. I guess it happens to everyone, but sometimes, when I was on the outside, I got so caught up in just living the day-to-day that I never really gave my life that much thought.

Before I got in here, I would have said that I had a pretty good marriage. We had our ups and downs like anyone else, but I never thought that it would ever change. I always figured I'd end up a widow—that Mongrel would have one accident too many and there'd be a biker funeral and that would be that.

But, being in here, I've had all this time to think about it. I wasn't really happy for a long time. Sometimes I felt like I couldn't breathe, being married to Mongrel. I think sometimes I felt more like a prisoner in my own home than I do in here.

♦     ♦     ♦

A new guard starts this evening—a rookie. You can tell the ones who are new because they won't leave you alone. They think that because you're sitting by yourself in your cell, there's something wrong—that you're depressed. They come up to your door and look in with that really concerned look.

"Are you all right, Margaret?" she asks.

"I'm fine."

"You look a little down," she says.

"I'm fine."

"You know, if you need to talk to someone, I'm here for you," she says.

"That's great," I say, looking her dead in the eye.

"So, you're all right?" she says.

"Look, sweetheart, sometimes I really like to be on my own—just sitting here thinking my own thoughts. It's not because I'm depressed, all right? I just want to spend some time with me."

"Oh sure, Margaret, but if you do need someone, just shout," she says.

"Absolutely," I say. "You'll be the first one."

◆　　◆　　◆

I'm not sure why he did it, but without him I wouldn't have been able to see Chrissie. It meant a lot, and I owe him. He's in his office. I stand at the door.

"You can come in," he says.

"It's all right, I'm just here for a few minutes."

"Okay," he says.

Neither of us says anything for a minute or so. It's a bit awkward. Then he talks.

"You know how I get results in here?" he says.

"Nope."

"I never believe anyone's as stupid as they pretend to be."

"Hmm. I appreciate what you did the other night."

"Johanna was out of line."

"I thought you guys always stuck together."

"Not always," he says.

"How come you work in a prison?"

"Because people on the outside are too mean."

"Really?"

"Yeah. You met anyone in here who's deep-down mean?"

"You mean besides Johanna?"

"Guards don't count." He laughs.

◆      ◆      ◆

It's the fourth meeting of Freedom Anonymous. Big Dee chairs.

"Welcome to the Last Resort meeting of Freedom Anonymous," she says. "I'm your chairperson for this time. So, what's up?"

"Well, you know," says Darlene, "I found out that the Christmas open house is the second week in December. It seems like a long time away but it ain't really, you know, 'cause you know how time can fly, especially when you're having a good time—like in here, ha, ha."

"Anyways," says Darlene, "I think that planning it around that time is our best bet, you know, 'cause it gets kinda confusing with all the visitors and all. Plus, like I said before, they don't use the regular doors—so there's less security, or at least there's more people for the security there is. You know what I mean?"

We all nod.

"Plus, with all the visitors' cars, they won't be able to keep track of the getaway car so easy, you know?"

"I think Darlene's got a point, you know," I say, winking at Big Dee.

"Sounds like a plan to me," says Sam. "Okay, so I got the word out through a few of the gals in minimum that we want to see Carley. The grapevine being what it is, we should see her real soon. She'll set up a meeting with Darlene and she'll be our outside contact. We gotta get on this outside stuff real quick."

"You know, I've been wondering about something," I say.

"Yeah, like what?" says Sam.

"Well, I was talking to Stella the other day, you know, about escaping . . ."

"You didn't fuckin' talk to Stella about our plans?" Sam's looking real hard at me.

"No, no," I say, "I was just kind of talking about what if—just conversation."

"What do you mean, conversation?"

"I mean I was just talking about the idea of escaping, not our plan or anything."

"Jesus, Maggie!"

"Look, I just talked to her about what if. And she tells me this story about how this guy, from one of the local tribes, escaped from a maximum security prison somewhere. He ends up getting all this help from the Indians—they move him around—give him a place to hide out, food, you know. They like nothing better than to fuck with the white man."

"I can relate," says Big Dee.

"Besides," I say, "she knows we're up to something. She practically said as much. I think we should talk to her."

"Oh sure," says Big Dee. "Now we get us an Indian."

"Why not?" says Darlene. "I'm part Indian."

"Oh yeah?" says Big Dee, letting out a whoop and slapping her thigh. "Which part? Your little finger?" She laughs again and gets up out of her chair. "I got to tell you all something real true. See the palms of my hands, how much lighter they is? That's because I'm part white, ha, ha. Shit, I heard it all."

"Fuck you," says Darlene, but she's laughing.

"All right, we all figured out what color we are?" says Sam. "Let's get back to the fucking plan."

◆    ◆    ◆

## STEP 4
# MADE A SEARCHING AND FEARLESS MORAL INVENTORY OF OURSELVES.

Big Dee asks Tony to come in for the first part of our meeting. She says it makes us look less suspicious—like it's a real twelve-step meeting. He explains what taking a moral inventory means. He says it's kind of like a spring cleaning, only of your whole life. Sam says it sounds like when she does a complete clean-up and overhaul of her bike.

Darlene says she'd be too embarrassed to do an inventory since she's a hooker, but Tony says that there's nothing to be ashamed of.

"Oh yeah?" says Darlene, and goes on to talk about the time she gave these two business guys blow jobs. Sam's pissed off now.

"So the third john is doing me from behind. I hear this moaning, you know, and one of them, I think it was the overweight one, falls onto the boardroom table clutching at his chest like he's having a heart attack, you know, just as the head honcho walks in the door. So they're all trying to whip up their pants without catching their dicks in their flies, you know . . ."

Tony's cool, but you can tell he's starting to get a bit uncomfortable.

"I think I'll leave you ladies to your meeting. Thanks for letting me drop in," he says, as he heads for the door.

"Anytime, Tony," says Sam.

"Now, where were we?" says Darlene, as the door closes.

"You were talking about giving some guys blow jobs," says Sam.

"Principles before personalities," says Big Dee.

"Easy for you to say," says Sam.

"Not so easy," says Big Dee. "Big words."

◆　　　◆　　　◆

I'm not so sure about looking at my past. Some things are best left alone. Besides, nothing can be changed now. I never believed that it was any good, looking backward. I remember that old story about the woman who was warned not to look behind her or she'd turn into a pillar of salt. But she couldn't stop herself. I guess she was just too curious. She did it, and she turned into a pillar of salt. I always wondered why it was salt. Why not a pillar of sugar? or cement? or marble?

And then I thought that maybe it was the salt from all the tears she'd cried in her life—all of her grief brought into that moment in time. I don't want to remember all the sadness.

◆　　　◆　　　◆

"I don't see the point of it." I'm talking to Big Dee. "What good does it do to dig up all that old shit again? And then write it down?"

"Beats me, sugar," she says.

"Besides, I can't remember half of it, and the half I do remember is so stupid, I wish I didn't remember it."

"I 'member everything," says Big Dee.

"Really?" I say.

"Sure," she says. "I see my whole life like a picture show. I look back, see exacly how it was, and who's there, and what they wearing. I get lots of time to think in here. I don't read like you do, so I spend my time thinking back and trying to make some sense of it. Like a crystal ball—the more you look, the more you see. I go back and each time I look at some old story, I see it a little different. Because I change all the time inside. And when I change inside, then everything on the outside don't look the same neither. You know what I'm sayin'?"

"Maybe," I say.

◆   ◆   ◆

What I do remember is that he comes into the kitchen, dragging his stiff leg, and flops down hard on a chair. I'm baking brownies. I've just taken them out of the oven. He sits at the table and he starts to cry. I don't know what to do. The only time I ever saw him cry was when Chrissie was born. And that was a different kind of crying.

But this is crying from way deep inside. It's a horrible sound— ragged and broken. I can't look at him. I know I should feel sorry for him, but I don't. I'm feeling too sorry for myself. It's like all the years of being pissed off and disappointed bubble up inside me and I can't turn around. I look down at my hands. They're holding onto the counter so hard that my knuckles are white.

I look out the window for what seems like a long time. Everything's frozen. It's like the whole thing is stuck in time, and then there's this shot. Bang. I don't even know if I've been hit. I turn my head, but my hands won't let go of the counter. I see his eyes looking right at me and then they're looking at nothing at all. When I come to, I still have my arms around him and I'm covered in his blood.

◆   ◆   ◆

## XIII: DEATH

Stella likes to pull a tarot card when she comes to visit me. But she's always afraid she's going to pull Death. Death never bothers me. I actually like it. There's this mask, maybe African, beside a dark blue sky with a moon way up high, and full. That picture already gives you a feeling.

And then, on the right, there's this woman sitting, all lit blue, covered in a shawl, maybe looking a bit like death. And there's a river flowing past her, which gives the idea that there really isn't any death, just a long unbroken strand that twists and turns.

There's a snake at the bottom, shedding its skin. I guess it means that nothing ever stays the same. Everything comes to an end. The snake sheds its skin for a new one. The tree loses its leaves. And death makes us sad. But it also sets us free.

◆   ◆   ◆

The word must have got out fast because Carley's in for a visit before the next meeting. Darlene shares the news over boiled chicken and peas. She looks over her shoulder.

"Okay, so Carley's in," says Darlene. "She's going to contact some friends. See about a place for us to lay low the first couple of weeks. She says that's when they do the most heavy searching, you know? She says after two weeks they kind of chill out a little, and then we might be able to move around."

"Shit," says Sam, "I gotta get the Harley out."

"Why not just wear a sign that says 'Arrest me'?" says Darlene. "Every cop in the city knows your bike."

"Yeah, well, I got a plan. I was lying on my bunk last night thinking and I came up with this idea. I tape up the tank. Then I brush on a layer or two of Bondo or White Lightning. Then I sand it down. Then I spray a coat of primer. Then a couple of coats of paint. Then I can take her across the line when I'm well and for sure out of danger. Then strip it all off. So's I don't lose my paint job of Marilyn on the tank."

"Sounds like a lot of work," I say.

"What about me?" says Darlene.

"What about you?" says Sam.

"You just going to leave me behind?" she says.

"Yeah, right behind me on the bike. What the fuck do you think, Darlene? What kinda partner do you take me for? Of course you're with me. I didn't think I had to say it."

"Well, I wasn't sure, you know," says Darlene.

"So, now you are," says Sam.

"All right," says Big Dee. "You lovers all straight now? Let's be thinking about the big picture—okay?

"So," says Darlene, "Carley figures the open house is the best time, too, you know. Because of all the confusion around the joint, and the people and the cars. She also thinks it might be a good idea for her to come in, looking a bit different, like in disguise. Nothing too weird. It's easy enough for her 'cause she's got more wigs than—"

"Good evening, ladies," says Johanna. "Didn't catch you in the middle of making plans, did I?"

Everyone's looking down at the table.

"You pretty funny," says Big Dee, slapping her leg. "Plans? What you think, girls? Maybe we just do that. Ha, ha. Make an escape plan. You got a shovel, Sam?"

"Fresh out of shovels," says Sam.

"Guess we just stay tight then," says Big Dee, as Johanna walks away.

"Pass the boiled chicken," says Sam loudly, then "son of a bitch" under her breath.

◆　　◆　　◆

Boiled chicken. I could never figure why anyone would boil it. Seemed to me that all the good stuff ended up in the water and you got left with this flavorless, stringy dead chicken.

Chrissie loved fried chicken. She'd never let me take the skin off. She said it was the best part. She had her favorite recipe. The last time I made it was just before I came here.

## CHRISSIE'S FAVORITE FIERY GINGER CHICKEN

8–10 chicken thighs (bone in)
Ginger (fresh) in very fine slices—enough to completely cover the bottom of large fry pan
Olive oil
2 tablespoons soy sauce
2 tablespoons Hoys sweet chili sauce, or to taste
2 tablespoons real maple syrup

Heat a thin coat of olive oil in fry pan. Cover bottom of pan with thin slices of fresh ginger. Sauté for a minute.

Lay thighs (skin-side down, to start) on bed of ginger.

Now mix together soy sauce, chili sauce, and maple syrup. Brush over all the thighs. There should be enough of this mixture to make a nice bubbling sauce. Cover and cook until one side of chicken is golden brown. Then turn the thighs over and brush with the sauce. (You may need to mix up a bit more. It's easy.) Cover and cook until golden.

Serve on a bed of basmati rice.

◆    ◆    ◆

Stella has a cellmate as of yesterday—a little Asian gal named Chan. Darlene overheard a guard talking. It seems that Chan arrived at the airport with close to ten kilos of heroin taped to her body. She can only speak Chinese. She follows Stella around like a puppy.

"Can't get rid of her," says Stella, shaking her head. She looks over at Chan and Chan smiles.

"God, the poor thing," I say. "Bad enough being here, let alone not being able to understand what anyone's saying. She's got nobody to talk to."

"She talk a lot to me," says Stella.

"Really? What does she say?" I ask.

"No idea, she don't speak English," she says.

I look at Chan, who's holding onto Stella like she's afraid of losing her.

"Hi," I say, "I'm Maggie."

"I Maggie," says Chan.

"No, no, *my* name Maggie, *you* name Chan," I say.

"You nay Chan," says Chan with a big smile.

"Close enough," I say.

"What am I going to do?" says Stella. "She don't let me go to the bathroom alone."

"She's scared," I say. "She looks awfully young to be in here, don't you think?"

"Guard say she twenty-something. Hard to tell with Chinese," says Stella.

◆　　◆　　◆

## STEP FIVE

ADMITTED TO GOD, TO OURSELVES, AND TO ANOTHER HUMAN BEING THE EXACT NATURE OF OUR ESCAPE PLAN.

Big Dee isn't any too happy when Stella turns up at the next meeting with Chan glued to her side.

"What she doin' here?" says Big Dee. "This here's a closed meeting. No new members."

"We've already been through all this, Big Dee. Stella knew all along what we were up to. Besides, she says she can set up something to help us on the outside—after the escape."

"I'm not talking about Stella. I mean her—the Chinese."

"Won't leave me," says Stella. "Starts to cry if I try to get away."

"Well, I don't like it," says Big Dee.

"Hey," I say, "what's the diff? She can't speak English."

"Who says?" says Big Dee.

"I says. I tried to talk to her," I say.

"Maybe she playin' dumb," says Big Dee.

"C'mon, Big Dee," says Sam. "The kid's right off the boat. Probably got a few hundred dollars and a promise that she'd get set up here and be able to bring her family over later. She's just a mule. If she'd made it through, they'd probably just have taken the drugs off her and shot her in the head. This way, she gets to live for a couple of years before she gets sent back."

"What happens then?" I ask.

"She gets sent back. Then, if she makes it alive out of the airport in Hong Kong, she'll be real lucky. Easier to kill her than to take the risk that she'll testify against some gang members. Either way, she's looking at a short life."

"That's gross," I say, looking at Chan. She smiles back.

"That's life," says Sam. "Can't do the time, don't do the crime."

"All right," says Big Dee. "I don't like it, but we got a meeting here and we don't have a ton of time till December, so we take a chance on her."

"Okay, well, first off, you know," says Darlene, "we gotta play it more cool and not talk outside of this room, 'cause I just about shit myself when Johanna said that yesterday. I mean, I didn't see her comin' from nowheres."

"She's sneaky, that bitch," I say.

"She don't trust nobody," says Sam.

"I don't trust her," says Big Dee.

"Anyways," says Darlene, "let's get back on track. Okay, Carley talked to Wilson Featherstone. He's a friend of a friend of Stella's, you know. He come up with a plan that sounds pretty good. Instead of taking the road out—which is risky, you know—we just get out of the prison grounds, then we cut through the bush on foot to the river.

"Him and his brother are going to leave some boats or something waiting for us. We cross over. It's just a short piece of water but he says there's a bit of a current. The highway's right there on the other side.

"So, in that way, you know, we can get away from the prison area real fast and double back on the highway, so's we're going in the opposite direction to what the police might think. Then we'll head up out of town to the reserve. He figures the cops will be looking first around the prison, you know, then around the yard, and then on the road to the prison. They won't think we were so organized as to have a boat and all."

"Sounds complicated," I say.

"Excape ain't suppose to be easy," says Big Dee, "else everyone do it."

◆      ◆      ◆

It takes most of a week, on and off, to do my fourth step. It's a lot harder than I would have thought. Thirty-five pages. It's amazing what comes up. I never believed in looking back. The past was the past. Mostly, I just blamed Mongrel for what didn't work. But the more I wrote, the more I could see that that's what I did the whole time I was married to him.

Mongrel used to tell me that he wasn't to blame for all my unhappiness. He'd go away for a couple of weeks and I'd be miserable the whole time and blaming him. He said it didn't make any sense because he wasn't even there.

But the truth was, he was there. He was there inside my head. I was running everything over and over and getting more and more pissed off. And when he got back home, he had to pay for it.

And near the end, I knew he was in a lot of pain because of how things had changed. He was never going to be the same. I just wouldn't see it from his side. I thought he was being selfish. There he was, in his forties, feeling sorry for himself because he couldn't ride his bike anymore.

But riding was his life. For him, being out on the highway was freedom. He rode proud. I loved to ride with him. I remember how it was, sitting behind him, my thighs tight up against his, and even after all the years we were married, I still always wanted him, especially when he just got off the bike. He was on fire then.

But after the last accident, the one that wrecked up his leg, he didn't want to touch me anymore. I think a big part of what kept him wanting to have sex was riding that fucking bike. And when he couldn't ride anymore, he just parked the bike in the shed and parked himself in front of the television.

◆　　　◆　　　◆

The hardest part about the fifth step is that you have to tell someone about all the stuff you wrote in the fourth. I'm not too comfortable about a few things, especially telling them to a third party. Me and my higher power—all right. But like they say in the book, it doesn't count unless you have that third leg to make it stand.

I don't have much choice about who to talk to. No way I'll talk to a minister. And you need someone who's been in the program for at least a few years. I ask Tony. He says okay.

"I guess I tried to talk to him, but we never talked that much about stuff. Not about things that mattered, anyways. Too many years of partying and riding and raising kids and dogs and visiting him in the hospital and working in diners. It all went by and somehow we just never talked about anything really. I can see that a lot of it was my fault. I didn't talk to him because I didn't think he'd understand."

"Why not?" says Tony.

"I don't know. There were things that we didn't know how to do together, even after all the years we were married. I didn't think he would understand certain things. Not because he wasn't smart—he was. But he was street smart, you know?

"He knew stuff naturally. He had a sense about things. That's how he made so much money. That's how he could take such good care of me and the kids. He had a sweetness about him. He wasn't mean. I was the mean one."

"So, now it's all your fault?" he says.

"Maybe not all, but a lot of it. You know I have a son?"

"I know from your file, but you've never talked about him."

"He won't have anything to do with me."

"I wondered about that," says Tony.

"Well, he hasn't come to see me because he thinks I did it. He thinks I killed his father. See . . . I don't feel good about this. I don't even know if I can talk about it."

"It doesn't go beyond these walls," says Tony.

"I fucked around on Mongrel," I say. "That's why Max thinks I killed him. Max knew about it. He was only thirteen. Mongrel was off riding. He'd been gone for a few weeks. I was mad at him, as usual—leaving me behind to take care of business.

"So, one of his buddies drops by to visit, thinking that Mongrel's around. He brings a twenty-six of Cuervo Gold. One thing leads to another and we end up in bed.

"Max was supposed to be at school, but he got sick and came home early. He caught us in bed. He hated me after that. He never told Mongrel, but Mongrel found out. Max never let me touch him again."

◆　　◆　　◆

## FIVE OF CUPS: DISAPPOINTMENT

Everything seems to be broken when you first look at the card. And I think about breaking things when I was little, and how bad it felt. Like breaking a favorite glass. Or a necklace. Or a friendship.

I can't figure out the roses in the upper part of the card, except that one is wilted. It's like no matter how beautiful something is, it dies. And you get to feel disappointment.

Disappointment is made up of broken dreams. But sometimes disappointment is some magic force tapping you on the shoulder, reminding you to live right now and not in some never-never land in the future. The present is like one of the jars in the picture. It holds water. The future is a broken glass that can't hold anything but air.

◆　　◆　　◆

Sam and Darlene are going at it. Something about Darlene getting a call from an ex. Sam starts calling her names. Big Dee's eyes go up and she shakes her head.

"Trouble in paradise," she mutters.

"Fuck you," shouts Darlene, "and—*rip, rip, rip*—fuck your fucking Harleys."

*Whack.*

Darlene is crying now.

"You love your fucking bike more than you love me."

"That's because it's less trouble than you. It don't fucking talk back or fuck some other bike when I ain't looking."

"It was just an old friend."

"Bullshit!"

Big Dee makes a face.

"Fuck you," shouts Darlene.

"Fuck you, too," yells Sam.

Something gets thrown, hits the wall, *bam*, bounces on the floor. Big Dee winces.

"I knew they's due for one," she says. "It been way too quiet round here."

"Relationships can be a drag. I don't think it's good, this living so close, especially in a relationship. I think I'd have shot Mongrel a lot sooner if he hadn't taken off on his bike for weeks at a time," I say.

"You want to run that by me one more time?" says Big Dee.

"I said you need space in a relationship or you want to kill the other person."

"But you said you shoot him," says Big Dee.

"I did not," I say.

"Yeah, you did," she says.

◆　　◆　　◆

I wasn't really in love with Mongrel when I married him. I was still in love with my first boyfriend, Danny. But I could see what being married to *him* would be. At least, I thought I could.

He had no sense when it came to money. He lived from day to day. He didn't care if he got a pay cheque. He just smiled and believed the universe would give him what he needed. And it did, if you didn't count rent and things like that. The way I saw it, I'd be working my butt off getting old and bitter and he'd just smile and think the world was a great place.

Mongrel was different. He loved making money. He had this pride thing about taking care of his old lady. I weighed love against security. I'd already seen, just looking around me, what love could do to you. It could almost kill you. I settled for security.

But marriage is sneaky. It's like this bunch of little things that, year by year, you don't pay attention to. You sweep them under the carpet. Or just the day-to-day keeps you so busy that you don't see what's happening to you until practically half your lifetime's gone by, and even then it takes a shock, like death, to wake you up.

Mongrel's death woke me up big time.

◆          ◆          ◆

Stella's burning sage again—trying to cleanse her cell and especially her cellmate. Chan storms around brushing the smoke away, screeching stuff in Chinese.

"What you doin', Stella?" shouts Big Dee. "Tryin' to kill that poor girl?"

"Room needs cleansing," says Stella. "So does she."

"I think she needs calming more than cleansing," I say. Chan is jammed in the corner of the room, pinching her nose shut and spitting at Stella.

"Don't spit," says Stella, shaking her finger at Chan. Chan gives Stella the finger.

"She learn a few things," says Big Dee, laughing.

◆          ◆          ◆

Pretty much all I think about now is the escape. Maybe it's just crazy. It seemed like a good idea at the time, but now that we're really on it, I'm starting to get cold feet. What happens if we don't make it? What if we get caught right away? What if someone gets hurt? What if the natives don't show up on time? Or the boat fucks up? Or we have a breakdown on the highway? Or we get a speeding ticket and get caught that way? Or someone on the reserve turns us in?

There's so many ways it could mess up—so many places for mistakes. Too many people to think about. Sometimes the plan seems to be perfectly in place and I can see it all. I can see us making it and laughing at the other end, free. Then, when I'm having a bad day, it looks impossible and all I see is the five of us in shackles serving an extra ten years for attempting.

"You think we got a hope in hell?" I ask Big Dee.

"I don't know," says Big Dee.

"Do you go hot and cold on it?"

"I sure do," she says.

"You think guys do that when they got a plan?" I ask.

"I ain't never figured out what guys are thinking when they doing something," says Big Dee.

"They gotta have doubts," I say.

"Sometimes it easier if you not too smart, you know?" she says. "Easier if you don't think too much about it and just do. I think that why us women has so much trouble. We think too much about stuff. Try to figure it out. Try to make it make sense. But there ain't no sense to most of what happen, far as I can tell. It just happen."

"Where do you want to go, if we make it?" I ask.

"Well, all I want is to warm my bones. Go to Florida. Sit in some big orange orchard and eat a bunch of sweet Florida oranges. I'm holding that picture in my head."

"Mongrel and I went there once," I say. "Down the Keys. The water was turquoise. The dope was terrible. And we stayed drunk the whole time we were there."

"Let's us go there, Maggie," says Big Dee, her eyes lit up. "Let's us all go to Florida."

◆     ◆     ◆

The bad news I find out about Florida, from the encyclopedia is that it gets hit by hurricanes and tornadoes every year that rip houses into toothpicks and leave people wandering around in a tailspin for weeks.

The good news, as Big Dee says, is that there's oranges and it hardly ever goes below freezing.

◆    ◆    ◆

Chan's glaring at Stella. Sam isn't talking to Darlene. Big Dee's acting like she got PMS. Johanna's on the warpath. And it's boiled chicken again for dinner.

"I hates boil chicken," says Big Dee, poking at her plate.

Nobody says anything. Sam pushes food into her mouth and chews loudly. She's doing it to bug Darlene because Darlene can't stand it when Sam eats with her mouth open.

Darlene hits the volume button on her Walkman. It's practically loud enough to dance to. Chan cuts her food up into tiny pieces, then picks it up with her fingers and places it carefully in her mouth. Stella's looking at her as though she'd like to wring her neck.

"The only thing I hates more than boil chicken is a room full of gals not saying nothing," says Big Dee.

"Everyone's in a bad mood, Big Dee," I say.

"Could've fool me," she says.

"Turn that damn music down," says Sam, yanking on Darlene's headphones.

"Fuck you," says Darlene.

"And how are the ladies tonight?" says Johanna in that tone she uses when she's looking for trouble. Nobody even looks at her.

"She end up facedown in a ditch if she live on the reserve," says Stella after Johanna's gone.

"Maybe we boil her up for dinner," says Big Dee.

Sam starts to laugh. She's got one of those laughs that's catching. Next thing, Stella's got her hand over her mouth and her body's shaking. Big Dee swats her thigh and lets out a holler. Chan has a laugh that sounds like a horse whinnying. It makes me laugh even harder. Darlene looks up and stares around the table.

"What the fuck you all laughing about?" she says too loudly, because she's got her Walkman on full blast. She yanks off the headphones.

Big Dee has tears rolling down her face by now and Sam is snorting between roars of laughter.

"You're snorting," says Darlene.

"Who cares?" says Sam, letting out another snort. Chan looks at her, eyes wide, and makes another whinny. Stella practically falls off her chair. I'm holding my stomach. Johanna comes stomping back over to the table.

"All right," she says, "what's so goddam funny?"

"Boil chicken," says Big Dee, and everyone howls.

◆　　　◆　　　◆

Mongrel used to boil chicken before he put it on the barbecue. The first time he did it, I told him it would spoil the chicken, but he told me to shut up until I'd tried it. So I did. He was right. Mongrel wasn't much of a cook, but he was dynamite at barbecuing. He said that the secret to a good barbecue is the sauce. He used to say you could barbecue a rubber tire with his sauce and it would taste great.

## MONGREL'S BARBIE-Q SAUCE THAT WOULD MAKE A RUBBER TIRE TASTE GREAT

1 cup Heinz ketchup

1 teaspoon cocoa

1 teaspoon lemon juice

1/4 cup maple syrup

1/2 cup soy sauce

1/4 cup Hoys sweet chili sauce

1-1/2 teaspoons olive oil

1 teaspoon Tabasco

1/2 teaspoon crushed chili peppers

1/2 teaspoon cayenne pepper

3 cloves garlic

1 tablespoon Worcestershire sauce

Mix all ingredients in a pot and simmer for 20 minutes.

◆　　◆　　◆

"Key West?" says Sam. "Think you could find a place that's farther away?"

"Isn't it in California?" says Darlene.

"Hell, no," says Big Dee. "It's close to Cuba. In Florida—way over and down the east coast. Real interesting little place. Lots of weird people live there. I remember one time when I was there, the mayor of Key West, he waterski almost all the way to Cuba."

"What the hell for?" says Sam.

"I don't know. Make some point or other," says Big Dee.

"Why we going there?" asks Stella.

"'Cause there's palm trees and it never get cold, and when it rain, it don't last forever the way it do here," says Big Dee.

"What about the hurricanes?" I ask.

"There's hurricanes?" says Darlene.

"Nothin's perfect," says Big Dee.

◆    ◆    ◆

## STEP SIX

WERE ENTIRELY READY TO HAVE GOD REMOVE ALL THE DEFECTS IN OUR ESCAPE PLAN.

"You looking for the bad, Maggie. How you supposed to feel better when you only look at what wrong with you?"

"If I don't look at what's wrong with me, how can I ask for it to be removed? Do you think I'm bad-tempered?"

"Once in a while."

"Resentful?"

"Uh-huh."

"Really?"

"Uh-huh."

"Selfish?"

"Maybe a little."

"Dishonest?"

"Sometimes."

"When have I been dishonest?"

"You want my opinion or no?" says Big Dee.

"I don't know."

"See, you don't even want other people to be honest."

"Hey, what do you really know about Florida?" I ask.

"I was raised down south," says Big Dee. "I know them Keys like the back of my hand—'specially Key West. My second old man played piano in a club there for fifteen years, maybe more. We all live over in Black Town."

"Where's that?" I ask.

"In Key West. See, you wouldn't understand. It's the South, honey. The blacks got one side of town. And the whites got the good part. Pretty much the way it always goes. Black Town's run-down. Mostly poor people. Not much work there.

"But my man worked most all the time. He got the voice make people want to come back and hear him more. Plus he shine on a room—flirt and wink at the ladies. He remember everybody's name."

"Where's he now?" I ask.

"Probably still there, squishin' palmetto bugs on the sidewalk, if he not dead from drinkin'. I ain't talk to him in a long time. He got no phone. Sometimes I think I send him a postcard or something. But I don't think he can read. Didn't used to be able."

◆　　　◆　　　◆

I like to read now. I didn't used to. Not until I went back to school. It was wintertime and it was raining a lot. I needed to get out of the house. Plus Mongrel and I had had this bad scene, but that's another story. I saw this ad for night school.

I don't know why I never saw those ads before. I just didn't. There was this one course that taught you about how to appreciate good books. No credit or anything, and you didn't have to have any background courses to do it. I hadn't even finished high school.

The guy who taught the course looked okay, judging by his picture. Some people put in pictures of themselves from twenty years ago. You spend the first half hour with them trying to get used to how much they don't look like their picture. Anyways, he had a beard.

The first night, he asked us what we liked to read most. Everybody talked about this book or that one. I didn't actually remember any book I'd read, so I said *People* magazine. Everyone cracked up. He asked me how come I liked it. So, I said something about how I got to meet all these people I wouldn't normally meet. And I saw a little how they lived and what they did.

There was always something about some ordinary person who did something. Someone who broke out. Who got away. Like you hear about people winning the lottery and what they did after they won it. In *People* magazine, you got to know someone in Boise, Idaho, who did something good or had something good happen to them.

I'm interested in people. Or, at least, I'm interested in reading about them. That's what I learned in that class. With books, I got this keyhole that I could look through and see all kinds of people's lives. That's what books are to me now.

Reading books probably saved my marriage. Books always made a lot more sense than real life. When things got bad, I'd just get a good book. I kept in touch with the guy who taught the course. His name was Doug. He said I could phone him anytime I needed to know what to read next.

◆　　　◆　　　◆

Stella says that the medicine wheel is like a book—a book about the spiritual path. You can understand it in your head, but each person lives it differently and there are no two identical paths.

"See, we are both on the path," says Stella. "And here we are in jail. For some reason, we meet on our journey and spend some time together. But probably only for a while. If we were on the outside right now, we'd never talk to each other."

"Probably not," I say.

"You ever talk to an Indian before?" she asks.

"I don't know. Maybe."

"Do you want to be different?" says Stella.

"What do you mean?"

"Like a better person."

"I guess I want to be more."

"So, you decided to take the journey?"

"I guess so," I say. "But it doesn't seem so much like I decided. It just seemed to happen."

"There are no accidents, Maggie. The path has a lot of patience. It's always there for them who decide to travel it."

"I don't think I have a lot of patience," I say.

"You learn it in here," says Stella.

◆　　◆　　◆

"We need money," says Sam. "If we're gonna head to Florida, we can't just take off flat broke. There's five of us. We gotta eat and sleep."

"No money here," says Stella.

"No reserve on the reserve?" says Sam. She doesn't say it in a mean way.

"Maybe better than money," says Stella. "We got the Indian pipeline. We get taken care of on the way. Stop in. Eat up. Sleep. I can pay my way."

"Okay," says Sam.

"What about you, Maggie?"

"I got some money from the sale of the house. Plus a bunch in deposit boxes. Chrissie would have to do the bank stuff, so I guess that means she'd have to know what we're doing."

"No way," says Big Dee.

"Chrissie would never tell. She'd go to jail before she'd do that. She could handle cops when she was three years old. I'd tell her, Now if they ask for Mongrel, or your dad, or some other name, you just tell them he left a few hours ago. She could do it. Three years old. She was a crack-up. The cops loved her."

"Never mind," says Sam. "You got some money and that's what counts. We'll figure how to get our hands on it later. Right now, we're just seein' what we got. How 'bout you, Big Dee? You got anything?"

"I got me a little stash down acrossed the border. Enough to get me to the Keys. Once I'm there, I got no trouble at all."

"Okay," says Sam. "How 'bout you, Darlene?"

"Well," says Darlene, "I never was much on saving, but I can pull a hundred just about anytime, just about anywhere. I could be like the Johnny Cash machine—get cash from the johns, ha, ha."

"I got a problem with that," says Sam.

"Let's not get into it now," says Big Dee.

Sam looks over at Chan, who's got her arm draped around Stella. "What about you, Chan? You got some money?" Sam winks at the rest of us.

"My nay Chan," says Chan, beaming.

◆　　　◆　　　◆

Buying a house was my idea. We'd lived in more rentals than I wanted to remember. Most of the moves happened because we'd come home and find an eviction notice nailed to the door.

The main thing for Mongrel was that there had to be an easy way to get from the outside to the living room. That was because in the cold months he liked to work on the Harley in the living room. And even with a tarp under the bike, the oil always ended up on the carpeting underneath. Then the landlord would drop around for a visit.

"You make too much noise," says the landlord.

"Oh yeah?" says Mongrel, towering over some little guy.

"What's that thing?"

"That *thing* is a Harley-Davidson, and a Harley-Davidson ain't no *thing*," says Mongrel, tapping his finger on the guy's chest.

"No bikes in the house," says the landlord. Then he sees the grease all over the furniture.

"No good. You're out!"

"Fuck you," says Mongrel.

"You leave now," says the landlord.

"You bet your sweet ass."

"You pay the back rent."

"Guess again, peckerhead," says Mongrel, practically slamming the door off its hinges.

Then we have to take the basement apart because Mongrel has all this stuff for growing down there. Halogen lamps and special wiring. Not to mention the plants, which are already three feet tall and stinking to high heaven. We have to move them all without meeting the Law. Plus the kids are upset. It was enough to drive me nuts.

It's me who finally talks him into buying a house.

"Honey, think about it."

"You got five minutes before the game starts, Mags, so make it good."

"Okay. You have your own basement to work on the bike anytime you want. You don't have to worry about some beige carpet."

"What about the crop?"

"Rent another place."

"It's expensive."

"We've got enough. And we're also not waking up in the middle of the night thinking we heard someone at the door."

"Good."

"And the kids get to feel settled. Stay at the same school for more than six months."

"Guilt? Good one, Mags! Anything else?"

"Yeah, it's ours. We don't have some asshole landlord walking up to our door telling us where we can and where we can't put the Harley."

"Sold to the gal with the cute smile. All right, Mags, I'll buy you a house. Now go get me a beer. The game's coming on."

Of course, I didn't say anything about how, if he was in an accident and got killed, I wanted something to fall back on.

◆　　　◆　　　◆

Johanna's suspicious. She doesn't say as much, but you can see it in the way she looks at us. She does little things, like appear out of nowhere when we're talking.

"I can smell her," says Stella.

"Smell like trouble," says Big Dee.

"Speak of the devil," I say.

"Well, well, ladies," says Johanna. "Why is it that every time I come up here, you're all heads together at this table? Call me suspicious, but I have this sneaking hunch that you're up to something."

"Damn," says Big Dee, "you catch us right in the middle of plannin' the great train robbery. Ain't that so, Stella?"

"Uh-huh," says Stella.

"Actually, Johanna, we heard your birthday was coming up, so we was planning a surprise party," says Darlene.

"My birthday, for your information, was at the beginning of September."

"I might have known she was a Virgo," says Darlene when Johanna's out of earshot. "You couldn't pull a needle out of her asshole with . . ."

"The jaws of life," says Sam.

◆　　◆　　◆

It's Big Dee who wants the name change. She says Last Resort sounds negative. She thinks we should be called the United Nations.

"Call us the United Nations," she says with a laugh. "We got every color in the rainbow."

"Plus lesbian, don't forget," says Sam.

"How about the Politically Correct Chain Gang?" I say.

A few chuckles.

"I like the Rainbow Warriors," says Stella.

"I already saw that somewhere," I say.

"Shit, too bad," says Stella.

"Look," says Sam, "We're the Freedom Anonymous group. That's good enough for me."

"All right," says Big Dee. "Just a thought."

◆　　◆　　◆

The first time I saw a black person, he was walking down a city sidewalk somewhere we were visiting on vacation. I couldn't stop looking at him. My mother had to yank me and tell me to stop staring.

◆　　◆　　◆

The hardest part was losing my best friend, Josie. At least for a while. It was my own fault. When Mongrel killed himself, I wasn't myself for a while. I guess I came unglued and Josie got the worst of it.

I just wanted someone to make it all better, to stop all the craziness. First Mongrel kills himself. Then they think I did it. It was way too much to handle without getting really stressed out.

Josie tried to help, but the more she did, the more I wanted. I didn't want just a friend. I wanted a mother who could kiss it better. And when I got taken in as a murder suspect, I completely lost it. I was so pissed off and crazy, I turned on her like a snake. I got to give her credit, though—she hung in for quite a while before she decided enough was enough. I used to say that she deserted me, but now, since I've had time to think about it, I guess I deserted myself.

◆　　　◆　　　◆

I miss Chrissie and Max.

I miss the smell of the forest after it rains.

I miss going outside on a sunny day.

I miss dropping by a friend's place for a beer.

I miss cooking and eating my own food.

I miss our dogs.

I miss sleeping in a soft bed with my own sheets. I miss walking to the store.

I miss my books.

I miss talking on the phone.

I miss my privacy.

I miss going to movies.

I miss riding my bicycle.

I miss door handles.

I miss working in the garden.

I miss the smell of a pie, fresh out of the oven.

I miss some of my clothes.

I miss being alone.

I miss the quiet.

I miss lying in bed on Sunday morning with my arms around my old man.

I miss Mongrel.

◆     ◆     ◆

I see Tony on Sunday. He's sitting in his office reading. I watch him from the door for a few minutes before he looks up. I didn't like him at first and I think he picked up on it. Maybe I was looking at him through Mongrel's eyes. Mongrel thought AA was for assholes. He called it Assholes Anonymous. For me, disagreeing with his likes and dislikes wasn't worth the trouble. If he didn't like AA, I didn't either. It made life easier.

Tony's actually kind of good-looking, if you see him from the right angle. He has nice eyes, kind of greeny blue or maybe just green. They change every time I see him. He looks right at you when you're talking and you get the feeling that he really is listening to what you're saying. Not just staring at you without a clue.

I didn't notice the first couple of times that he had a tattoo on his arm. Maybe it was up too high and his shirt covered it. It's a skull with a snake running through it. Not a bad job. Fairly small. If my father had seen it, he'd have written Tony off, though.

He has a nice voice, kind of husky, like he's smoked too many cigarettes or too much dope for too long. I've always been attracted to certain voices. Mongrel had a soft voice for such a tough-looking guy. Whenever Chrissie or Max fell and hurt themselves, he had a way of talking to them that made everything better. There were times when I was so unhappy he'd come over to where I was sitting and he'd pick me up and carry me to the big window in the living room that looked out onto the bay.

"See, Mags, look at that pretty picture."

"I'm not in the mood to be happy, Mongrel."

"I know you're not, but baby, you're bringing down the whole house."

"I'm not doing it on purpose."

"Well, I'm starting to wear out on it, babe."

"Mongrel, why am I so unhappy sometimes?"

"I don't know, Mags. I bought you this nice house. I gave you two kids. You got an old man who takes good care of you."

"It's not that."

"Well then, what is it?"

"I don't know, Mongrel. If I knew, I wouldn't be like this."

◆　　◆　　◆

"Hey, Margaret." He looks up.

"Hey, Tony," I say.

"You been standing there long?"

"A few minutes."

"Did you want to talk to me about something?" he says.

"Well . . ."

"What is it?" he asks.

"I don't know."

"Something's bothering you?"

"Lots is bothering me. I'm in prison."

"But that's not what it's about."

"No."

"Are we playing twenty questions?" He smiles.

"Look, I'm sorry about how I've been, all right?"

Tony just looks at me. I hate dead air.

"I mean, I don't know why I was the way I was. It wasn't your fault. I just took it out on you."

"It's all right, Margaret. You've been going through a lot. It's your first year. I cut you some slack."

"Anyway, the other gals really like you. Well, except for Sam, but that's only because you're a guy."

Tony smiles at that.

More dead air.

"I like you, too," I say.

◆       ◆       ◆

"What you so happy about?" says Big Dee.

"Me?" I say.

"No, Maggie, not you," she says, "that person sitting just behind you on that bunk. Of course I'm talkin' to you. Who else I gonna talk to unless to myself?"

"I don't know. I'm just feeling good."

"Hmmm," says Big Dee.

"Maybe it's because I did that fourth step and got all that stuff off my chest. There's something about writing stuff down that really helps. I mean, you feel lighter. Then I did my fifth with Tony," I say.

"Hmmm."

"Or maybe it's because I really believe we're going to get out of here," I say.

"Hmmm."

"Or maybe I'm just having a good day," I say.

"Hmmm," says Big Dee, looking at me suspiciously. "It seem to me that every time you come back from Mr. Tony's office, you jumpin' around like a cat on a hot stove."

"Don't be ridiculous," I say.

"Then how come you got a shiny red face?" she says.

"Maybe hot flashes," I say.

"More like hot pants," she says.

◆　　　◆　　　◆

The seventh meeting of Freedom Anonymous meets in the usual place. Two of the gals are missing.

"Where's Stella?" I say.

"She's in seg," says Sam.

"Stella's in segregation? What the hell did she do?"

"She took a swing at Johanna," says Darlene.

"You're shittin' me."

"Wish I was," says Sam.

"How long's she in for?"

"At least a couple of days."

"What about Chan?" I say.

"She's in seg, too," says Darlene.

"No!" I say.

"Yeah, it seems that Johanna tried to restrain Stella, which is no small job, you know, if you've ever seen Stella in a brawl. I heard she took on the cops one time when she was three sheets to the wind and it took ten of them to keep her down. Anyways, Chan don't know what's going on except her buddy's getting held, so she comes flying at Johanna, swinging like a monkey. Johanna had them both thrown in," says Sam.

"Shit," I say.

"Yeah, well, you know," says Darlene.

"Anyways, we got a meeting to run, so I guess we run it without Stella," says Sam.

## STEP SEVEN
# HUMBLY ASKED HIM TO REMOVE OUR SHORT-COMINGS.

"That's a good one for you, Sam," says Darlene.

"Which part—the humbly or the shortcomings?" says Sam.

"Take your pick," says Darlene.

"All right, you two," says Big Dee. "How I see it, what we humbly need to do is ask him to remove all the stuff in our way so's we can excape."

"Right on," says Darlene.

"You don't think it's going to be a bit tricky for us, seeing as how we're a group of five. Especially with Big Dee," I say.

"What about me?" says Big Dee.

"Well, for one, there's not many six-foot-tall giant black women in this part of the world," I say.

"So?" says Big Dee.

"So, that's something we have to think about when we're doing our planning," I say.

"We could dress you like a guy, you know?" says Darlene.

"Sure," says Sam. "They'll be looking for five women, and Big Dee and I could be guys."

"Except you already look like a guy," says Darlene. "You don't think the police would be smart enough to get a description, do you? You'd be better off in a dress."

"No way," says Sam.

"It's just for the escape, you know," says Darlene.

"Hey, Sam, I bet you'd look real cute in a little sundress," I say, giving Big Dee a wink.

"In your dreams," says Sam.

◆　　　◆　　　◆

I wake up from a dream about fudge. I can almost taste it. I remember my mother making it in the winter. I got to scrape out the pot. The fudge was still warm. I'd end up with it all over my hands and my face. We got the recipe from the label on the can of evaporated milk.

## YUMMY FIVE-MINUTE FUDGE

2/3 cup evaporated milk
1-2/3 cups sugar
1-1/2 cups miniature marshmallows
1-1/2 cups semi-sweet chocolate chips
1/2 cup chopped walnuts (optional)
1 teaspoon vanilla

Put milk and sugar into saucepan on low heat. Bring to a boil. Cook 5 minutes, stirring all the time.

Remove from heat. Add marshmallows, nuts, chocolate chips, and vanilla. Stir with a wooden spoon until chocolate and marshmallows have completely melted.

Pour into a buttered pan. When cool, cut into squares. (I mark the squares while the fudge is still warm. Then, when it's cold, the squares are easier to cut.)

◆　　◆　　◆

### ACTOR: MAN OF WANDS

You have to hide your real face when you're in prison. You pretend one thing on the outside and feel something else on the inside. If you don't play the role, you spend a lot of time in segregation.

The top part of the card looks like lightning. There's a Japanese actor with a white face and tiny lips. An African mask. The sword fighter's face is hidden. You can only see a shadow.

Actors change their faces, hiding everything. We all do it. We're like eagles, flying high on what might happen, but always looking down for the slightest movement.

The five of us are actors now. We pass the time and plan the steps we have to take. We go over and over the details, looking for possible trip-ups—where we might go wrong. It's not a game anymore. The stakes are too high. The roles are tricky and they keep changing.

To the people who walk around us and see us every day, we show a wooden face, smiling, as if nothing's happening. But don't look too closely at any of our hands because they might be shaking. The tarot says it's the trembling hand that holds the mask in place.

◆　　　◆　　　◆

"A Harley-Davidson is a piece of living, moving art," says Sam.

"God, sometimes you sound like Mongrel," I say.

Sometimes she does sound like Mongrel, although I don't think I ever remember him using the word art. He didn't know much about it. He thought it was for decoration, which was women's work. He left that up to me. The only time he ever actually bought any was when we took a trip down to Mexico.

Mongrel would never leave the bike alone for one minute during the trip. He said he'd put money on the fact that the Mexicans would have it stripped down and all the parts sold before we had time to finish our tamales.

He would only stay in ground floor adobes where he could keep the bike inside. He paid a kid to watch the bike when we went to the beach, telling him that if anything—and that meant anything at all—happened to his Harley-Davidson, the kid wouldn't have any *huevos* when he grew up. This was all done with sign language, with Mongrel making these hacking actions around the area of the poor kid's balls.

He'd hand the kid a few hundred pesos. Then, when we got a few feet away, he'd turn around and grab his crotch, just to make sure the kid got the point.

We took turns shopping. Mongrel liked big silver pieces inlaid with coral and turquoise—dealers' stones. One time he came out with this huge thing wrapped in brown paper. I asked him what it was and all he'd say was that it was a major score. He didn't want to let me look at it until we got back to where we were staying. I'm holding onto him with one hand, bouncing down these potholed streets on the bike, and trying to hold onto the package with the other. He makes me promise not to look until he has it set up in the main room.

"All right, Mags," he says. "Come on in."

Sitting up on top of the table, blinking like a Christmas tree, is this black velvet painting of a biker chick with huge tits sitting nude on a Harley. The painting comes with a battery, so the woman's nipples flicker. Red. On and off. I have to wonder how many days I'll be able to stand watching the damn thing before I start kicking the dog around or yelling at the kids. It's really irritating. On. Off. On. Off.

"What do you think?" He beams.

I don't want to spoil a great vacation. But I'm thinking maybe I missed something about Mongrel. I mean, I thought I had him pretty well figured out. It's not like he had great taste or anything, but I'd never seen him go this low before.

"It's interesting, I guess," I say.

"You don't like it?" he says.

"I didn't say that. I just . . ."

"Look, Mags, tell me the truth. If you don't like it, you don't like it."

"All right, Mongrel," I say, "I'll tell you the truth. I don't like it. I think it's a piece of trash."

"Good," he says. "That's what I wanted to hear, 'cause I'm going to give this piece of shit to that sonofabitch Carl who fucked me on that dope deal. I'll tell him it's a peace offering. I can't wait to see his weaselly little face when he sees it. Ha, ha."

◆　　◆　　◆

You do learn patience in prison. You have to. Everything that should take two days takes weeks. If you need something right away, it comes later. I sometimes wonder if it's part of the punishment—the waiting, the red tape, all the paperwork it takes and the forms you have to fill out just to get something really simple. Like books.

I'm trying to bring some better books into the library, some of the ones I read when I took that reading appreciation course. I'm trying to get in contact with Doug, the teacher I had. He said he'd help me. He knew a lot of good books.

Right now, I could kill for a really good book. Maybe it's because I need an escape from the tension. Something to take my mind off the escape. You get inside a book and you get outside your own head for a while.

My mind is giving me the most trouble. One day it seems to be all right, and I can see the world and my life as making some kind of sense. And then, no warning or anything, I wake up shaking and I wonder how the hell I got here. That's when nothing makes sense and I feel like I'm way in over my head.

I dream of flying. I'm running away from someone or something. My heart is beating a mile a minute. I can feel whatever it is closing in on me. I feel the panic gripping my chest. My legs get heavy. I don't know if I can make it. I don't know where I'm going. But I keep moving until I come to the edge of a cliff.

If whatever it is catches me, it's death for sure. I know it. I look down and know that, if I jump, it's also death. There's no time to think. I decide to hell with it, and I jump. As I raise my arms to throw myself off, I'm lifted up. I have wings. I can fly.

◆    ◆    ◆

Stella got out of seg this morning. I can hear her pacing around her cell. She was smudging with sage earlier, trying to get rid of the bad energy and her anger. I stand outside her cell.

"You all right, Stell?" I ask.

"Not so good," she says.

"You want some company?" I say.

"I'm pretty bad company right now," she says.

"I don't mind."

"Okay. Come in," she says. I light a smoke and hold the pack out to Stella. She takes one and I light it. She takes a drag and blows the smoke at the ceiling.

"I'm sorry, Stella."

"You didn't do nothing."

"I know. I'm just sorry you're feeling shitty."

"I'll be okay," she says.

"I had a dream last night," I say.

"Oh yeah?"

"I dreamed I was a bird. I got away."

"Hmmm. Good dream."

"It felt so great," I say. "You know how it is in a dream when you fly? There's a part of you that knows you can't do this, but you're doing it anyway. I love that feeling."

"You remember what direction you fly?" she says.

"I don't know. Well, hold on. Yeah, I must have been flying south because of the position of the sun."

"On the medicine wheel, south is the place of the heart—of feelings for others, great passion and love. But it's not the love you have for a brother or a child—it's romantic love."

"Not much chance of that happening in here," I say.

"Maybe not. Maybe so. Anyways, whatever it is, you gotta learn to control your feelings. You gotta be careful not to fall in love too easily. The elders say that, even with love, you got to be disciplined. You know what I mean? Don't lose your head."

"Over a piece of tail," I say.

"Ha, ha. Pretty funny," says Stella.

"Were you all right in seg?"

"I was all right. Not at first, maybe. I was real mad. But later on, yeah, when I got quiet—you know, quiet in my body. I stopped pacing back and forth. And then I got quiet in my head. Stopped the fighting. And then I put a picture of an eagle inside my head and I breathed. I looked at the eagle and I breathed."

"Funny how we both saw birds."

"Hmmm," says Stella.

"You didn't get lonely?"

"Sure, but sometimes it's good to be alone for a few days. I took some time to go inside. I looked at some things I don't like much. Stuff inside me I don't like to admit. I got a big problem with booze, eh?"

"Yeah, I know. I'm sorry."

"Not your fault," she says.

"I don't mean it like that. Well, maybe I do. If it hadn't been for us, you'd probably never have a problem with booze."

"Can't change history," she says.

"I guess not. Can't even seem to learn from it," I say.

◆　　　◆　　　◆

Johanna's been real quiet lately. Makes me think she's up to something. I wait until Jim's on shift.

"Hey, Jim," I say.

"Yo, Maggie," he says.

"What's with Johanna? She's been real quiet lately. Anything up?"

"Well, just between you, me, and the fence post, she thinks you guys are up to something. She was trying to get your unit bust up. Send one or two of you over to some other unit. That's what I heard, anyway."

"What have we done?" I say.

"Beats me," he says. "She says you all go quiet whenever she comes around. When inmates go quiet all the time, they're up to something. She got that out of some report she's reading."

"We go quiet because we can't stand her. And she knows it. She couldn't really break us up, could she?"

"I don't think so, Maggie. Hey, don't worry. Johanna's always seeing shit that ain't there. It's her nature. She's done it before."

"Broken up units?"

"Tried to," he says.

"And?"

"No luck so far," says Jim.

"Do you think we're acting suspicious?" I ask.

"Not on my shift," he says.

"I mean, what could we be doing, anyway? Except maybe planning to murder her. Only problem would be where to dump the body."

"I could help with that," says Jim.

◆　　◆　　◆

Stella calls me into her cell. She pulls me toward her and speaks in a whisper.

"She's faking," says Stella.

"Who is?" I say.

"Chan."

"What do you mean?"

"She talk in her sleep last night."

"Chan?"

"Yeah, of course. Who you think I'm talking about?"

"Well, Stella, lots of people talk in their sleep," I say.

"Yeah, but she talk English," says Stella.

"You're shittin' me."

"Nope," says Stella.

"What did she say?"

"She said lots of things. About the drugs. Telling them to leave her alone—not to hurt her. She was speaking some Chinese, too. But mostly English."

"Fuck," I say.

"What're we gonna do, eh?" says Stella.

"We got a meeting tonight. I'll talk to the others first."

"Okay," says Stella.

◆　　◆　　◆

"I told you. I told you we shouldn't trust her. I never trust no China-man. They always up to sneaky stuff."

"Oh, for chrissake, Big Dee," I say.

"That's the truth. She lie and she been at the meetings. She can speak English. That mean she knows what we doing. The rest of us all in this together. Not her. We don't know nothin' about her. Could be a plant. Maybe she talkin' to Johanna. How we suppose to know?"

"No way she's talking to Johanna."

"What do you know? You all say she just fine, but I say no, and you tell me she just off the boat."

"Well, we were wrong. Now we got us a problem. What are we going to do about it? That's the question."

"We boil her like they do that damn chicken. One less Chinese in this world ain't gonna make no difference."

"Jesus, Big Dee!"

"Fine for you, Maggie. You white. Chinese treat you okay mostly. You ever see how they look at us blacks? They think we all just some kind of animals—maybe one step above apes or something. They don't treat us like no equal. Only people worse than whites is yellow, far as I'm concern."

◆　　　◆　　　◆

We're all in the meeting room when Stella arrives with Chan.

"Hey, Stella," says everyone.

"Hey," says Stella.

"Hey, Chan." Everyone's looking at her. No one's smiling.

"My nay Chan," says Chan, smiling brightly.

"Your name Trouble," says Big Dee.

Chan doesn't blink. Everyone keeps staring at her. Finally, Sam stands up and walks over in front of her.

"So, Chan," she says, "you can cut the crap because we all know you speak English."

Chan looks up at Sam with a smile on her face.

"And wipe that fucking smile off your sneaky little face before I wipe it off for you. You was talkin' in your sleep last night, honey. Stella heard you. You was talkin' English. Savvy?"

Chan's eyes drop. She puts her hands up in front of her face, like she's going to get hit or something.

"Shit, I ain't gonna hit you," says Sam. "What the hell am I supposed to do here?" She looks around at the rest of us.

"I don't say nothing," says Chan.

"You never talked to Johanna?"

"No, never."

"You sure?"

Chan nods her head up and down. She's shaking.

"Okay, well, we don't have a hell of a lot of choice, unless we put a pillow over your head when you're sleeping. See, you know something you're not supposed to know. Either we get rid of you or you come in with us. We been workin' real hard on this plan and we don't need no fuck-ups right now. Got it?"

"I'm not rat," says Chan.

"Could've fool me," says Big Dee.

"No, I'm not. I promise. I don't say anything," says Chan.

"Now that make me feel just fine," says Big Dee. "You promise? How I suppose to know you not lyin'?"

"No, not lying," says Chan.

"You already did," says Darlene. "You been conning us for the past two weeks."

"I'm afraid," says Chan.

"Of who?" I say.

"Maybe you kill me," says Chan.

"Maybe we still do," says Big Dee.

"No, I go with you. I can help, too."

"How?" says Stella.

"I make ID," says Chan.

"What do you mean?" says Sam.

"I make phony paper for everybody," says Chan.

"You know how?" asks Darlene.

"I specialize," says Chan.

◆     ◆     ◆

Within forty-eight hours, Chan has a driver's licence for Stella, photograph and all.

"How the hell did you do it?" says Sam.

"Not so hard," says Chan. "I go to school yesterday morning. I know my teacher, Judy, always put her purse in file cabinet. When she go to the bathroom, I sneak in and take the card. Then I wait for Stella. When she go out, I take her photographs. Sorry, cut up a nice one."

"It's all right," says Stella, shaking her head as she looks at the ID.

"Now you let me come with you?" says Chan, smiling.

"Well, it's nice work," says Sam. "But you can't steal any more ID in here or someone's gonna get suspicious."

"No problem. I have connection. They can bring me cards from outside. I just steal to show you. Now you believe me. I specialize."

◆     ◆     ◆

"I told you they was sneaky," says Big Dee, as we go back into our cell for lock-up.

"She's a gold mine," I say.

"Yellow gold," says Big Dee.

◆     ◆     ◆

## STEP EIGHT
MADE A LIST OF ALL PERSONS WE WERE ABOUT TO HARM WHEN ESCAPING, AND BECAME WILL-ING TO MAKE AMENDS TO THEM ALL.

I hate saying I'm sorry. It makes me feel like I made a mistake and the other person is getting off scot-free. I wouldn't mind saying I was sorry if I thought the other person would, too.

What happens when you say you're sorry is the other person just says all right, even if they had as much to do with the problem as you did. So, you end up going away pissed off and sorry that you ever said a damn thing.

Take for instance this thing with Johanna. Maybe I'm partly to blame for it. I know she was a bitch, but maybe I was, too. Maybe I always looked at her like she was a bitch and she knew I was looking at her that way, so she got pissed off because she doesn't like being looked at that way. But still, she *is* a bitch.

So, I just don't get how that's my fault. How come I have to be the one who says I'm sorry? And what if, say, I *do* go up to her and make amends, and she just laughs in my face. Then I really get to feel like an asshole.

◆     ◆     ◆

"I don't buy this Step Eight. I mean, there must be special cases," I say.

"The step says all persons, Margaret," says Tony. "We're willing to make amends to *all* persons we have harmed."

"Yeah, except who harmed who here? She harmed me. What the hell did I do?"

"I don't know. But I do know it takes two to create a conflict."

"Whose side are you on, anyway?"

"It's not about sides, Margaret. It's about conflict."

"That woman's a bitch of the first order. I'm not making any fucking amends to her."

"Nobody said you had to. Or at least not now. Why don't you wait until you've cooled down a bit?"

"I don't need to cool down. She shouldn't be working here. She fucks with the inmates. And you know it. You just sit there, letting it happen. That makes you part of the problem."

"You know that's not true."

"Well, I just don't like where you're at."

"How come we got here? I don't have a problem with you, and you don't have one with me. I don't know what to tell you. You two have an issue. It needs to be resolved. But the truth is, she's got the power."

"It's not fair."

"No, it's not. But hey, Margaret, life isn't fair."

"I hate it in here."

"I know. It's not a good place."

"I want to go home."

"Come here," he says. He takes my hand. His hand's warm. "I can't fix anything. All I can do is hear you out. You're pushing too hard right now. You need to back off a little. Take some time. It won't always feel like this. It won't, Margaret. Trust me."

I'm looking at his mouth when he's talking. I've never really looked at it before. I don't really hear what he's saying. I just know I want him. I want him to hold me. I want him to kiss me.

"I want you to kiss me," I say.

He stops talking but he keeps holding my hand.

"I can't do that," he says.

"Yes, you can," I say.

I lean over and kiss him softly. He doesn't pull away. I can feel his breathing change. My tongue touches his upper lip. Then I feel his tongue touch mine.

"Margaret, I can't do this."

"You're doing it," I say.

"But I shouldn't," he says, taking my head in his hands and kissing me again.

◆　　◆　　◆

"Your hair a mess and your lipstick all over your face," says Big Dee.

"You got too much imagination and not enough to do with it," I say, wiping my mouth on my sleeve.

"How dumb you think I is?" says Big Dee.

"I don't know. How dumb is you?"

"Don't fuck with me, Maggie," she says.

"I ain't fucking with you, Big Dee."

"How come you avoidin' the subject?"

"Because I don't like it."

"I'll bet," she says.

I start shuffling my cards. I can feel her eyes on me. She does this little humming before she starts to sing to herself, loud enough for me to hear.

"You must remember this, A kiss is just a kiss," she croons.

"Fuck off, Big Dee."

"Just singing," she says.

"Well, I never heard you sing that song before, and I've heard most of your songs at least a hundred times," I say.

"You know, Maggie the Cat, what you doin' ain't too smart. What I know is that when you get yourself tied up with a man, you ain't thinkin' straight no more. You start thinkin' with your pussy and it be a long way from your brain. You know what I sayin'?"

"So, what's your point, Big Dee? You think—even if it is true, which it ain't—that me having a little fun on the side is going to get in the way of our escape? Huh? You think some guy is more important to me than freedom?"

"Maybe not right now," says Big Dee, "but you let it get bigger and then you get yourself caught between two things. And then it gets hard. I know what I's talkin' about."

"Yeah, yeah," I say.

"You mark my words," says Big Dee.

◆     ◆     ◆

You never know
When love is going to catch you
Right in the middle of nowhere
With your pants down
And your lipstick off
Your soul somewheres
Back there
Off guard
Dreaming of the real thing
With wet kisses
And hot nights
As sweet as magnolia
That's love.

◆　　◆　　◆

## THREE OF CUPS: LOVE

This card doesn't look like love to me. But then, when I look at all the parts of it, it makes sense. The background looks like crashing waves—like a storm. And love can be stormy, all right. Then there's a vase with flowers pouring out of it. And some roses in the center. There's a blue fish on the card. I don't think of love when I look at fish. This one looks like a tropical fish—a guppy.

We used to have a tank full of them. One of Mongrel's crazy projects—collecting tropical fish. One time he had this angel fish. It was huge. It used to bully all the other fish. It even ate some of them. One time Mongrel caught it eating a bunch of newborn guppies. He got so mad at that angel fish, he reached right into the aquarium, yanked it out, and threw it out the window. There was snow on the ground. That fish was worth a fortune.

Anyway, love is tricky. You give yourself or you give up yourself. Love makes you fly like a bird or it holds you tight, just like shackles. It can make you howl at the moon or race crazy to the edge of a cliff and throw yourself off. The first moments of love are, plain and simple, nuts.

◆　　◆　　◆

Mongrel said he fell in love with me at first sight. He said it saved a lot of time. I didn't really love him at first. I liked the attention, though. He moved in a cloud of noise. Loud pipes. A fat bike. Roaring in, then roaring out again. And he talked loud. And when he made love to me, he roared like an animal when he came.

When we were married, it was always noisy. The television blaring. The stereo full blast. His friends shouting at each other, even when they were standing right close to each other. I used to wonder if they all had hearing problems from years of riding Harleys.

"Why do you guys always yell at each other?" I ask.

"We ain't yelling. We're talking."

"Well, how come you have to talk so loud?"

"Because we're guys," says Mongrel.

"But why?"

"What the fuck does it matter why?"

"I'm just curious."

"When I stop taking good care of you, then you can start bitching about stuff like how loud I talk. In the meantime, don't worry your sweet ass about how come guys talk too loud. We're different. We got dicks. Don't try to figure it out. You'll just give yourself a headache. Come here," he says.

"I'm not in the mood," I say.

"I know just how to fix that," he says.

◆　　◆　　◆

Mongrel said I gave the best damn blow jobs in the universe. I took it as a compliment. Of course, I did wonder how he'd know that unless he was getting them somewhere else and they weren't as good. But I let it slide. Besides, I liked doing it. Not all women do, I guess. Even some of my friends, other biker chicks, would talk about it like it was some kind of major chore they only did on special occasions, like their old man's birthday or if he bought them something.

I thought it had something to do with trust—I mean, it's a pretty touchy position for a guy if you consider how much damage you could do with one good chomp. Anyways, I liked Mongrel's cock. It had a nice shape. It wasn't too big, but then I never was a size queen.

◆　　◆　　◆

Stella has a visit from Wilson Featherstone, one of the guys on the rez. He's our main connection for the escape. He's going to be doing the driving after we get across the water. He came up with this plan for us to get to the other side in these inflatable kayaks.

"Inflatable *kayaks?*" says Big Dee. "You pullin' on my fat leg. I don't even know how I gets into one, let alone haul my ass across the water."

"It's easy," says Stella. "Same as canoe, eh?"

"Now, that make me feel a whole lot better," says Big Dee. "'Cause I'm sure you seen lots of photographs in them history books of us blacks paddling canoes. I'm from the South. Closest thing I know to a boat be a raft, which is pretty near impossible to tip over—not that I ever be on one."

"Don't worry," says Sam, "we'll help you."

"This is real nice," says Big Dee. "Now I know that instead of wasting ten years of my life in this prison, I'm going to die by drownding in a blow-up canoe."

"Kayak," says Stella.

"Like I know the difference?" says Big Dee.

"I can draw you a picture," says Stella, and she draws this picture. "See?" she says.

"That a kayak?" says Big Dee.

"Yup," says Stella.

"You think I'm going to put myself in that little thing, you out of your mind, and that's the truth," she says.

"It's perfectly safe," I say, "or they wouldn't be able to sell them."

"Oh sure. They sell guns, don't they?" says Big Dee.

◆　　◆　　◆

## STEP NINE

MADE DIRECT AMENDS TO SUCH PEOPLE YOU MESSED UP WHEN YOU ESCAPED FROM PRISON, EXCEPT WHEN TO DO SO WOULD INJURE THEM OR OTHERS EVEN MORE.

"Pride goes before a fall," says Big Dee.

"If your pride goes, you fall is more like it," I say.

"Twistin' it don't make it right."

"Easy for you to say."

"Only easy 'cause it ain't my ass in the sling," she says.

"I told myself, if you're going to do this, you have to make amends to one of the big ones first. I can't make amends to Mongrel, because he's dead. And Max won't have anything to do with me. He won't answer my letters. I tried to call him the other day—he hung up. And the rest are kinda small potatoes. So I guess it's Johanna, right?"

"It's your life."

"What if she just laughs?"

"She do what she do, Maggie. That ain't your problem."

"What is my problem?"

"Pride."

"Oh, please."

"Look, Maggie, you want to say you sorry, then you go right ahead. You don't want to, then don't. It just fine by me, no matter what you do. But you drivin' yourself crazy doing all this should I, shouldn't I. And pretty soon you drive me crazy, too. Either do it or don't do it, but stop talking about it. You givin' me some kind of headache."

◆    ◆    ◆

My pride got me into a lot of trouble. Even when it was completely clear that I was in the wrong, I'd hang on. I hated being made to feel humble. I never said I was sorry. I wasn't built that way. Mongrel never said it either. He said that sorry wasn't in his dictionary, except when someone fucked him over. Then they were going to be some sorry asshole or he'd never sleep again.

One time, this other grower gave him what were supposed to be primo seeds—the best of the best. Mongrel came home with a matchbox full and tales of how we would have to get an account in a Swiss bank—not that he ever put his money in a bank. After wasting half a season babying these plants, they turned out to be not worth a pile of bleached rat shit, as he put it.

Three years later, when everyone had forgotten the story, Mongrel put the word out that he'd got hold of these exotic black opium poppy seeds. He said he'd slid them by customs on some trip from Thailand.

The same guy who fucked Mongrel over was practically willing to sacrifice his first born to get a flat of them, and it was no gift— he paid top dollar. It took at least a couple of months before he realized that he'd got a back acre full of stinging nettles. Mongrel loved that story.

❦    ❦    ❦

Stella says that there's nothing but a lot of false pride in the world today—that for pride to work, it has to be balanced with the same amount of humility. She says that the chiefs in the old days worked to keep that balance.

"You see it in their faces, in their eyes. You look at them old photographs, eh? They don't look down."

"I thought looking down was a sign of humility," I say.

"Nope. Their eyes look straight ahead. Following a vision. That's what a chief was like, Maggie, back before things got all screwed up."

"By us, is that what you're saying?"

"Well, it's true. Always someone come from somewheres and take what belongs to the people who been there for a long time. That don't ever change."

"You believe in karma?" I ask.

"Maybe. Sometimes I do. It depends on how you're using it, eh."

"How I see it, it's like if you do something bad, then something bad happens to you. You steal—someone steals from you. You beat on dogs this lifetime, maybe you get to come back as a dog in your next lifetime. Then you get beat on."

"I don't believe that. Us Indians didn't do nothing wrong as far as I can see. We maybe did some things bad but not so's we deserve what happened to our people. We'd have to be real evil to get something as bad as the whiteman."

"That's a bit heavy, Stella."

"Maybe. You know, the medicine wheel works with the shape of a circle and the thought of many cycles. What comes around, goes around."

"I guess we'll get ours then, right?"

"I guess you will."

◆　　　◆　　　◆

The medicine wheel says the nearer you get to a goal, the more difficult the journey becomes. You have to be able to hang in there, even when it's hard and painful. Actually, the hard and painful times are when you really need to keep going. Thunder and lightning come from the West, the home of the Thunder Beings— the bringers of power. Like the power to heal and the power to see and know.

◆　　◆　　◆

Sam brings an atlas from the library to the next meeting.

"We gotta see where we're going. It's just too up in the air for me. Now, where we going to go first?"

Stella leans over and puts her finger on the map.

"Okay. We go right off first thing to the reserve up at Mount Currie. Take the Duffy Lake road," she says.

"I thought it was closed in the winter," says Sam.

"Only if there's avalanches," says Stella.

"Avalanches?" says Big Dee. You can see the whites of her eyes.

"Not always," says Stella.

"That real good," says Big Dee, shaking her head. "But what if there is one?"

"We use snowmobiles," says Stella.

"Kayaks and then snowmobiles?" says Big Dee. "Uh-huh. Sure."

"Maybe not snowmobiles," says Stella.

"I don't like the idea of coming back down through the city before we cross the border," says Darlene.

"We don't need to," says Sam. "Look, we go east, cut down through Manning Park. It's great in the winter."

"Mongrel and I took the kids there one winter," I say. "Great skiing."

"Oh, now we be skiing?" says Big Dee.

"I like to see snow," says Chan.

"I prefer to see palm trees," says Big Dee.

"Where are we going to cross over?" says Darlene.

"I think right here," says Sam. "Small border crossing. Easier to get through. I got some biker friends, live near Twisp. We can stay there for a few nights."

"All six of us?" says Darlene.

"They're bikers," I say.

◆　　◆　　◆

Johanna came by our unit this afternoon. I did my best to smile. My face felt like it was made out of cement. She looked at me real strange. Stella just sat there shaking her head and smiling. I glared at her.

"What's so fucking funny?" I say.

"Only people I know who can smile with their mouth and hate with their eyes is the whiteman," she says.

"That's a load of crap!"

"It's true, Maggie. You just can't see it."

"Yeah, well, while you're busy putting down the whiteman, he's paying your rent."

"Sure, after he steals our land," she says.

"I didn't steal your goddam land, Stella. I wasn't even here when the Indians pissed away their land or however it happened. And I sure as hell can't go back and fix the stuff I never did. It's like my old man killing himself—I can't go back and fix that either. Besides, all this shit happened a long time ago," I say.

"Doesn't seem so long for us," says Stella.

"Well, it's getting stale," I say.

"Still pretty fresh for me," says Stella.

"You know, Stella, we're not gonna make it out of here unless we all work together on it. We won't do what it takes if we hate each other."

"I don't hate you, Maggie," says Stella.

"Could've fooled me."

"I just hate white people sometimes," she says.

"Well, the last time I looked, that's what color I was."

◆　　　◆　　　◆

There's a power blow-out at noon. It's off for a full two hours. Something must have gone wrong with the back-up. The doors have to be keyed. The guards are nervous. They lock all of us in our cells. It's so quiet. There are no generators. No announcements over the loudspeakers. No doors clanging shut. No buzz from the lights. No hum from the ventilation system, which never stops making noise all day and all night. And it's dark. It feels like heaven.

"Big Dee?"

"Uh-huh?"

"It's so quiet."

"Uh-huh," she says.

We sit in the silence. I think about how I've got so used to all that noise all the time. It makes me wonder what other things I'm getting used to. Maybe this is part of what one of the counselors talked about—becoming institutionalized? That's what she called it. You get so used to everything that you can't deal with the outside world anymore. I wonder if that's what is happening to Big Dee?

"Maggie?"

"Yeah, Big Dee?"

"Where are you?"

"I'm right here."

"Could you come over here?"

"Sure," I say, feeling my way in the dark.

Big Dee is curled up in the corner of her bunk. She reaches out and her hand finds me. She's shaking all over.

"What's the matter, Big Dee?" I say.

"Nothin'," she says.

"You're shaking like a leaf."

I put my arm around her broad shoulder. I can hear her breathing— shallow.

"It's all right," I say. "It won't last forever, Big Dee. It's just a power failure. Come on, now, you take a deep breath and relax."

Big Dee swallows. I put my hand on her cheek. It's wet.

"You're crying. You don't like the dark, do you?"

"I'm afraid of it, Maggie."

"Don't be afraid, I'm right here."

"You won't leave me?"

"No, I won't."

◆    ◆    ◆

"Maybe it's a sign from our higher power," says Sam.

The power failure has taken on a life of its own. It adds a new wrinkle to the escape plan. What if we could create a power failure—during the open house? The timing would have to be perfect.

"But how could we cause a power failure?" says Darlene.

"We can't," says Sam.

"So why we talkin' about it?" says Big Dee.

"Because we get someone on the outside to cause it," says Sam.

"This is getting way too complicated," I say.

"What did you think an escape was going to be, Maggie—a laydown? We just slip out the back door and scoot? Of course it's complicated." says Sam.

"Simple's sometimes better, eh," says Stella.

"Yeah, well, guns worked better'n bows and arrows, at least for winning the West," says Sam.

"War ain't over yet," says Stella, looking Sam dead in the eye.

◆        ◆        ◆

I've been going regularly for special counseling with Tony. Very special. I barely get in the door before I've got his shirt halfway unbuttoned. There's something real exciting about sneaky sex. I can't wait to get him on the floor. Partway through, I get this thought.

"You ever done this before?" I ask.

"Huh?" Tony stops moving. His eyes focus. "What do you mean, Margaret? You were here three days ago."

"I don't mean with me."

"Whoa. Where are you going?"

"I'm just curious. I want to know. Am I the only inmate you've ever screwed?"

"Well, now that I'm completely out of the mood . . . I can't believe you're asking me that question. What do you take me for?"

"I'm just asking."

"You're just asking me if I screw around. Basically, you want to know if I'm a pig. How many inmates do I fuck each week? Is that what you want to know?"

"Hey, I didn't want to think I was just, you know, one in a string."

"One in a string? I've never done this before. I shouldn't be doing it now. It's against all the rules. It's against my own personal rules, too. I'd lose my job in a heartbeat if anyone found out."

"Does Johanna know?"

"Of course not. But she suspects something. I don't know what she thinks."

"Is that why she rides my ass all the time?"

"I don't know, Margaret."

"Well, I don't know either," I say.

"Look, you make it sound as if this is part of my job. Don't you know how difficult this is for me?"

"What about me?"

"All right, it's hard on both of us. This isn't a perfect situation. Having to make love on the floor isn't my idea of comfort. But it's all we've got right now."

"It's all we've got, period. I'm probably not getting out of here for at least ten years. You really think you can keep this going for that long?" I say.

"I can't see that far down the road."

"I can. Maybe you're just not in for the long haul."

◆　　◆　　◆

I dreamed about Mongrel. It must have been before the accident because he wasn't limping. I was baking something. He came up the stairs with one of his guns in his hand. It wasn't unusual—he was always cleaning them. He put the gun on the counter and he came over and kissed me. He sat down at the kitchen table and lit a joint. Then he told me that he'd met someone else the last time he went out on the road.

He described her in full detail. I could feel my stomach tightening into a knot. He talked about her as though I was just some casual acquaintance—as though I wouldn't feel anything. I turned around to hide my face and I saw the gun sitting there. I walked over to it and picked it up. I looked at it like it was something I'd never seen before. It was heavy. I had to hold it with both hands.

I slowly swung it around until it was pointing directly at his chest. He laughed and said I would never be able to do it because I loved him too much. I told him it wasn't true, that in fact I'd never loved him and that I was in love with his best friend. His face went dark and he started to get out of the chair. I knew if I didn't kill him he would kill me. So I pulled the trigger.

◆　　◆　　◆

## XII: HANGED MAN

Circles repeat themselves. Water spins in a circular motion, looking like the inside of a tornado. In the upper corner a bird's neck, long and thin, forms another circle. A pair of hands enclose the reflection of a woman's face. And the red flower is reflected in the water, too. Things I don't understand.

The hanged man is the symbol of the law of reversal. The card is supposed to show that success will happen, but in the complete opposite way to what you expect. You can't use force. You have to surrender.

When you feel walled in, when you're in prison, you have to wait it out. It's like you're in the middle of nowhere, so you have to accept your limitations. You have to surrender the face you've been putting on. It's like the "dark night of the soul" that has to come before new life. This is the time when you have to be on the same track as the great spirit of the universe.

◆　　　◆　　　◆

"Mom, I can't believe you're doing this," Chrissie says.

"Keep your voice down, honey. This is a prison."

"But where are you going to go?" she whispers.

"We're not sure yet. I'll let you know."

"But how will I see you?"

"We'll figure that out later."

"Mom, you're crazy."

"It goes with the territory. You don't seem to understand that I could be in here for life."

"But you might get off!"

"And pigs might fly. Look, Chrissie, if I thought there was a hope in hell that I was going to get off, I'd stay. But the evidence is stacked against me. I've already thought it through. Lots of times.

"Now, honey, I need you to get me some money, all right? You know where it is. You can do it. I want you to go across the border and over the Cascades. You take it across the border the way your dad used to do the drugs. You remember?"

"Of course," sighs Chrissie.

"All right, now, you're going to take the money to some friends of Sam's. She's one of the gals who's going with us. Her friends live in this small town across the Cascades called Twisp. Okay? Don't cross the border at Blaine. There's too much heat. Also, I think you should do it in installments. Don't do it all at once, just in case you get stopped. We don't want to lose it all. But I have to have the money. Now, will you do it?"

"I guess so," says Chrissie. "But what if they catch me?"

"Who's going to catch you?"

"I don't know. Sometimes you have bad luck. They're spot-checking. You know the drill. God, Mom, I just don't know how you can be trying an escape."

"Don't use that word," I say, looking over my shoulder.

"There's no one there," whispers Chrissie. "God, Mom, do you know what you're doing?"

"No. But I didn't on the outside either."

◆     ◆     ◆

I like to read my recipes. It's not as though I can make anything in here, but it feels good just thinking about the food. I plan whole meals, complicated ones with lots of dishes. I can see the table all decorated with flowers from the garden.

I don't know what to do about Max. I can't let him know I'm leaving, and I won't be able to see him if we make it—at least, not for a while. I worry about him, wonder if he's eating all right. I always felt a special bond with him all the time he was growing up. I guess it was to compensate for the fact that he and his dad weren't that close. Mongrel favored Chrissie. I knew he did, so I had to even things out.

I think about him when I get to the recipes that were his favorites. He could eat a whole batch of chocolate chip cookies if I didn't watch him. When he was sick, I'd always make a special batch just for him. I swear they made him well.

## MAX'S FAVORITE CHOCOLATE CHIP COOKIES

> 3/4 cup butter-type Crisco
> 1-1/4 cups brown sugar (lightly packed)
> 1 egg
> 2 tablespoons milk
> 2 teaspoons vanilla
> 1-1/2 cups flour
> 1 teaspoon salt
> 3/4 teaspoon baking soda
> 1 cup chocolate chips
> 1 cup chopped walnuts

Preheat oven to 375°.

Cream Crisco and brown sugar until light.

Add egg, milk, and vanilla and beat 1 minute.

Combine flour, salt, and soda and add to creamed mixture gradually.

Stir in chocolate chips and nuts.

Drop dough by spoonfuls onto ungreased cookie sheets.

Bake at 375° for 8–10 minutes.

Cool for 2 minutes, then remove from cookie sheet and place on rack.

◆ ◆ ◆

## STEP TEN
CONTINUED TO TAKE PERSONAL INVENTORY AND PLAN THE ESCAPE, AND WHEN WE WERE READY PROMPTLY ADMITTED IT.

◆ ◆ ◆

The Christmas open house is getting closer and the jail is getting really busy. I don't know how we could've tried to pull this off at any other time. The excitement around us is a perfect cover for our own excitement. Carley's been in, talking to Sam. Darlene's jealous. She's worried that Sam might be having an affair with Carley. Chrissie got a good hunk of money over the border. She said it was easy. Like father, like daughter.

Stella's got what she calls the motel accommodation all organized with the Native band.

Chan has most of the fake IDs finished. She's also working some connection for the power failure—a family friend who owes a big favor to some other family friend. It's all too complicated for me. I don't even try to figure it out. But whoever this guy is, he's willing to pay off his debt by blasting a hole in the right place at the right time so that we'll have a power failure.

Darlene managed somehow to get a look at the schedule for the open house—where the guards are going to be. Who's on. Who's off.

Big Dee is what we call quality control because all she does is bitch about how nothing is going to work and look for holes in the plan. Which is important, actually. She's found a few good ones.

"So what," she says. "You get some guy to blow the generator on the outside, you think they got no back-up in here? Just because something went wrong last time don't mean it going to go wrong again. I mean, where you think you are? This here is maximum security. Everything electric. They got some other generator somewheres."

"I think Big Dee's got a point," I say.

"Hell, we don't want to do all this in the dark anyways," says Sam. "Just make things harder for us if we can't see nothin'. Probably make the guards all nervous and they end up hauling out their guns and shooting someone by accident."

"You don't need explosion?" says Chan.

"Now, let's not throw out the baby with the soup kitchen," says Sam. "I think we could use the power failure as a diversion. It'll throw the guards off a bit. Add some confusion. We'll be fine as long as we're not confused, and we won't be 'cause we'll be expecting it."

◆　　◆　　◆

"Everything's connected," I say. "Everything gets held together by these tiny little invisible threads. Even when it doesn't seem to make any sense, it all makes some kind of sense."

I'm doing Stella's cards.

## SIX OF WANDS: TRUST

"Six of Wands. That one's about trust, Stella. It's about skydiving into life. You might have to learn how to trust more. It's like kids and dogs—they're so naturally trusting. Maybe it's like seeing yourself as someone on a flying trapeze. You go flying through the air and you have to trust that the other person, whoever it is, is going to catch you, right on the second. Because you can't count on just you.

"So, see here, the way the cards lie? You have some dark energy around trust. You need to trust somebody. You have to let go of the idea that it's all up to you. Otherwise, you'll wear yourself out."

"Why the hell should I trust anyone, eh?" says Stella.

"I don't know. Maybe it just makes life a bit easier is all," I say. "Got any more questions?"

"You think we gonna make it?"

I lay my hands on the cards and take a deep breath. I fan them out and there's a natural split over on the right. Stella reaches over and pulls out a card. She lays it face down.

"Turn it over," I say.

"I don't want to." She shakes her head, her arms folded across her chest.

"Go on," I say.

She hesitates, and then reaches and flips the card over.

Death.

Stella's face looks like a dark cloud.

"Shit," she says.

"It's not what you think, Stella. Death comes before a new beginning. No death—no freedom."

◆　　　◆　　　◆

The closest we came to losing our freedom was the time Mongrel decided we should go to Mexico for a holiday. It was the middle of winter and pouring rain.

"Mags," says Mongrel, hitting the mute on the TV remote, "how many days of solid fucking rain has it been?"

"I don't know. Quite a few," I say.

"Come over here and look at this," he says, kicking off one of his boots. I go over.

"Is that webbing growing between my fucking toes? Gimme the phone," he says.

I get him the phone. He dials. Next thing you know, he's leased a van and we're on our way to Mexico, kids in the back, stereo blasting.

The Canada/U.S. border is easy because Mongrel has a connection. He knows who's on shift and just glides through, have a nice trip, thank you, officer.

The U.S./Mexico border is a little more tense and it isn't easier with Mongrel's barnyard Spanish. Now there's looks over shoulders, an exchange of pesos, big smiles, a squeezing of hands, amigo, ha, ha, mucho calor, si si, adios, waves for the kids and guapa, guapa you wife.

All the time I'm grilling Mongrel.

"You *didn't* bring any dope across the border, did you?"

"Mags, relax, we're here for a nice holiday, okay? Don't start. Put on that nice bikini I bought you. You kids go to the beach. Your mother and I have business to discuss. Vamos!"

We stay in Mazatlán until the blue bottles or Portuguese man-of-wars arrive—they're the most vicious stinging jellyfish. Mongrel is playing beach soccer with Max and a bunch of local kids when he steps on one.

"Holy fuck, I've been poisoned," screams Mongrel, jumping up and down on one foot as he tries to hold the other. "Mags, for chrissake, do something!"

Of course, the kids think he's hilarious, this wild man with hair all the way down his back, jumping around in circles, holding onto one foot. He takes a swing at the kids to make them shut up and they scatter, shrieking with laughter, Mongrel kicking sand at them and cursing their mothers.

"Mags, I'm dyin'! Fuck off, you little wetbacks. Mags, cut my fucking foot off before it spreads! Fuck! Jesus! Max, git your sorry ass over here, pronto. Owww! Mags, *do something!*"

That night we're on a ferry to the Baja, Mongrel limping and cursing the Mexicans for having the jam to leave dangerous, life-threatening slime lying around on public beaches. There's no way in hell he'll stay in a place like Mazatlán. Period.

We're up on the deck. The sun is setting but the air is still warm.

Max and Chrissie are tearing around with a couple of other kids they hooked up with.

"I've never felt fucking pain like that before," says Mongrel.

"It must have been awful," I say.

"I shoulda brought some morphine with me," he says.

"Probably lucky you didn't."

"Anyone else on deck right now?"

"Nope," I say, thinking he wants to get it on. There's something about hot weather that just makes him horny all the time.

"Probably safe to fire up a doob, then," he says, sliding a joint into his mouth.

"What are you doing?" I say.

"What does it look like?" he says.

"You can't smoke dope in the open like this. This is Mexico."

"Hell I can't," says Mongrel, snapping a wooden match aflame with his thumbnail.

The next morning, on arrival, our van is pulled off to the side and four federales proceed to rip it apart. The kids think it's great fun. Mongrel pulls a deck chair off the roof and lies out in the sun, smoking a fat cigar, making bad jokes with the police. I sit on the curb, fuming. I'm seeing pictures of my whole family rotting away in some filthy, rat-infested Mexican prison, my daughter sold as a hooker.

"You fucking asshole," I hiss at Mongrel, my eyes two thin slits.

"Relax, mama mia, it's all under control," says Mongrel, laughing.

"You promised," I snarl.

Two hours later, the Mexicans—because they can't find

anything—try to put the van back together. Of course, Mongrel has to help them. The head honcho stands to the side glaring at the van, then at Mongrel. He knows there's drugs somewhere in the vehicle, but he can't risk being made a complete fool of.

Mongrel offers him a cigar. I know Mongrel—he's really rubbing it in. The federale takes it and walks real stiff over to his car, gets in, and peels out, leaving two black strips of rubber. He's pissed.

Freedom.

◆　　◆　　◆

"I ain't settin' my black ass in no kayak," says Big Dee. "An' that be final."

"Then how do we get across the water?" I ask.

"How 'bout we use a real boat? With a motor?" says Big Dee.

"How we going to find that?" says Sam.

"Well, it seem to me that if them Indians can find kayaks, they can find a damn boat," says Big Dee.

"I'll talk to Wilson Featherstone. See what he can do," says Stella.

"Well, you better step on it, Stella. We're running out of time."

"Can't run out of time," says Stella. "Time endless."

"That why you always late?" says Big Dee.

"Not late," says Stella smiling, "just on Indian time."

"Better not use it for the escape," says Darlene, "or we'll be doin' hard time for a real long time—a real long time even for Indians."

◆　　◆　　◆

I'm having trouble sleeping. If I'm not thinking about the escape then I'm thinking about Tony. If I'm not thinking about him, I'm thinking about Mongrel. When I'm not wondering about Mongrel, I'm wondering about the trial.

My trial date has been set for January—not that I intend to be there. I don't kid myself about what's going to happen. I know how it looks. A crazy wife who's heading into the menopause and screwing around murders her abusive, semi-crippled biker husband, who's been screwing around on her. Even her son thinks she did it. And her husband's friends, too. And some of hers.

I thought I had lots of friends, working at Lou's and all. I thought there were at least a few people I could count on. But when something like this happens, you get to see who your real friends are. And you find out you really don't have that many. One of the only people I know for sure is on my team is my lawyer, and that's only because she's gonna make money on it either way. Of course, she makes more if she wins. And Chrissie's on my team. And Tony. And the gals here at the prison, naturally.

◆　　◆　　◆

Tim was Mongrel's best buddy. They'd met in Winthrop one year. I should have known better when I saw that he showed up every second time with a different woman, but lust is blind and stupid. And he was smooth.

Mongrel never suspected anything, or if he did, he never let it show. He was always inviting Tim over.

"Hey, Mags, throw a couple more spuds in the pot," he says. "Tim's coming over with his new old lady."

"Which one?" I ask.

"The new one," he says.

"The redhead?" I ask.

"No, the new one. The one with the big jugs and the even bigger divorce settlement."

"I don't think I know that one," I say.

"Well, you will. She's coming for dinner tonight."

◆　　　◆　　　◆

I don't see Tony for a week. Maybe it's for the better. Leave him out of the situation. Plus it gets Big Dee off my case. She's been looking sideways at me as it is. Asks me last night how come I'm not doing counseling with Tony. I said I was getting bored. She drops down an eyebrow and goes hmmm, like she always does when she doesn't buy it. She's got one of the best bullshit detectors I've ever seen.

Jim comes by after lock-up. Says Tony wants to see me. Big Dee gets a little smile on her face which I tell her she might think about wiping off.

I don't feel too good when I get to his door. He waits until I'm inside.

"So, what's up, Margaret?"

"Not much."

"I don't understand."

"What's to understand?"

"Look, let's not play games. The last time I saw you, we made love right here and you couldn't wait to see me again. Then I don't see you all week. Suddenly, everything's changed. I don't get it. What happened between then and now?"

"I did some thinking."

"You did some thinking?"

"Yeah."

"You didn't think I might be interested in the process, did you? I'm involved in this, too, Margaret. This isn't just some fling I'm having. What the hell's going on?"

"It's got nowhere to go, Tony. We've already been through this. I keep going back and forth—"

"Sounds more like in and out, Margaret, and right now you're out."

"I don't know where I am."

"Do you want out?"

"I don't know."

"Why do I feel like I'm missing something, here? I thought I was getting to know you. I thought we were talking."

"We were."

"And now?"

"Look, Tony, I just thought if I stayed away, I'd stop thinking about you. Really, I did. I tried to stop. I just couldn't. I don't want to hurt you, but I also don't want to get hurt either."

"Jesus, Margaret, as I already said, there are no guarantees. I could die tomorrow. Or you could. But if you play it so safe that you never get hurt, you never get loved either."

"Yeah, well, it's easy for you to say all this stuff. You get to leave every day. What do I know about what you do on the outside?"

"You want to know? I go home. I think about you. I make some dinner. I think about you. Then I read or I watch some TV or I see friends, but every time there's a gap in the conversation, I think about you."

"I thought only I did that."

"Don't stay away from me, Margaret."

◆    ◆    ◆

I never was much for math but the numbers keep coming up. Twenty-five for life. Ten with good behavior, which probably doesn't include escaping. Minus one for the year already served. That makes nine. Times that by three hundred and sixty-five days and you get three thousand, two hundred and eighty-four days or seventy-eight thousand, eight hundred and forty hours. No matter which way you cut it, it's a fuck of a lot of time. You don't even want to know the minutes.

And nine years might as well be a lifetime, things change so fast. I'll be old. If it wasn't for television, I'd think the whole world was a prison. It's like when it's raining, and you can't imagine that somewhere else the sun's shining. That's how it feels. It feels like everyone must be in prison.

◆    ◆    ◆

Mongrel did his time in Folsom. Just before Max was born. A bust. Mongrel always figured it was a setup—that someone put the finger on him. But the law had had their eye on him for quite a while. It was just a matter of time before they landed on him. In his case, he was lucky. He'd just moved a shitload of stuff and was waiting for some more, so they could barely make a trafficking charge on him. And, of course, he got himself the best lawyer money could buy.

Mongrel never took to Max the way he should have. He missed that first year. It was as though he couldn't accept that he had a son. It was like a story to him. And when Mongrel did see him, Max was already formed in some way that he didn't need his dad. They never were that close.

Mongrel never stopped dealing, even in the joint. He just became the supplier in prison. It's like he never skipped a beat. I only went to work because I was bored all the time at home. I didn't have to. Mongrel was making good money in prison. He sent a stack of hundreds to us every couple of weeks—like clockwork.

◆　　　◆　　　◆

I'm not really sure anymore how it happened. I've gone over it so many times in my head that I'm starting to get confused. I know I was baking brownies—hash brownies. But I don't remember if I'd just put them in the oven. No. I must have been taking them out because I offered one to Mongrel and he refused.

I remember that, because he never refused anything with drugs in it. I don't think he was ever straight. First thing in the morning, he'd roll over and fire up a joint. He said it took the edge off life.

He must have come upstairs from the basement. He was limping real bad from the last accident. He knew he'd never walk right again. He had a gun in his hand. He said that life wasn't worth living. I tried to talk him down.

At some point, he aimed the gun at me. I felt like the world had gone all crystal and there was this blue tinge to everything. I could hear the blood pounding in my head. I think I stopped breathing.

Then he told me that he knew about me and Tim —that he'd known for a long time. I closed my eyes, and when the shot rang out, I stood there, waiting for the pain, but nothing happened except this terrible ringing in my ears. I must have passed out. When I came to, he was still sitting in the chair with his eyes wide open. They looked like glass marbles. I crawled across the kitchen floor and wrapped myself around his legs.

◆　　◆　　◆

## STEP ELEVEN

SOUGHT THROUGH PRAYER AND MEDITATION TO IMPROVE OUR CONSCIOUS CONTACT WITH GOD AS WE UNDERSTOOD HER, PRAYING ONLY FOR KNOWLEDGE OF HOW TO GET THE HECK OUT OF HERE WITHOUT HURTING ANYONE AND THE POWER TO CARRY OUT OUR PLAN.

We've made it to Step Eleven. Everyone's quiet tonight. The pressure's on. If everything goes as planned, we should be out of here in ten days. Big Dee's getting cold feet.

"I think you all should go without me," she says.

"Why?" says Sam.

"'Cause I'm black."

"So?" says Stella.

"So, not so many blacks around here," says Big Dee.

"So?" says Stella

"So, I sticks out like a sore thumb."

"We're not going without you, Big Dee," I say. "What about Florida? And no rain? And those juicy oranges?"

"Seem like just dreams," says Big Dee.

"Everything start from dreams," says Chan, nodding her head. "You come, Big Dee. We like you."

Big Dee drops her head. Tears are running down her cheeks. Chan looks over at her and then at the rest of us.

"What did I say wrong?" she says.

"What's wrong, Big Dee?" says Darlene.

"There's nothin' wrong," says Big Dee, "just never had nobody say that to me before."

◆　　◆　　◆

Tony knows I'm lying to him, I'm sure. Not about caring about him. I *do* care about him. Quite a lot. But he thinks I'm excited about the open house, which, of course, is true but not for the reason he thinks.

"You seem distracted, Margaret," he says.

"It's just the open house. So much to do. All the planning."

"What planning?" he says.

"Well, not really the planning, but you have to have everything organized, you know, the logistics and all."

"I didn't realize it was so complicated," he says.

"Well, it is and it's not. It's just that it comes at a time of year when I have a lot on my mind. I mean, Mongrel shot himself last year on the anniversary of President Kennedy's assassination. Do you think he chose that day intentionally?"

"I don't know, Margaret."

"Do I talk too much about Mongrel?"

"Sometimes," says Tony.

"I'm kind of all over the place right now. Being in here. Going up for murder. I mean, I would never have guessed I'd be part of what I thought only happened on afternoon television or in the *National Enquirer*. I still wake up thinking I'm having a bad dream."

"It can't last forever," says Tony.

"Nothing does. Has anyone ever escaped from here before?" I say.

"You're *not* thinking of escaping, are you?" says Tony.

"Of course not," I say. "It's just a question. You know—curiosity."

"In fact, there was an escape—about two years ago. A couple of women actually made it over the fence. I don't think anyone to this day knows how they did it."

"Did they get away?"

"One did. The other one got caught almost immediately. She went directly to her best friend's house."

"Hmmm, dumb. What happened to the one who got away?" I say.

"She got away," says Tony.

"She never came back?" I say.

"No, she never did," he says.

"Wow, that's great," I say.

"I guess so," says Tony, looking at me.

◆　　◆　　◆

Mongrel said the menopause turned women into barracudas with eight rows of teeth. He thought they should have to wear an alarm system to warn people when they were in "the change."

I tell Big Dee and she says Mongrel should have had to wear an alarm to warn people that he was so stupid.

"I wish men had to go through menopause," I say.

"Well," says Big Dee, "I don't know. But you think on this one. How come if us women suppose to get so mean and ornery when we get in the change, most all the killing and violence gets done by men? You ever think on that? Make me think that men must be in the change all their lives, they act so damn fool ignorant and mean. What you laughin' at?"

◆　　◆　　◆

## EIGHT OF WORLDS: CHANGE

I guess the change of life is like any change. The card shows the changing of the seasons, from orange leaves of fall to icy blue snow. The planets and how they change in the sky. The chameleon that changes colors depending on where it's sitting. Change can't be stopped or even slowed down much. Mostly, I've been afraid of it. I'd rather stay with something that doesn't work all that well than do something new. The only time I've ever changed is when I've been forced to, like this past year.

◆　　◆　　◆

Johanna came by this morning, wearing one of her shit-eating smiles.

"How are you girls this morning?" she says.

"Pretty good, considering where we is," says Big Dee.

"That's good," says Johanna, "Seen Darlene?"

"She around," says Big Dee. "Ask Sam."

"Oh yes, Sam," says Johanna.

"You talking about me?" says Sam, coming down the corridor.

"Well, yes, I was," says Johanna, "but actually I was wanting to talk to Darlene."

"You got a message for Darlene, I'll pass it on," says Sam.

"Good. You can tell her that she's moving to Unit C this afternoon."

"What's that?"

"I said Darlene's moving."

"How come she's being moved?" says Sam.

"I thought maybe she needed a change of scenery," says Johanna.

"She's my woman."

"You know we don't encourage that kind of relationship," says Johanna.

"You're fucking with me, Johanna," says Sam.

"I'm not sure I get your point."

"Sam, let it go," says Big Dee.

"You know exactly what I'm talking about," says Sam.

"I hope that's not a threatening tone I hear in your voice."

"Sam, it ain't worth it," says Stella.

"I think you might need a little lock-up time in your cell," says Johanna.

"She be fine," says Big Dee.

Johanna moves toward Sam but Big Dee steps between them.

"I said she be fine," says Big Dee.

◆　　　◆　　　◆

Rice pudding was my favorite comfort food. I used to make it when Mongrel and I had a fight and he'd go off somewhere. Or if Max didn't come home. Or when Chrissie turned thirteen and came home pregnant. It caught me so off guard that I made enough for the whole family and ate it all myself. Then I threw up.

## RICE PUDDING FOR COMFORT

1/3 cup Monarch Pearl rice
1/4 cup sugar
2-1/2 cups milk
Butter
Nutmeg

Pour the rice, sugar, and milk into a small casserole dish and give them a stir.

Put 4 pats of butter (about the size of the end of your thumb) around the inside rim of the casserole dish. The butter will melt into the rice in the oven. Sprinkle 1/4 teaspoon or so of nutmeg on top of the mixture.

Bake at 325° for about 2 hours. After about half an hour, take the casserole dish out and give the pudding a stir or the rice will clump together.

When done, the rice pudding should have a nice golden scum on top. In our house, there were scum lovers and scum haters. Mongrel and Chrissie hated scum. Max and I loved it. Also, some people like to put raisins in their rice pudding. I think it's better without.

◆　　◆　　◆

Darlene left the unit this afternoon. She was a mess. She almost got herself put in seg. Sam managed to talk her down. All we need now is for one of us to end up in segregation and we won't get out of here. As it is, we're going to have trouble getting through to Darlene now. She'll be able to get to the last meeting before we go, but that's all. There's still lots of small details to be taken care of.

Stella talked to Wilson Featherstone. He's got connections with some guy who runs a tugboat up the river we have to cross. He's going to leave a small motorboat on our side about an hour before the electrical failure. I guess he got the message that inflatable kayaks were out.

"How small?" says Big Dee.

"He says it'll take six people," says Stella.

"Six what-size people?" says Big Dee.

"Six medium-size people, I guess," says Stella.

"Well, I'm an extra-large-size person," says Big Dee.

"Yeah, but Chan here is an extra-small size," says Sam, laughing.

"Not so small," says Chan, pulling back her shoulders.

"Hardly big enough for a snack, if I was a cannibal," says Big Dee, looking at Chan, whose eyes go wide. "Which I is *not*!"

◆　　◆　　◆

Stella says that in the medicine wheel, darkness comes from the West. It's the direction of the unknown, of meditation or maybe prayer. She also says it's the direction of testing—where your will is taken to its breaking point.

"See, Maggie, the nearer you come to where you want to go, the harder the journey is, eh? Because of that, you need the gift of perseverance. So you have to learn how to toughen yourself so you can stick to the challenge, even though it's difficult. Sometimes painful."

She points west just like she's looking out a window, except we don't have one.

"It's the direction of thunder and lightning—of power. Power to see and power to know. It's from this direction that we have to learn to use power, but only in ways that are in harmony with the teachings of the Sacred Tree."

"What you on about?" says Big Dee.

"Talking about Indian stuff," says Stella. "We need to find our animal spirits. Then the spirit of that animal will help you. It also lets you know what position you are in the band or tribe. I know my animal already. I found out a long time ago."

"Well, maybe it didn't help you that much—you still in here," says Big Dee.

"Oh, it helped me a lot," says Stella. "Without it I would be dead now, and that's for sure."

"What's your spirit then?" says Big Dee.

"I'm the eagle," says Stella.

"What does that mean?" I say.

"It's my job to watch over everything, because I see from a higher place. For the escape, I'll be the leader."

"Why you?"

"Because I've been chosen."

"By who?"

"The eagle leads," says Stella.

"I thought we were all equal," I say.

"Every band needs a chief," says Stella.

"Yeah, but how come you get to be the chief?"

"It's my turn, eh?" says Stella.

◆　　◆　　◆

When Chrissie came home pregnant, I expected Mongrel to hit the roof. But he didn't. He told Max to go outside and play.

"Max, get your butt outa here. Go play outside for a while, would ya?"

"I don't want to," says Max.

"You ain't got no choice. Scram! Mags, get me a beer."

Mongrel sits down across from Chrissie, who by now has tears running down her face. She won't even look at me. Mongrel reaches up and wipes her face with his hands. Now, instead of tears there are two black grease marks. He takes Chrissie's hands in his.

"Okay, Chrissie, now what you want us to do about this baby?"

"I don't want an abortion."

"Okay, kiddo, so you don't want an abortion. Now I want to know what it is you do want."

"I don't want to be pregnant."

"Well, I get that. But you are. So we gotta decide what's best for everyone, okay? And that means all of us, even Max."

Chrissie says she's maybe not ready to have a baby and bring it up on her own. Mongrel says he agrees. She says maybe she could stay with us until she has the baby, then give it up for adoption.

"Yeah, of course you can stay. This is your fucking home," says Mongrel. "But you already know that giving it up ain't gonna be easy."

"I know," says Chrissie.

"Max, get your ass in here. I know you're behind the door!" Max slinks in, red in the face.

"Your sister's pregnant. We're fine about it. You got that?"

Max nods.

"And it ain't anyone else's business, so keep your mouth shut about it or you won't be able to sit on your sorry ass for a month. Not a word. You got it?"

Max nods again.

"So, that's it," says Mongrel. "Mags, where's that beer?"

◆　　　◆　　　◆

"I got a bad feeling about this," says Sam.

"It's only for a few days, a week, tops," I say.

"You don't know Darlene," she says.

"She'll be at the next meeting," I say.

"She's no good on her own. She can't sleep. She gets scared. She always got to have someone. I don't even think she cares if it's a man or a woman. She just can't stand to be alone."

"Maybe she's stronger than you think," I say.

"I don't know," says Sam. "You know, even when we was fighting she would never go to sleep without putting her arms around me. I'd wake up in the middle of the night, and she'd be crying. I'd ask what's wrong and she'd say, Just hold me, Sam, just hold me or I won't be able to make it another day."

◆　　　◆　　　◆

"I guess I can't be a elephant," says Big Dee.

"Sorry, no elephant in the medicine wheel," says Stella.

"No hippopotamus either, I suppose," says Big Dee.

"Nope," says Stella.

"Well, what *is* on that wheel?" she says.

"Mouse," says Stella.

"Now that suit me just fine." Big Dee laughs.

"Ha, ha," says Stella.

"Hey, how 'bout a bear?" says Big Dee.

"Bear— that's a good one," says Stella.

"How good?" says Big Dee.

"The black bear is one of the teachers of the West. It has great strength, but not just from the outside, like muscles. Its strength comes from deep inside. Bears go into their caves and hibernate. And the bear person closes herself off from others to get vision. To be alone. To see things that other people can't see. The black bear is special. I think it's perfect for you."

"Okay, I's a black bear," says Big Dee.

◆　　　◆　　　◆

Tony's gone quiet. He keeps staring at me. It makes me uncomfortable. I want to talk to him but I don't want to slip up—not now. I don't want my real feelings to show. I don't want any of this to get in the way of the escape.

"There's something wrong, isn't there?" says Tony.

"No, there isn't. I'm just having a bad day."

"You're not telling the truth, Margaret. I can feel it."

I don't know what to say. He's never talked to me like this before. I feel my stomach go tight. I can't look him in the eye.

"If you don't want to be with me, just tell me."

"It's not that, Tony."

"Well, what is it then? There's something going on. I can sense it. It's like I'm losing you—like you're leaving me."

"How can I leave you, Tony? I'm a prisoner. This is a jail."

"You're not telling me something, Margaret," says Tony.

I reach over and take his hand.

"I'm sorry, Tony," I say.

"You going to run, aren't you?"

I look up at him. He's looking hard at me.

"Are you going alone?"

"Yeah, of course."

"I could stop you," he says.

"I know you could."

"But you know I won't."

"I'm not leaving to get away from you, Tony. I didn't expect any of this to happen. I didn't want to fall in love. It couldn't have happened at a worse time. I just know I couldn't make it for ten years in here. It's not because of you. I just don't think I'm built for it."

"Margaret, do you have any idea what you're doing?" he says.

"No, I don't, but I don't have any choice."

Tony takes my hand and lays it on his face. He's looking at me and nodding.

"God, Margaret. I don't know what to tell you. It's such a crazy risk to take. You could get yourself shot."

"I'm not using a gun, Tony," I say.

"The guards have guns, for chrissake."

"I just gotta hope they don't use them, that's all."

He kisses my hand. I put my face in his hair. It smells clean. I never want to forget this smell.

"I'll get in touch with you later, when I'm settled somewhere."

"You can't do that, Margaret. You leave here, you leave me."

"Don't say that."

"It's over if you do this."

"Why?" I say.

"Because this isn't a storybook. This is real life. It's a prison escape. What are you thinking? It's not going to be like before. You're never going to be free to talk to me, or the rest of your family, or your friends. You're going to be a fugitive. You don't understand the implications of what you're getting into."

"I don't want to hear this," I say.

"Fine, but you're going to find out when you leave here, if you make it. It'll be all over. You'll have to start a new life."

"I'll deal with it when I get to it," I say.

"You'll have to," says Tony.

◆　　　◆　　　◆

"He won't," I say.

"I can't believe what I'm hearin'," says Big Dee. "We one week away from jackrabbit parole and you tell someone on the other side?"

"He's not on the other side," I say.

"Hell he ain't," says Big Dee. "He's a counselor. He's friends with the guards."

"So what? He's not going to say anything—he as much as gave me his word."

"Well, now, that makes it all right. He give you his word. Jesus, Maggie, I never met no man ever kept no word he ever make."

"Tony's different," I say.

"So was my second husband. He was a Baptist minister. That don't mean he didn't lie like a sidewalk."

"Well, I trust him," I say.

"You's fuckin' him," she says.

"That's not true," I say.

"Is so," she says. "You think we can't hear you in the coffee room?"

"What are you talking about?" I say.

"Tony's office right next door to the coffee room and there be some air pipes or something. Anyways, we hear you two ooh-oohin' in there. We all thought it pretty funny."

"You're full of shit, Big Dee," I say.

"Oh yeah? Well, how come Tony always say 'Ye-e-e-ssss' and then laugh when he comin'?" says Big Dee.

I glare at her.

"Well?" she says. "Don't he? Ye-e-e-cssss, ha, ha, ha."

"Fuck you," I say.

"And by the way, for your information, Miss Hot Pants, it ain't the first time he screw someone there. We heard that noise before, so think on that."

"What the hell are you saying?"

"Just a word to the wise," she says.

◆   ◆   ◆

## STEP TWELVE

HAVING HAD A SPIRITUAL AWAKENING AS THE RESULT OF THE ESCAPE, WE TRIED TO CARRY THE MESSAGE TO OTHERS AND PRACTICE THESE PRINCIPLES IN ALL OUR AFFAIRS.

It's the last meeting before we do the run. You can slice the energy in the room with a knife.

"You're sure your friend will do the power cut?" says Sam.

"He has to," says Chan.

"And he'll be on time?" says Sam.

"He always on time," says Chan.

"Not like Stella," says Big Dee.

Stella smiles, but it's not quite straight on her face.

"Where's Darlene?" says Stella.

"She has to come from the other unit," I say.

"Well, we ain't got all night," says Big Dee.

"Who's covering the door?" I say.

"Me and Darlene is," says Big Dee. "Her friend, whatever her name, going to come from the outside and cover the guards. Bring some friends with her, too, I think. They don't come in, though. Wait for the power failure, then come—"

The door opens. Everyone shuts up real fast. It's Tony.

"I need to talk to you, Margaret," he says.

Big Dee glares at me. I get up and go to the door. Tony's standing there. He looks pale.

"You told them," I say.

"No, Margaret, I didn't."

"That's good. Now, I got something I need to talk to you about."

"Can't it wait?"

"No, it can't. Big Dee told me something interesting. It seems they could hear us through the pipes. It seems they also heard you before I got in, with someone else."

"What? That's not true. I only moved into that office about a month before you got here. I used to be way the hell and gone over by Unit C. Shit, why am I defending myself? Look, this is getting crazy. I'm not here for this. A real bad thing has happened to one of the girls."

"Who?"

"Darlene."

"What happened to her?"

"She OD'd."

"No way, Tony, where is she?"

"She's dead, Margaret. They found her in her cell just an hour ago. Heroin. It wasn't an accident."

"Oh God. Oh poor Darlene. Oh Jesus, Tony, what are we going to do? What am I going to tell Sam?" I can feel the blood leaving my head. "I got to sit down. I'm feeling sick."

Tony grabs me as I slide to the floor.

◆　　◆　　◆

When the shot rang out, I stood there waiting for the pain to hit. I don't know how long I waited. All I know is that I couldn't move. It was like my whole body had turned to cement. But my eyes looked out the window and saw this red-winged blackbird. It flew away at the sound of the shot. And my ears were ringing from the explosion. I wasn't breathing.

I looked down and saw my hands gripping the countertop. They were completely white. I heard a sound coming out of my throat. It didn't sound like me at all. It wasn't a cry or a scream. It was this strange sound, like a wounded animal. And then I turned around and saw Mongrel sitting in the chair. He was looking at me and his chest was covered with blood.

"No. Oh no, Mongrel," I heard myself say before I slid to the floor.

◆　　◆　　◆

"I'm Maggie the Cat. I'm the cougar," I say. The room is real quiet.

"I'm the black bear," says Big Dee.

"I'm the eagle," says Stella.

"I am a mouse," says Chan.

"I'm the wild horse," says Sam.

"We're here to mourn the death of our friend and sister, Darlene. It couldn't have happened at a worse time, not that there's ever a good one. But it happened, and now we got to deal with it. I chose a symbol for her because she reminded me of a rose. A rose is delicate and it has a beautiful smell. But it also has sharp thorns that hurt anyone who tries to take and own its beauty. That's what she was like. We're also trying our best to be with you, Sam, at this time which is so hard for you."

"They shouldn't have put her in that other unit. She wasn't no good on her own," says Sam.

"You right," says Big Dee.

"What am I going to do?" says Sam.

"You got to let it out," says Big Dee.

"I'm feel like I'm going crazy," says Sam. "I'm gonna kill that fucking Johanna." She starts toward the door.

Big Dee grabs her.

"You ain't goin' nowhere the way you feeling right now," says Big Dee.

"Let me go," says Sam.

"I can't hold her alone. Help me, Stella. Gimme that blanket, Chan. Ball it up, quick," says Big Dee. "Okay, I hold her. You help me, Maggie. Chan, you put that blanket over her face. Now, Sam, we your friends. We not trying to hurt you. But you can't go out there. You way out of control. You let it out into that blanket. You wail as loud as you can. You get that poison out of your body. Come on, girl. You let it out."

Sam starts to shake all over. Then it comes. It's a terrible sound. She screams and screams. We all hold her tight as her body breaks with sobs. And then all of us are crying. Crying for Darlene, and for Sam. I guess we're crying a bit for ourselves, too.

◆　　◆　　◆

When Mongrel died, I must have held onto him for a long time. I guess I thought that if I stayed there long enough he'd just wake up and everything would be the way it was before. I might have stayed there forever if it hadn't been for Max. I realized he'd be coming home from school. And I didn't want him to see his father like that. I didn't want him to have that empty body covered with blood as his last memory of his dad.

◆　　◆　　◆

This day had to come. Strange, I slept through the night. I sit on the edge of my bunk and look at my hands. They're perfectly still. I look over at Big Dee and she just quietly nods at me.

"We gonna make it," she says.

"That's right." I say. "What about Sam?"

"Sam be all right," says Big Dee. "Stella looking after her."

"I haven't seen Johanna, have you?"

"No, I ain't," says Big Dee.

"She shouldn't have . . ."

"Shhh," says Big Dee, "we don't waste no energy on her. Not today."

◆　　◆　　◆

Normally, the guards would break us up. They don't like tight groups talking low. But Darlene's death has given us some cover, if you can find one bit of good news in it. The guards leave us alone.

"People start to come to the open house maybe five-thirty or so," says Stella. "That will give us about an hour and a half before the place is crowded. Carley says she'll come at six. She's expecting to see Darlene at the door. Sorry, Sam. I got to say her name, eh."

"It's okay," says Sam.

"So that means that Big Dee will meet her, but don't say nothing about Darlene because we don't want Carley freakin' out. She'll find out about Darlene soon enough. All right?"

"How we gonna be sure about how it'll look at the gate?" I say.

"Nothing is for sure," says Stella. "We're just counting on it being like it was last year. If there's some big changes, we'll have to change the plan as it goes along."

"Shit," I say. "I don't like that."

"Change is good," says Chan.

"Says who?" says Big Dee.

"Listen up," says Stella. "You got to remember to think about your animal spirit. If you get scared, or you can't see your way, call to it. It will help you. Don't try to do this all on your own."

"How do we do that?" I ask.

"Just ask it. Anyone who goes on a journey to make themselves better will be helped. Teachers will appear when needed. Spirit protectors will watch over you."

"I'm getting scared," says Big Dee.

"Good," says Stella. "That means you aren't dead. Anybody got a smoke?"

◆　　◆　　◆

The flower shop looks like Christmas—all full of bright decorations and flower arrangements, made by the inmates for sale to the public. There's two tables of food. Cheeses and cold meats and fruits and stuff from the bakery. It looks great. I haven't seen food like this for a while.

Chan did the food display and it looks as good as anything you'd see on the outside. She stands beside it proudly.

"What you think?" she says, beaming.

"It's really beautiful, Chan," I say.

"Think so, really?"

"Yeah, I sure do."

"Feel scared," she says.

"Me, too," I say.

"Want a cookie? Chocolate chip," she says.

"I'm not hungry," I say.

"Me, too," she says.

◆　　◆　　◆

Big Dee stands in the corridor. She's one of the greeters. She tells the visitors, mostly women, where they can find the flower shop or the bakery or the hairdresser's or the tailor shop. Maybe it's just my imagination, but the place seems to be swarming with guards. Every time I turn around, there's one in my face.

"Sam," I say, "come here."

"What?" she says.

"Is it just me, or is this joint full of guards?"

"It's a prison, Maggie. Haven't you noticed them before?"

"What time is it?" I say.

"You asked me two minutes ago," she says.

"Well, I'm freaked out," I say.

"Get over it," she says. "We need you to be cool."

"I'm cool," I say.

"Could'a fooled me," she says.

◆　　◆　　◆

In Mexico, after the federales finally put the van back together, I knew there was dope in there somewhere.

Mongrel slowly gets up from his deck chair, stretches, and throws the chair on top of the van.

Then he shakes all the guys' hands and he gives each one a cigar. He even gets me to take pictures of all of them with him in the middle, big smile, arms around them. They love him. They all wave as we drive away, the kids waving back. I sit in the front seat. I'm pissed.

"All right, Mongrel, where is it?"

"Where is what, Mags, my little chiquita banana?"

"Don't be a fucking asshole, Mongrel. Where's that dope?"

"Relax, Mags, we're on holiday," he says.

"You just about landed your whole fucking family in some shithole Mexican jail."

"Let me tell you something, Mags. If I ever landed my family in some wetback fucking joint, you can be pretty fuckin' sure that I'd also be getting their little butts out pronto. I ever not take care of you? All of you?"

"Sometimes," I say.

"Not very fuckin' often," he says.

"No, not very often," I say.

"How 'bout we stop in at the swankest place in La Paz and I buy you a new dress and take you out for dinner and champagne? You like that, baby?"

"Mongrel . . ."

"C'mon, Mags. Let's have fun. Don't you still love your old man?"

"We could have got caught," I say.

"But we didn't," he says. "That's the fuckin' point, Mags. We didn't. I took care of it. All right. Now, get over here and sit up close to me."

I slide over and he puts his arm around me, his free hand cradling my breast.

"You know what I want right now?" he says.

"Let me guess," I say.

"You're real cute when you get mad, you know?"

"Fuck you," I say.

"That's what I want," he says.

"Where's the dope?" I say.

"In the deck chair." He laughs.

"Where?" I say.

"In the aluminum tubing," he says.

"You're fuckin' crazy," I say.

"Nah, they're just fuckin' dumb."

"I suppose you think you're real cool?"

"I am, Mags. I am cool."

◆     ◆     ◆

At five minutes past six, there's still no Carley. Stella comes over to me.

"Carley part Indian?" says Stella.

"I don't know," I say. "Why?"

"She's late," says Stella.

"Not only Indians are late, Stella," I say.

"It's a joke," says Stella.

"I'm not late," says this woman who looks like a librarian.

"Who the fuck are you?" says Stella.

"I'm Carley."

"Got some ID?" says Stella.

"Don't be funny," says Carley. "Everything under control?"

"So far," I say.

"I know about Darlene," she says.

"Shit, how did you find out?" says Stella.

"Ear to the ground," says Carley. "I'm part Indian."

"Christ," says Stella, "twenty years ago nobody wanted to be Indian. Now everybody wants to be one."

"Yeah, well, you better be ready for this. There's three guys in a van in the lot, real close to the door. When the lights go, that's their signal to come in. They'll create a diversion on the outside and get their . . . and that display over there is just gorgeous. Did you girls do that?"

Two guards walk by. They smile at us. We smile back.

"Well, they seem awfully nice," says Carley.

"Oh, they're the best," I say.

◆　　　◆　　　◆

## FIVE OF WANDS: OPPRESSION

I was looking at this card last night. Not that I pulled it. I just looked at it. All about nets and fences and shackles and traps and knots. Behind bars, you can't see clearly. It's like your vision becomes small because there's so little to see. And when you can't see, it's like your mind is in prison, too. And your emotions are frozen. They shackle your body, and handcuff your activities. And when you're trapped, your spirit begins to crack.

But the message is to look through any small doorways you can. And don't give in. Or give up. You never really know what freedom is until you've been in prison.

◆　　　◆　　　◆

Mongrel hadn't talked to me in what seemed like weeks. The school phoned to tell me that Max had been caught smoking dope in the can. The dog had come in stinking of rotten fish and had rolled all over the carpet. It was a bad day. I decided to bake some brownies.

I didn't even hear him come in but when I turned around Mongrel was standing in the kitchen doorway. I didn't see the gun in his hand.

"Who was that on the phone?" he says.

"The school," I say.

"Not Tim?" he says.

"No, Mongrel, it wasn't Tim. It was the school phoning to say that your son was caught smoking dope in the boys' can."

"My son?"

"Yes, your son."

"How can I be sure he's mine?" he says.

"Jesus, Mongrel, it's not like you haven't done your share of fucking around."

"You know, Mags, there's quite a few countries in the world where, if a man caught his old lady screwing some other guy, he could kill her, bam, no questions asked."

"Is that what you're going to do?" I ask. Then I see the gun. I don't know what makes me do it, but I turn around and stare out the kitchen window. I'm gripping the counter so hard that my knuckles are white.

"In any case," I say, "if that's what you want to do, you'll have to shoot me in the back."

Everything goes still except my heart, which is pounding so hard I'm sure he can hear it. Then there's this loud crack and my arms go slack and I feel this warm liquid running down my legs. I look down and realize that I've peed all over myself and the floor.

◆　　　◆　　　◆

The lights go out so suddenly, I'm paralyzed. All I remember is that Stella gives me a shove when the back-up power comes on. After that, it's like walking through molasses. Everything is happening around me, but it seems so slow. I just keep my focus on getting out that door.

Out of the corner of my eye, I see Sam take Johanna's gun and tell everyone to get down on the floor. Then there's this shot and a lot of screaming. Then I'm at the door and running. I can't believe I can run this fast. I feel like I could run forever.

"This way, Maggie."

"I can't see a goddam thing," I say.

"Follow my voice."

I follow.

"Over here."

Within seconds, it seems, I find the boat. Except for the moonlight, I never could've seen a man standing beside it.

"Who are you?" I gasp, out of breath.

"I'm Wilson Featherstone."

"How did you know my name?" I say.

"I don't know it," he says.

"You told me to follow your voice."

"Not me," says Wilson. "Where are the others?"

"They're coming." My chest hurts like I'm going to have a heart attack.

Next, there's a crashing through the bush.

"Jesus, Lord, help me!" It's Big Dee.

"Over here, Big Dee."

"Oh my heart. Oh sweet Jesus. Oh Lord, take me. Take me now."

"Get in the fucking boat, Big Dee."

"Oh help me, Jesus, I can't get in that thing," she says.

"Get in!"

Wilson helps her into the boat.

Chan is next.

"Sam and Stella are coming," she says. "You all go. I don't go."

"What the fuck are you talking about, Chan?"

"They can kill me. You go. I stay."

"Git your yellow ass in this boat," says Big Dee.

"No, I can make them confuse. I can run different way. Start yelling."

"The fuck you do." Big Dee almost tips the boat over when she grabs Chan and hauls her in.

Sam and Stella fall through the bushes. Sam still has the gun in her hand.

"Jesus, fuck, get going! I shot Johanna."

"You fucking what?" I hiss.

"We gotta get the fuck out of here."

We're falling all over trying to get into the boat. The boat is rocking.

"Jesus, Lord, save me!" Big Dee's crying at the back of the boat.

"Get under the tarp," says Wilson.

"No way," says Big Dee.

"Get the fuck under," I say.

"I's scared of the dark," says Big Dee.

"And I'm scared of the fucking electric chair," says Sam.

◆　　◆　　◆

If I learned one important lesson from Tim, it was that you should always pay attention to how a man treats the women before you, because that's the way he's going to treat you. Period. No exceptions. Of course, I was too stupid to pay attention to the information.

He told me one time that one of his ex old ladies had cracked him over the head with a ball-peen hammer. At the time, I thought it was pretty gross. But by the end of our affair, I felt like cutting his balls off and putting them in a meat grinder.

Even his ex-wife put the knife in the day he lost custody of his kids. We had just come back from a ride. I was at his house. Mongrel was in jail. The phone rings.

Tim picks the phone up, says hello, and then his face goes dark. He hangs up.

"Who was that?" I say.

"My fucking kids."

"Short conversation."

"Yeah."

"What did they say?"

"You're fired!" he says.

◆　　　◆　　　◆

"You really shoot Johanna?" says Big Dee.

"I had to," says Sam.

"I thought we weren't gonna use fucking weapons," says Stella.

"She fuckin' killed Darlene," says Sam.

"Fuck," I say, "we're fucked now."

"She fuckin' had it comin'," says Sam.

"You ladies talk real bad," says Wilson.

"Yeah, well, fuck you," says Sam.

The sirens are wailing now. We can hear the voices. Wilson pushes the boat off. It moves silently through the water.

"Hey, Wilson," I whisper, "how come this boat's so quiet?"

"Fuckin' electric motor," he says.

◆       ◆       ◆

I'm pruning the rose bush when an unmarked car pulls up in front of our house. Being the wife of a biker and a dealer, I know how to identify a cop car from a hundred yards with my eyes closed.

First of all, cops always slump over to one side when they drive. Same as taxi drivers. Probably something to do with the fact that their ass gets sore from being sat on all day.

Also, they don't drive the same way as everyone else. They kind of skulk along—sneaky. They don't park either—they kind of slide into the curb. Anyway, having cops show up at our house wasn't an altogether new experience. Mongrel always told me to play dumb when cops asked questions. He said they liked you a lot more if you didn't seem to be smarter than they were.

"Are you Margaret Hoffer?" one of them says.

"Who wants to know?" I say.

"We do."

"And who are you?"

"I'm Constable Baker and this is Constable Dunn."

"Nice to meet you boys. Got badges?"

"Yes, we do," they say, pulling out two real shiny badges. "Now, are you Margaret Hoffer?"

"I guess I am," I say.

"You're under arrest for the murder of Marvin, otherwise known as Mongrel, Hoffer.

◆     ◆     ◆

"I's scared," says Big Dee.

"We'll be out of the dark soon," I say.

"I don't know how to swim."

"We ain't swimmin', for fuck's sake. We're in a boat," says Stella.

◆     ◆     ◆

## SACRED OBJECTS

Stella told me, before we left, that when you go on a journey, especially a spiritual one, it's good to look for a sacred object to carry with you. The object isn't so important in itself, but you can use it to remind you that you're on the path.

The object could look ordinary to anyone else, but to the finder it carries a special meaning. It might be something simple, like a pebble or a feather. Or it might be special and rare, like a hand-carved jade dragon.

Just before I got into the boat, I saw something shiny on the ground. I picked it up and stuck it in my pocket. Later on, I saw that it was a beer cap from a bottle of Corona. Mexican beer. Mongrel's favorite. I had to wonder if he wasn't there somewhere, helping me that night.

◆     ◆     ◆

Max was the collector. When he was little, he was always coming home with something. A robin's egg. A two-tone rock. An eagle feather. He seemed to have a natural feeling for the magic found inside things. He would run home, hands holding some new treasure he couldn't wait to show me.

"Guess what I found?" he says.

"A dinosaur nostril," I say.

"Mo-o-om!"

"All right, what?"

"Close your eyes."

"You put a snake in my hands, you're dead meat."

"Are they closed tight?"

"They're closed, for chrissake."

"Okay—open."

I see a package in my hands.

"What is it?" I ask.

"Money," says Max.

"Really?" I say.

"Yup," says Max.

"How much?" I say, peeling back the wrapper. It's a stack of thousands.

"I don't know. I didn't count it."

"Where did you find this, Max?" I say.

"In the bush."

"On our property?"

"I don't know."

"Can you keep a secret?" I say.

"Sure," he says.

"This is a lot of money. Now, if you don't tell anyone, especially your dad, we'll get you something real nice at the Kmart next time we go there. Maybe like a bike or something?"

"Wow, sure," says Max.

"And I'll make your favorite chocolate chip cookies, too.

"Wow," says Max.

◆　　◆　　◆

When we get to the other side and out from under the tarp, we can see the cop car lights flashing. It looks like Christmas. Hell, it *is* Christmas. There are colored lights all over the place, not that I'm paying much attention to them.

Wilson gets us out of the boat fast and then points to a van parked off the side of the highway. He hands the keys to Sam.

"I got to take this boat downriver. You get Stella to tell you how to get to the reserve."

"We gotta drive ourselves?" says Sam.

"Yeah, we don't want to be in the same car as you guys. You're fugitives. We'll end up in jail. No thanks. See you back on the rez. Oh, I almost forgot to tell you, Stella, you can't use the Duffy Lake road."

"What?" says Stella. "How come?"

"Road closed. Avalanche."

"Where the fuck we supposed to go then?"

"Brackendale. There's a medicine woman there. She's a Coast Salish. She'll be waiting for you. Drive safe, okay? It's my cousin's van. He'll kill me if you smash it up. You get caught, you tell the cops you stole it. Okay?"

"Yeah, okay. Hey, Wilson, thanks," says Stella.

"Well, let's get the fuck out of here," says Sam.

"Everyone in the back. Get under those blankets. And keep your mouths shut if I get pulled over. Jesus, look at those lights, eh? Merry Christmas!"

◆　　◆　　◆

# PART TWO

# OUTSIDE

IT IS NOT UNTIL THE NEXT MORNING THAT WE KNOW WE'VE DONE IT.
I'm not sure exactly where we are. It was hard to tell last night, being
under a blanket in the dark, praying all the way. But I know for sure
we aren't in prison now. It's way too quiet.

"I couldn't sleep," says Big Dee.

"Me neither," I say. "Way too much adrenaline."

"Too quiet for me," she says.

"Yeah, and I like it that way, so shut the fuck up, will you?"
Sam says.

Chan's huddled in a corner, chewing on a fingernail, looking a bit
shocked. Stella's the only one sleeping.

"This don't look much better than my cell—maybe worse," says
Sam, lighting up a smoke as she looks around.

"It's just temporary," I say.

"Praise be," says Big Dee.

"You want some coffee down there?" It's a voice from the top of
the stairs.

"Right on!" says Sam. "Who the hell's that?" she whispers.

"It's the medicine woman," I say.

"Oh, great, so now we're in a fucking Western movie," says Sam.

◆　　　◆　　　◆

I left everything behind except my cards and my scissors that I sneaked out of the salon, and the beer cap. I took the cards because I couldn't imagine being without them. I need something to read or at least to look at—to make me think. I hated leaving some of my clothes, but it wasn't as bad as when I left for prison.

I never realized how many things I had until I had to leave them all behind. I didn't know how all my things were so much a part of me. They surrounded me and made me feel safe. But when I went to prison, I had nothing.

Then I noticed that I started to collect things and put them together in my cell. Stuff from the flower shop. Pictures from magazines. I started to make the cell into my own place. Like Sam with her Harleys. Sam's cell was . . . well, it was Sam's all right. No doubt about it. She had her own style.

Stella's cell was pretty empty. She wasn't much on decorating. A few photographs stuck on the wall with Scotch tape. A tape deck with some cassettes. An ashtray for cigarettes or burning sage. Funny to think about this now. But we all left behind our precious things. Except me—I didn't leave my cards.

Mongrel would've brought a pound of coffee and an ounce of weed. He had his own special coffee blend—his secret blend. He took it with him everywhere.

"If there's one thing I can't stand," he'd say, after we had a coffee in some diner on the road, "it's bad fucking coffee. Like, I don't get it. It takes exactly the same amount of time to make a bad cup as it does to make a good one. So, I don't get it. Do you get it, Mags?"

"No, honey, I don't get it, but then I thought it was a pretty all right cup."

"That shit we just drunk. Pretty all right? Mags, you losin' it on me? That was pure unadultagrated shit."

"Unadulterated."

"Who the fuck cares?"

"I do."

"It's just a fucking word."

"It's just fucking coffee."

◆　　　◆　　　◆

## MONGREL'S ULTRA-SPECIAL JO
(specially blended by Ric at Continental Coffee)

1/4 pound Dark French
1/4 pound Jamaican Blue Mountain
1/4 pound Pure Yemen Mocha
1/4 pound Java Celeres Kollosi

(Optional: a gram of the finest hash, powdered. This part of the blend was supplied by Mongrel, not by the people at Continental Coffee.)

◆　　　◆　　　◆

I hate arguing. I hate how my body feels when I'm doing it. Everything starts to tense up. I can feel it here in my jaw first, right around where the words are going to come out.

I'm not so much afraid of what I might hear. I'm afraid of what I might say. I get mean when I'm pissed off. I was a lot meaner than Mongrel. He was too lazy to be mean. He got to "fuck you" before any real damage was done. He probably saved our marriage with that phrase.

"Fuck you, Mags!" And that was usually the end of it. He'd stomp out the door and then the bike would roar and he'd drive out the road on his back tire. Sometimes he came back the next day. Sometimes he didn't come back for a week or two.

◆ ◆ ◆

The first cup of coffee we drank that morning was the best-tasting cup I'd ever had.

"Shit, this here's great coffee," says Sam.

"Um-hmm!" says Big Dee, rolling her eyes.

"Tastes like heaven," I say.

"Tastes like freedom," says Stella.

◆ ◆ ◆

There's no tarot card for freedom in my deck. I guess oppression is close enough.

◆ ◆ ◆

We're free.

"We made it," says Sam. "We fucking bust out of maximum."

She starts laughing. Big Dee follows right behind. Chan gets that whinny of hers going and I can't help myself, I'm laughing, too. Stella just sits and shakes her head with a goofy smile on her face. Half her teeth are missing.

It seems like we're never going to stop until I notice that one of the laughs doesn't sound right. One by one the laughs go away, and then all that's left is the sound of Sam crying.

"Darlene didn't make it," Sam talking.

"No, honey, she didn't," says Big Dee.

◆　　◆　　◆

Lucky thing it's Christmas because we can come upstairs. We're in this basement that's been converted into a suite. It's on the reserve up at Brackendale. There are so many relatives coming and going and bringing their friends and kids that we can take turns coming up for a while. We get introduced as different members of other families and friends.

Big Dee only comes upstairs at night because she's so obvious. But she doesn't mind because they've got a big-screen TV and they don't mind her taking over the remote.

The living room is full of stuff. I look at it now and all I can think is, how would you store it all? They'd better hope they never have to do time.

When I went to jail, I put a lot of my things in storage and then

Chrissie took a lot for me—the really special things. I let a bunch go. Now I can't even remember half of it. It's sitting in boxes in some basement, maybe even getting more valuable. Like wine.

"Man, they got a lotta shit up there," I say.

"Lot of nice shit," says Big Dee.

"Nice family pictures," says Chan. "I miss my pictures."

"Where are they?" says Big Dee.

"Back home. In my country. Only have one, now. Me and my sister. Want to look?"

"Why not?" says Big Dee. "I ain't goin' nowhere."

◆    ◆    ◆

Shoe, the medicine woman, lives in a quiet spot separated from the rest of the houses on the reserve. She says she needs her privacy.

"What kind of a name is Shoe?" says Big Dee. "I ain't never hear of no woman called a shoe. You know what a shoe is? I think I heard about it from someone somewheres in jail. Maybe only in the men's joint, down in the South.

"It's this box in the shape of a shoe, and if you fuck up real bad or they don't like you, you get put in there. You can't stand up and you can't lay down and you stay doubled over and they keep you in there for days. Sun beating down. It break real hard men, that one. They call it the shoe."

"How come we're talking about jail?" says Stella.

"'Cause we already talk about the coffee," says Big Dee.

"Well, can't we talk about something else?" says Sam.

"Like what?" I say.

"I don't know, Harleys or something."

Groans all around.

"Whatsa matter with Harleys?" says Sam.

"I like Harley," says Chan.

"Atta girl," says Sam, giving Chan the thumbs up. "Hey, you guys. Did I tell you I had Carley get through to my friend, the one who rides, and she's gonna take my bike—well, after she paints over the tank—down across the border to my friend's place so's I can ride?"

"I think you may have told us that," says Stella.

"Maybe 'bout twenty times," says Big Dee.

"Yeah, well, fuck you guys. It's more exciting than talkin' about recipes."

"Hey, we got us a good one for boil chicken," says Big Dee.

"Boil chicken, prison-style," I say.

"We ain't gonna be eating that shit no more," says Sam.

◆　　◆　　◆

After Mongrel got out of Folsom, we got invited to dinner at the house of one of the guards. He'd got tight with Mongrel. He was what they call a weak cop. Without him, Mongrel couldn't have done business as usual in the joint. The truth was, this guard brought a lot of the dope in for Mongrel.

He and his wife lived in Sacramento in this huge house with five rottweilers. The sound of those animals when you came to the door was enough to make your blood run cold. They sounded like they were going to rip your throat out.

"Jesus, Mongrel, what's he got in there?"

"Dogs, I hope," says Mongrel.

"Hey, come on in," says John. "Don't mind the babies. Their bark is way worse than their bite. At least, so far, ha, ha."

Their house was like a zoo. They had more animals than you could count. In the living room, there was this big glass-top table and you'd look through the glass at this big snake. There were little cages all over with different animals—most of them exotic.

I asked his wife, Sadie, who was this hippy chick, how they ever went on holidays with all those animals to feed. She got this dreamy look on her face and said they took separate vacations. She said they liked different things. She liked to sit on the beach and make beaded necklaces. He liked to collect animals and guns.

She cooked this really great dinner. Roast chicken, new potatoes and asparagus from her own garden. The salad was incredible. It had flowers in it. Mongrel wouldn't touch it. I thought the dressing was the best.

I couldn't help but notice that they had a Smith and Wesson just lying on the counter. I asked her if she always left it lying around like that, and she just laughed this spacy laugh and told me that ever since John had started working for the DEA, they never knew who was going to show up at the door, ha, ha. She also laughed when I asked for her recipe for the salad dressing. She said it was so simple.

## SPACY SADIE'S SIMPLE SALAD DRESSING

3 parts top-of-the-line cold-pressed virgin olive oil
1 part balsamic vinegar
Secret ingredient: Add one part salad cream (NOT mayonnaise) by Cross and Blackwell.

Beat with a fork until smooth and creamy.

For another version of this recipe, you can substitute raspberry vinegar for balsamic.

◆　　◆　　◆

"Jeez, we was on TV last night," Big Dee says. "Bad pictures. Made us look like criminals. You think they might try to get you to smile when they do them mug shots."

"Nobody ever smiles for a mug shot, Big Dee," says Sam.

"Why not?" she asks.

"Because by the time they're taking a fuckin' mug shot, you know you're up the creek. It's not a happy moment, if you know what I mean."

"Well, if you skatin' on thin ice, you might as well dance, I says," says Big Dee.

"So how come you didn't smile for your mug shot, Big Dee?" I say.

"I was pissed off."

"See," says Stella, "I never smile, I ain't got half my teeth. Look dumb."

"What'd they say about the escape?" I ask.

"Not much."

"What about Johanna?"

"Serious condition."

"Not dead?"

"Not yet."

◆　　◆　　◆

Mongrel's cellie at Folsom was a Hell's Angel called Icepick. He'd murdered a guy in front of at least twenty-five witnesses. He'd shoved a screwdriver under the guy's chin clear up to his brain. If he hadn't been an Angel, he'd have done life, but the Red and White got him a couple of too-smart lawyers.

It was a funny thing how, come the trial, none of the witnesses had seen anything. They said they were either in the can taking a leak or they were lining up an important shot at the pool table or they were just plain too shitfaced to remember anything.

Even the prosecution thought the guy who Icepick offed was a low-life scumbag. So, they called it a "wildlife killing." Of course, they had to give Icepick something, so they gave him three to five years for an unregistered weapon.

Mongrel loved that story.

"A wildlife killing," he says. "Can you believe it, Mags? A wildlife killing."

"Sounds about right to me."

"Man, that Icepick was some piece of work."

"Uh-huh."

"Even the fuckin' guards loved him. He never caused no grief neither. Always said 'sir.' Real polite. Straight up. They used to say it was a pleasure to have him in.

"'Course, you wouldn't want to fuck with him. He got to work on the warden's bike. He made the best weapons in Folsom. Wasn't afraid to use them neither."

◆　　◆　　◆

Shoe told us that if we were going to stay with her, we had to follow some of the traditions. She said that a few of the elders weren't too happy about us being on the reserve. And a few others were dead against it. Shoe kept them off by promising that we'd do some of the rituals to cleanse ourselves, seeing as how all of us were prisoners and some of us were murderers.

"I don't mind," says Sam. "It's probably just sitting around smokin' on a pipe or something."

"You watch too many cowboy movies," says Stella.

"So, what are we going to do then?" says Sam.

"Shoe's going to take you through a healing time. Some of it is spiritual. Some of it is physical."

"How physical?" says Big Dee.

"Better ask Shoe," says Stella. "She's the medicine woman."

◆　　◆　　◆

"So, first thing I got to ask is if any one of you is in your moon," says Shoe.

"In my moon? What that mean?" Big Dee looking suspicious.

"In your moon means your time of month, like having your period," says Stella.

"I'm all out of moons," says Big Dee.

Shoe smiles and pats Big Dee on the shoulder.

"That's okay. Now, tomorrow morning, before light, I come down and get you and we all go to the river. I borrow some warm clothes for you. You go into the water, all the way in."

"You shittin' me?" says Big Dee.

"No, you have to cleanse from jail. It's part of the physical cleansing. Don't have to stay in too long. Just go all the way in and then come out."

"But there's snow on the ground."

"Not much."

"Enough to freeze our asses off."

"No. No ice in the river right now."

Big Dee leans over close to my ear.

"Are you startin' to think that maybe prison wasn't so bad after all?"

"Stella will make sure that you are all ready for tomorrow morning. Maybe go to bed early tonight. Don't watch too much television, especially the Big One."

"You talkin' to me?" says Big Dee.

"Yes, I am talking to you," says Shoe. She's smiling.

◆　　　◆　　　◆

I tried to explain about the fingerprints. I didn't want Max to come home and see his father like that. The gun was still in Mongrel's hand when I came to. I didn't want this to be Max's last memory—his dad slumped over in a chair, blood all over his shirt and a gun in his hand. I took the gun and wiped it clean. I realize now it was a real stupid thing to do. But at the time, I was in shock. I mean, it's one thing to find someone who's killed himself, but it's another to be right there when he does it.

◆　　　◆　　　◆

"See, back in history, for the Coast Salish peoples, which are the peoples from around here, the cedar tree was the most important. It gave us wood to build our canoes, and we made our clothes out of it, and we made our temporary shelters with it. We didn't live in teepees."

We passed through a bunch of cedars on our way to the river. It was raining.

"I'm getting wet," says Big Dee.

"Not half as wet as you will be soon," I say.

"Shoe," says Big Dee, "this a absolute have-to?"

"Have-to," says Shoe.

The river is moving fast. If you're not careful, you could get swept away. Sam strides over to the edge of the water, buck naked. She puts her foot in.

"Shit," she says.

Big Dee touches the water with her foot.

"Holy Jesus, Lord."

Stella just walks in, ducks, and walks back out. She looks like something out of a nature movie. Her hair hangs all the way down her back. She's got these great tattoos. And she's got a body that most men would kill for—I mean, they'd want one like hers, give or take a few things.

Getting into that water is one of the hardest things I've ever done in my whole life. It's so cold it takes my breath away.

"Get your head under," says Shoe.

◆　　◆　　◆

Shoe has some interesting stuff on her walls. She collects things out of books, writes them out, and sticks them up. Actually, she puts them on the fridge first, stuck there by a fridge magnet given to her by one of her grandchildren.

If she likes what she put there well enough, it goes onto a cork board in the hall. And if she really likes it, she glues a piece of cardboard behind it and puts a frame on it and hangs it in the living room. This one is in the living room. It goes like this.

UNCERTAIN ADMISSION

The sky looks down on me in aimless blues
The sun glares at me with a questioning light
The mountains tower over me with uncertain shadows
The trees sway in the bewildered breeze
The deers dance in perplexed rhythms
The ants crawl around me in untrusting circles
The birds soar above me with doubtful dips and dives
They all, in their own way, ask the question

Who are you, who are you?
I have to admit to them to myself
I am an Indian.

Frances A. (Bazil) Katasse

I ask Shoe who this guy is, and she says the poem was written by some kid. He wasn't even sixteen when he wrote it.

I like Shoe's place. I feel comfortable here—welcome. I like the way people come and go. How they talk to each other. Laugh a lot. Tell lots of dumb jokes. They're kind.

The other morning, Shoe and I are sitting in the kitchen having a coffee. I'm looking out the window and I see this big bird sitting in a tree, maybe twenty-five yards from the house.

"Is that an eagle?" I ask.

"Yeah. That's a bald eagle."

"Wow, it's beautiful."

"Yes, it is."

"Stella says she's an eagle."

"Uh huh. Sounds right."

"Big Dee's a bear."

Shoe smiles and nods.

"Sam's having a hard time, Shoe. She needs some help."

"I know."

"Can you help her?"

"Only if she asks me to."

"She's very proud."

"I know that, too."

"I'll tell her to talk to you."

"Okay."

◆　　◆　　◆

I used to like reading murder mysteries. They took my mind off things. I liked trying to figure out who was guilty. I'd learn who all the characters were and then I'd put the book down and come up with my own idea about who did what. I wouldn't go back to the book until I had it all figured out, my way. Sometimes I was pretty close. But sometimes it was just as much fun being wrong.

I think if my case was put in a book, I'd probably say I was guilty. Tampering with evidence. A motive. That's why you have to be careful about evidence. It can be misleading. When you put everything together in a certain way, you can come up with a story.

But that's what it is, a story. And if your lawyer's story is better than the prosecution's story, then you get off. So, you better hope you got a lawyer who tells good ones. I didn't think my lawyer had it in her. Actually, I think she thought I was guilty, deep down, and it got in the way of her doing her job.

◆　　◆　　◆

"We got to do this three more times? I ain't doing it," says Big Dee.

"You have to, Big Dee."

"I don't have to do nothin'."

"They're doing us a major favor."

"Say what?"

"Look, Big Dee, they're letting us stay here. We need a place to chill."

"Chill is about right," she says.

"They're taking care of us until the heat dies down."

"Or I dies, whichever come first."

"It won't kill you, Big Dee."

"I don't get the point of it," she says.

"Shoe don't want prison energy on the rez," says Stella. "Some of us killed people. We got to be cleansed. The elders decided."

"Who the heck are these elders, anyway?" says Big Dee.

"The elders are the elders. They're the older people on the reserve. They know things. They seen a lot. We need to show them respect."

"Easy for you to do this cleansing," says Big Dee. "You're Indian."

"Not so easy the first time," says Stella.

"Oh yeah?" says Sam. "When was that?"

"Once when I was a kid. There were snow drifts up to here, eh. And once when I come out of jail—the first time."

"How many times you been in?" says Sam.

"Lost count," says Stella.

◆      ◆      ◆

## TWO OF WANDS: PURITY

Just looking at the picture on the card, I feel my body go cool. Snow on a branch in that white winter sun. A window that looks frosted. A white flower. Footsteps. And a hand holding onto a candle. The flame that burns and purifies.

That's what Shoe's making us do. Purification. The book says it's about being authentic and natural, true to yourself. Not worrying about what someone else thinks about you. Easy to say. Harder to do.

◆　　◆　　◆

Mongrel thought you could tell how good something was by the price. He figured the more expensive it was, the better it was and the more he wanted it. He never felt right about cheaping out on our wedding. He did a lot of things to make it up to me.

He never put his money in a bank, at least not in an account. Too easy to trace. He liked safety deposit boxes. He also liked diamonds. Small things. Easy to transport. Dogs couldn't smell them.

He thought of everything as an investment—how it might have more value later. He liked playing with money. And he was good at it. He played us into some pretty fancy cars and nice vacations.

One time, he was smuggling a bunch of diamonds over the border. I got this idea about how to smuggle them. I stuck all the diamonds onto a strip of masking tape. Then I put a second layer of masking tape over top of them. I made it into a loop big enough to slide my hand through. Next I covered this over with papier-mâché, but nicely so it was real smooth. Then I let it dry overnight, and the next day I painted the papier-mâché with flower designs. It looked so cool. A woman in Mexico City tried to buy it off me.

"But it's gorgeous and so unique," she says.

"You like it?" I say.

"I adore it. You must tell me where you got it."

"I made it, actually."

"Really? Do you sell them?"

"Sometimes."

"You must let me buy this one."

"It ain't for sale," says Mongrel, walking up with a Tecate in his hand. "I bought it for her in the Himalayas for our fifteenth wedding anniversary. It's got sentimental value, you know what I mean?" He looks at me. "Honey, you know you're not supposed to sell your things."

He turns to the woman.

"Look, lady, she's been like this most of her life. It runs in the family. She'd sell her hair if it wasn't nailed on. Has to take pills for it, if you know what I mean." He turns to me. "Honey, did you take your pills today?"

The woman is looking uncomfortable.

"Probably not," he says. "Sorry to disappoint you, ma'am."

When she's out of earshot, he grabs me by the arm.

"Don't fuck with me, Mags."

"I was just having some fun."

"Fuck fun," he says. "You lose that bracelet, I'll kill you."

"I'm not going to lose it."

"You got any fuckin' idea how much you're packing on that wrist?"

"I don't know, honey. How much?"

"A fuck of a lot, smartass."

"Well, then, maybe you could take us out to dinner at some nice restaurant?"

"Hell, with what you got in that bracelet, I could buy the fuckin' restaurant."

"I'll wear my white dress. And pretend to be your mistress."

"You ain't listenin' to me, Mags," says Mongrel.

"You ain't saying what I want to hear."

◆　　　◆　　　◆

"A medicine woman sees with the other eye and hears with the other ear." Shoe talking. "You can see normal, but if you see with the other eye, you see deep.

"You have your natural ear that hears all the sounds around you. But the other ear can hear the trees talking to each other, or the birds, or the animals.

"When I go to gather medicine, I don't just pick any plant. The plants tell me which ones to pick. They light up like a candle. And I can actually hear them and they're so happy to give themselves up.

"When I walk along, I see the medicine shining from a plant and I know it's the right one. Maybe this one doesn't light up, and I look way over there and those other plants do light up, but that's because my eye can see it. And I know that that medicine is going to work on the right person.

"So, when I make my medicine, you know, I'm like as if I'm in prayer all the way through. My whole body is so full of the spirit of the plants that I almost feel numb all over. When I'm busy making medicine in here, singing away, the lower part of my arms is numb from the power of the medicine. You can feel it in the room. My grandchildren can feel it. They know when I'm making medicine."

◆          ◆          ◆

Sam needed strong medicine. She was a mess, not only on account of Darlene dying, but also because she had too much time to think about it. A lot of time we were just hanging out—doing the spiritual stuff in the morning and then working on crafts in the afternoon. Shoe had us making them for the Christmas craft fair over at this gallery off the reserve in Brackendale.

Sam wasn't big on crafts. Instead, she took one look at Shoe's recreational vehicle and she went into overhaul mode. Shoe finally let her fool around with it. Shoe had abandoned the RV when it stopped working. Figured they'd get it fixed in the spring in time for the powwow in Omak.

"You gotta take better care of things," Sam says to Shoe. "Look at the color of this here oil. It's black. When was the last time you had a tune-up?"

"Maybe a couple of years ago, I don't know. Don't pay much attention to these things," says Shoe.

"Shit, Shoe, you're killing your pony."

"Just an old truck camper."

"No, it's a home on wheels. A way to get free for a while. I'd love to have one of these. You gotta love your vehicles, Shoe. They perform way better when they're loved."

"Most things do," says Shoe.

Sam stuck her head into the engine.

"Might have to call you the Turtle," says Shoe. "Always hiding behind something hard. Tough shell."

"Yeah, that's me," says Sam.

"Maybe not so good to do all the time."

"If it works, don't fuck with it. That's how I see it," says Sam.

"So, I guess it's working then?" says Shoe.

Sam comes out from under the hood. She looks at Shoe, who's moving the dirt around with the toe of her boot.

"No, I guess it ain't," says Sam, crossing her arms over her chest and leaning against the RV.

"Uh-huh. I see."

"I'm not much good at asking for help," says Sam.

"That's okay," says Shoe.

"I feel like my chest is going to explode. I got this bad pain right here."

"In your heart," says Shoe.

"I don't know. Maybe. I keep looking for her to be there—to be here, you know? I wake up and I expect her to be hanging onto me. And then I have to remember that she's never going to be."

"She might be gone, but her spirit's still here. She's gone to a better place. She's not running anymore."

"Maybe. But I'm still here and I'm still running. And everything hurts," says Sam.

"Maybe I can help you," says Shoe.

◆　　　◆　　　◆

When Chrissie gave up the baby, I had no idea it was going to be so hard on her. I still saw her as a baby herself. I thought she'd just want to take the easy way out. But I was wrong. She only had him for a few days, but she poured every ounce of love that she could into that little boy—probably enough for a lifetime.

It hurt Mongrel, too, even though he'd never cop to it. He just acted like he was pissed off about something else to cover up his feelings.

The whole thing brought back bad memories for him. His own mother left him with a foster family when he was only three. He said it didn't matter. One less asshole to buy presents for is how he put it. But there was something about it that put a knot in him.

He always acted weird around Mother's Day. The kids got me cards and things, but Mongrel took a beer and sat in front of the TV for the whole night. It happened like that every year.

Finally, me and the kids decided to have some fun with it. The kids decorated the TV. I made Mongrel's favorite dinner. We treated him like a king all night. It worked. He started to look forward to Mother's Day.

◆　　◆　　◆

"The cedar tree made our homes, our clothes, and our transportation. It was also our counselor. You can talk to a tree. Did you know that?"

That's what Shoe does with Sam. She takes her out into the forest, not far from the house, and tells her to pick the right tree for her. Sam walks over to it straightaway. Then Shoe tells her to kneel down and wrap her arms around the tree. And then tell the tree her story.

"I can't talk to a tree," says Sam. "I'd feel dumb."

"Don't know till you try."

"I need to be alone," says Sam.

"I'm going back to the house."

"What do I say?"

"Just say what's important."

Shoe comes back to the house and pours herself a coffee. She sits down at the kitchen table and starts a game of solitaire. Every once in a while, you can hear Sam. When she's really loud, Shoe nods. Then she just carries on with her game.

Once the moon comes out, high and full, it makes everything outside look blue. When Sam hasn't made any sound for a while, Shoe puts away the cards and puts on her parka.

"Make sure there's lots of hot coffee," she says. "Probably going to be up all night."

◆　　◆　　◆

## SIX OF CUPS: SORROW

The card for Sorrow is beautiful. It's dark, the color of dark pansies—rust and mauve. There's an overturned pot the color of sunset in Mexico. And flowers. This card is hard to understand. The more you look at it, the more you see. Sorrow has many levels.

Death and sorrow. Sorrow follows death. A time for purification, that's what Shoe says. Purification because you pour your sadness out, like water out of a jug. And letting that sadness out makes room for something new.

◆　　◆　　◆

I couldn't say goodbye to Tony. All I remember in the panic of it all, when everything seemed to be moving in slow motion, is that I saw him standing near the door. He was looking at me. Just looking.

"Maybe he could come up here," I say.

"You crazy?" says Big Dee.

"Danger," says Chan.

"They're not going to follow him."

"Why not?" says Sam.

"He's done work on the reserve before. Did a few meetings," I say.

"He's a risk," says Big Dee.

"Nobody comes here," says Stella. "The elders decide that."

"How come them elders do all the deciding?" Big Dee asks.

"Because that's the way it works here. They been around long enough to know not to make decisions too quick."

"Maybe that's how come the whiteman won the West," says Big Dee.

"It ain't over yet," says Stella.

◆　　◆　　◆

This is what the eagle saw: Sam kneeling in front of a big cedar, holding onto it, rocking back and forth. Then a sound comes out of her throat. Not much. Just a whimper. Maybe someone's name. Rocking. Swaying. The sound getting bigger.

Then something rips through her and she holds the tree even tighter—hanging on. The pain cuts through her body and she groans. She loses track of time. It seems like she's been there for hours when Shoe comes to get her, carrying a blanket.

"Put this around you. You're going to the sweat lodge now."

When they get back to the kitchen, we're all waiting. Sam looks different. She looks a bit worn out, but she's softer. Like she got rid of some heavy weight out there. Some of the toughness is gone.

"You okay?" says Big Dee.

"I'm okay." says Sam.

Chan runs over and puts her arms around Sam, patting her back like she was a baby and saying, Shush, shush. Sam's crying but she isn't making any sound. One by one, we go over and touch her, hold her. Shoe pours herself a coffee and waits.

◆     ◆     ◆

Mongrel never said he loved me. It wasn't his style. And I never said I loved him either, because I wasn't sure for a long time that I did. At least not when I first married him. But later on, there were times when I'd watch him working on his bike. That's when he was most happy—muttering to himself, cursing if he hurt himself. If it was sunny, I'd sit on the steps with a cup of coffee in my hands, watching him. He pretended not to notice. Pretended I wasn't there. Then, suddenly, he'd look up and smile like a little boy. That's when I loved him.

◆   ◆   ◆

When he walked up from the basement with a gun in his hand, I knew he wasn't joking. He'd come up on me with a gun before. One time, he came into the bedroom when I was undressing. He pointed a pistol at me.

"All right, lady, take all your clothes off."

I slowly start to take off my sweater.

"Where's your old man?" he said.

"Probably out screwing around with the neighbor's wife."

"Aw, shit, Mags, you're ruining it."

"All right, all right. My old man's coming home soon."

"How soon?"

"Real soon."

"I guess you'd better get your clothes off fast, then."

He lays the pistol down on the dresser and watches me. When I don't have anything on, he walks over and grabs me. He's wild.

But when he came up from the basement that day, he wasn't wild at all. He was scary. His voice was flat. He said he couldn't come up with a reason for living. I didn't know what to tell him. I couldn't come up with a reason for him to live either.

◆   ◆   ◆

"On the fourth day, you are born again," says Shoe. "You start over like it's day one, like a baby. A new life. You decide. You choose a tree or something that speaks to you, that calls to you. And on that tree or rock or whatever, you meditate. You talk about what you're going to do with your life. This is the way of showing you the path.

"And on the fourth day, you feel pretty good because you've decided what you're going to do with your life. You've decided which path you're going to take. Maybe it will be hard, but you'll be able to follow it.

"Sometimes, it's easier to see the changes on someone else. You look at them the last day of the cleansing, and you get this feeling there's a new light shining on them. And you can really tell they've changed. They feel different. They know exactly what it is for them—like, it comes to them.

"Maybe they've seen a vision of their life, or a dream. Their spirit helper has come to them in that dream, maybe a bear or an eagle. See, in real life, if a bear comes up to you, you'd probably run like a sonofabitch. But in a dream, if a bear comes to you, maybe it will rub against you or stand in front of you, but not in a scary way. Then you know that it's your spirit helper coming to show you the path."

◆　　◆　　◆

Twelve elders met last night to talk about the situation. Shoe tells us how it went.

"They're prisoners. They might bring problems to the reserve," said one of the elders.

"We're not to judge," said Shoe.

"Stella isn't one of ours," said another.

"Stella has done a lot for us. Besides, she's an Indian."

"What about the others? They're not Indian."

"They're traveling together. I promised Wilson Featherstone I'd help. He says that if someone's in trouble, they should at least be able to count on us Indians," Shoe said.

"Not criminals, though."

"How do we know what they did?"

"Some of them murdered people."

"We don't know why. Might have been self-defense."

"Maybe. Maybe not."

"I can look after them. It's my business. It's my home, eh?"

"Your home is on the reserve. What you do in your home touches all of us. Think about what you are doing, Shoe."

"I can't just throw them out."

"Maybe we can find them another place."

◆　　　◆　　　◆

"I seen her standing right there, just as clear as you, Maggie," Sam talking. "Darlene's standing there and she tells me everything's all right. I want to touch her. So I reach over and just before I touch her, I hear this noise. I blink, just a second, and she's gone. And this horse is standing there. But this time, it's real, because I touch it. It's a real horse."

"That was your spirit guide," says Shoe.

"I don't know," says Sam. "It looked like the real thing to me."

"Of course," says Shoe, "It *is* the real thing. Just a different kind of real." She lights a cigarette from the cigarette she's already smoking.

◆　　◆　　◆

"So, says Sam, "Where we gonna go?"

"Maybe over to the gallery," says Shoe.

"Brackendale?" I say.

"I think so," says Shoe, "You got to understand. It's Christmas time. The elders don't want no problems."

"Yeah, I can dig that," says Sam.

"Brackendale's just off the reserve. Big place. Lots of room. People always coming and going so you won't stick out. Except maybe the Big One." Shoe smiles over at Big Dee, who flashes her a peace sign.

"How come they're all right about it?"

"The guy who built it—you'll meet him tonight. Name's Thor. We did him a lot of favors over the years. Helped him build the gallery. He says you can stay and have Christmas dinner. He's a friend."

"What if someone sees us?"

"The gallery's closed to public on Christmas. His wife Dorte is going to cook a couple of turkeys. She's a great cook. Wish I was going."

"When do we leave here?"

"Tonight."

"Pretty sudden."

"Yup."

"We appreciate what you've done for us, Shoe."

"It's okay."

"You did more than you had to."

"It was easy for me. I like you. All of you. Oh, by the way, I got a plan. There's a bunch of us heading down to Omak in a few days. Going for the bingo. We can take the motor home, now that it's working, thanks to Sam here. Pretty good mechanic. We can hide all of you in the back."

"Are you crazy?" says Sam.

"I hope so."

"Ha, ha," says Big Dee.

"What about the border?" I say.

"We cross at Osoyoos. No problem there," says Shoe.

"What if they check the back?"

"Never check us Indians. They always ask the same questions. 'Where you going?' The border guy asks. We say we're going to the bingo or to the powwow. Or whatever. Then he asks if we got any liquor or cigarettes. We say no. What a stupid question. Why would anyone try to sneak booze and smokes across the American border, heading south. It don't make sense. You'd have to be real dumb to do that.

"Then he asks if we got any firearms. We all laugh and tell him, Nope, you got 'em all. Then he laughs and tells us to go through and hopes we have good luck at the bingo.

"One time, one of our kids asks if a bow and arrow is a firearm. That's the only time the border guy stops us—practically takes the whole motor home apart. He can't find no bow and arrow, though. So, he asks where it is, and the kid says he don't have one, just wanted to know if it counts as a firearm. The guy is really pissed off. We don't stop laughing all the way to Omak."

◆    ◆    ◆

Mongrel was real cool at borders, especially considering he was always packing something. He kept trying to find new ways to sneak stuff across.

"Hey, listen to this, Mags."

"I'm listening."

"Okay. You know how Jake's into bees?"

"Yeah."

"Okay. You know where he gets them from?"

"Yeah, he gets them from Oregon."

"That's right, Mags. And you know how they come here?"

"Nope."

"Well, I'm gonna tell you. They come up in cans. Cans of bees."

"Uh-huh, so what's your point?"

"My point is, I bring the dope across the border in bee cans."

"I don't get it."

"I can't see some border guard wanting to open up a can of bees, can you? Especially if we make sure a few dozen of them are flying around in the back."

"We've got a van, Mongrel."

"So?"

"So, I don't want to be driving down the highway with a few dozen bees flying around my head."

"So, I gotta work the bugs out of it."

"Pretty funny, Mongrel."

"Huh?"

◆    ◆    ◆

Mongrel did get into bees for a while. He kept the hives on the outside edge of a field where he was growing this special bud. He figured the bees were probably happy because they were stoned most of the time. He also believed the honey got you high.

We collected enough honey from two summers to last us for about ten years, if we hadn't given so much of it away. I started cooking and baking with honey instead of sugar. It was a little tricky at first. One of our favorite things was honey-butter. It was dead simple to make.

## ALMOST-GETS-YOU-HIGH HONEY-BUTTER

I can't believe how much mileage I've got out of this recipe, considering how simple it is.

> Butter (at room temperature)
> Honey (at room temperature)

Okay, now the thing is to make up only enough of the honey-butter to use in a week. Honey will last forever with nothing in it (I mean, they've found honey in the tombs of the Egyptian pharaohs—or was it honey that they wrapped them in? Anyways, it lasts a long time unadulterated), but if you put something into it, it spoils.

Measure the honey and butter, one part each, into a mixing bowl. Beat until smooth and light. Put into a jam jar.

Always keep the honey-butter in the fridge. It's great on toast, pancakes—anything that's warm.

◆    ◆    ◆

Everyone's quiet. We're packing up—not that there's much to pack. But Shoe and some of the people on the reserve have given us stuff for Christmas. Shoe found this old postcard with a horse on it, running wild. It was one of those old-fashioned hand-painted photographs. The colors were beautiful.

"And this is for you, Sam," says Shoe.

"Wow, cool postcard. Hey, look at this, Chan. Year of the Horse. That's you."

"No. I'm Year of the Pig," says Chan.

"Too bad," says Sam.

"No, pig's good. Nice character. Good friend. Very loyal."

"I wouldn't want to be no pig," says Big Dee.

"Why not?" says Chan.

"'Cause I'm a bear," says Big Dee.

"Me, too," says Shoe. "That's my animal spirit. My whole family is bears. And my husband's family is the eagle. He's lucky because there are lots of them around here."

"Stella's an eagle," says Chan.

"And you're a mouse," says Stella. "Nice little snack for an eagle." She winks at Chan.

◆    ◆    ◆

Stella says that the person who has the bear as her teacher is very strong. But strong from the inside. Something about how the bear hibernates. The person who is the bear has to go deep inside herself to learn things. And the learning comes from staying away from everybody. Staying alone to pray and to be tested.

♦    ♦    ♦

I sometimes wonder how my life would have been different if I'd married Danny, the guy I was in love with when I married Mongrel. You pay a price if you settle, at least that's what Josie said. She used to say she'd rather have nothing than settle for less. But after she was single for a long time, I think she changed her tune and settled. She never liked Mongrel very much. He couldn't stand her.

"I don't want that bitch in my house."

"Our house. And that bitch is my best friend."

"Fine. But I don't want her around when I'm here. She looks at me like I just crawled out from under a fuckin' rock. She's full of herself. Keep her the fuck away from me, Mags. She just might find herself needin' a nose job."

"Jesus, Mongrel."

"I ain't jokin'."

"Maybe if you were a little nicer to her."

"Fuck nice."

♦    ♦    ♦

It wasn't as if I never thought of killing Mongrel. I did. I mean, I wouldn't tell that to my lawyer. But I don't know anyone who's been married for a long time who hasn't thought about ways to off the old man or the old lady.

That's one of the reasons I liked reading detective novels. There were all these interesting ways to kill people, such as some poison that can't be traced in the body. I knew I could have fed Mongrel poison mushrooms. But everybody would know I'd done it because Mongrel knew his mushrooms. It went with the territory. Besides, I was too scared to have poison mushrooms in the house, because of the kids. You turn your back for a second and they've swallowed them. It wasn't worth it.

Josie and I were always trying to outdo each other, seeing who could come up with the best way to kill the old man. She went for gory deaths, like pushing him over a cliff into a rock canyon. Or arranging for a big boulder to fall on his head and crush his skull. Or setting up some freak hunting accident.

One time, when we were really stoned, we came up with this wild idea where we'd kill them both at the same time—a double accident. When Mongrel came in, we were rolling on the floor, holding our stomachs, practically peeing ourselves.

"What the fuck's so funny?" Mongrel said.

Josie's eyes went wide and then she let out a shriek of laughter. Mongrel turned around so fast, he left a skid mark of black rubber on the floor. Then he booted the door open. Bang. He was gone.

◆　　　◆　　　◆

Big Dee can't remember the last time she had Christmas dinner on the outside. For me, it's the first one without the kids. Sam doesn't have Darlene, but she's doing better. For Chan, it's a whole new experience. Stella's sitting by the fireplace, right at home, a big smile on her face.

Everybody has something to do. Sam keeps the wood chopped and the fire going. Chan goes out and picks up pinecones and cuts some holly. She decorates the tables. Big Dee keeps Thor out of the kitchen with her stories. I hang out in the kitchen with Dorte. Stella mostly just smokes cigarettes.

I love being in a kitchen again—all the buzz of making a big dinner. Lots of things to keep track of. What time to put the potatoes on so they're soft on the inside and brown and crackly on the outside. I always did roast potatoes, never mashed. Not at Christmas.

Everything smells wonderful. This is quality food. Not that prison shit. Not the cheap cut or the shortcut. The real thing.

When we finally get it all on the table, everybody goes quiet. We hold hands and Thor says a prayer about how the two most important things in life are food and friendship.

We tell stories over turkey and stuffing and cranberry sauce. We laugh with our mouths full. Every once in a while, one of us looks at the other and we hold there for a second, maybe smile. The potatoes are just right.

When dinner's over, a gal called Leslie takes out her guitar and plays for everyone. She writes her own stuff. She's real good. We sing Christmas carols and old songs. And I try to remember that I'm safe—at least for this day.

I don't think I'll ever forget this Christmas. I know for sure I won't forget the turkey stuffing. It's the best I've ever had.

## DORTE'S EXOTIC CHRISTMAS TURKEY STUFFING

Wild rice
Whole wheat bread

Butter

1 large onion

Poultry seasoning

Salt

Pepper

Pecans

Cashews

Pine nuts

Dried cranberries

Dates

Dried apricots

Cook up a cup of wild rice in advance.

Tear the bread into smallish pieces.

Put a gob of butter in a big fry pan. Sauté the onion for a few minutes on low heat. Dump in some of the bread and wild rice. Add poultry seasoning, salt, and pepper to taste. Add a handful of pecans, cashews, and pine nuts. Add a small handful of dried cranberries. Cut up 3 or 4 dates. Add. Cut into nice slices about 6 dried apricots. Add. Keep stirring all this to coat with butter and spices. Make sure it's not too dry. Add some more rice and bread. When it's just a bit too much to fill the turkey, then it's just the right amount.

Stuff the body cavity. I always put a bit in the neck cavity as well.

◆     ◆     ◆

Max came running into the house calling me. He didn't stop at the bedroom door. Our only rule was that if the door was closed, the bedroom was out of bounds because his dad and I were busy. But this was the middle of the afternoon and the door was open and he knew Mongrel was out of town.

He stopped at the bottom of the bed and looked at both of us. There was no expression on his face. Tim just leaned back and said, "You deal with it, it's your kid." I stared back at Max. There wasn't anything I could say. "I'm sorry." I think that's what I said. He turned around and ran out. He didn't come back for two days. When he did, he wouldn't look me in the eyes.

◆     ◆     ◆

### SIX OF WANDS: TRUST

I have a hard time looking at this card. It's all about how kids see the good in others. They're just naturally trusting. They trust that you're going to take care of them and not change things too fast on them. The card has a lot of different hands on it, touching, holding on, just holding. But there's this pair in the bottom left corner—two men shaking hands. Tim was Mongrel's best friend.

◆     ◆     ◆

We leave early. It's still dark outside. Stella rides up front with Shoe.

"We're taking one hell of a chance," says Big Dee.

"We got no choice," I say. "We got to cross the border somewhere."

"What if they stop us?"

"We deal with it. Look, Big Dee, we gotta really keep our heads out of what could go wrong. I don't want to make it happen."

"Well, I's scared."

"We're all scared, Big Dee."

"Not me," says Chan.

"Why not?"

"I know we get there."

"How?" says Big Dee.

"Just know. Got a feeling."

"Pull us a card, Maggie," says Sam.

"No way," I say. "I'm not going to take a chance and pick a bad one. Not that any of them are really bad. But some of them just sound bad. And a bad one right now could jinx everybody."

The closer we get to the border, the quieter it gets in the back of the RV. When the camper finally stops, we all hold our breath. The customs guy does his thing.

"Where you from?" he says.

"Brackendale, up past Squamish," says Shoe.

"Got any liquor or cigarettes?"

"Nope."

"Any firearms?"

"Nope. You got 'em all."

"Ha, ha. I guess we do. What about the bows and arrows?" he says.

"We traded them in for some Uzis," says Shoe.

"Jesus," says Big Dee under her breath. "What the hell she sayin'?"

"What's the purpose of your visit?"

"Going to the bingo down at Omak."

"Well, good luck. Hope you win something."

Shoe steps on the gas. We're all just looking at each other, not breathing. Stella sticks her head around from the front and gives a thumbs up.

"Shit," says Sam, "do they have to be so friendly?"

◆　　◆　　◆

Chan says she was born in Burma. Her mother died when she was just a baby. Her father was a drug runner in the Triangle. Chan was a mule, carrying drugs over borders from the time she was able to walk. Her father tried to get her away from the jungle by finding her a job with a rich family in Hong Kong. She took care of the children and cooked. But she hated Hong Kong. She loved the jungle. The freedom.

She found her way back to the drug trade. One day, she saw a picture of a snowcapped mountain in a country called Canada. She decided that was where she was going to go. From that moment on, she held that goal in her mind.

They promised her free passage, a place to stay, and enough money to get an apartment in Vancouver. There were mountains, just like the ones in her picture, right near the city. They said they'd try to find her father and send him over when she was settled. It was a dream come true. She'd never really seen snow except in pictures.

◆　　◆　　◆

We're across the border, heading for Twisp, Washington. Chan has her nose pressed against the window.

"What you lookin' at?" says Big Dee.

"Snow," says Chan.

"I hates snow."

"So white," says Chan.

"That probably why," says Big Dee.

"You never seen snow before?" I say.

"No, only in pictures," says Chan.

"Hey, Shoe, pull over."

"What's the matter?"

"Nothing. Chan's never seen snow before."

"No shit?"

Shoe pulls over to the side of the road and we all get out. Watching Chan is like watching a cat when it goes out for the first time in snow. It can't figure it out. So it starts to step on it, then it stops. Looks confused. Shakes a paw.

That's what Chan's like. She walks over to the side of the road, takes a big step, and goes in up to her thigh. She gets a look on her face that you just have to see. She puts her hand down to steady herself and it sinks in past her elbow. Stella's got her hand over her mouth trying not to laugh. Chan pulls her hand out.

"Cold!" she says, like it's a big surprise.

"'Course it's cold. It's snow," says Big Dee.

"I never think it was cold like this," says Chan, putting the snow to her lips.

"You got to know one important thing about snow, Chan," says Sam.

"What?"

"Never eat it if it's yellow."

"Ha, ha," says Big Dee.

"How 'bout snow angels? You ever make snow angels?" asks Stella.

"How the hell could she make snow angels if she ain't seen snow? Jesus, Stella."

"There are angels in the snow?" Chan is wide-eyed.

"Sure, watch," says Stella. She steps out into the fresh snow and falls on her back. She waves her arms and legs. Chan watches her every move. Then Stella gets up carefully. She's got snow all over her back.

"See, Chan, there's the snow angel."

"Where?" says Chan.

"Right there," says Stella. "See the head, and the wings, and the skirt?"

Chan looks and then she breaks into a smile.

"Why don't you try it?" says Stella. "Anyone can."

Next thing, I'm flat out making one. And Sam is, too.

"C'mon Big Dee."

"I hates snow." She hardly gets the words out when a snowball smacks her in the ass.

"Someone gonna die for that," she says, grabbing a handful of snow and throwing it at Sam. Sam ducks and it hits Chan. Chan scoops up a bunch and goes running after Stella, who's giggling like a little girl.

"Hurry up, you guys. We don't want to miss the bingo," says Shoe.

◆     ◆     ◆

Shoe doesn't tell us until we're in Omak that she's letting us take the RV.

"You're not serious," I say.

"Sure. We can hitch a ride back with some friends. We weren't going to use the RV till summer anyways. You might as well take it."

"But how do we get it back to you?"

"Maybe you can drop it off if you go to New Mexico. We got some friends there. Other places, too. Stella knows where. She come with us a few years back. Met them at the powwow down there. Maybe they might come up for the powwow up here. They could bring the RV with them. It don't matter. It'll come back one way or another."

"You saved our asses," I say.

"Well, you take care of my pony," says Shoe, looking over at Sam.

"You got it," says Sam.

"Okay, then," says Shoe.

It's a hard moment. Nobody wants to say goodbye. Finally, Shoe pats the RV and nods her head.

"Well, we gotta go. Don't want to miss the bingo," she says.

◆     ◆     ◆

Sam's bike is waiting for her when we get to Twisp. Debra and Carey, Sam's friends, have it stored in their garage.

"Jesus H. Christ!" Sam spinning in tight circles. "They fucked it up!"

"It looks great to me," I say.

"They painted over Marilyn!"

"Well, Sam, they couldn't bring it across the way it was. It would have been a dead giveaway."

"I know that, Maggie. But they were supposed to tape it up first, for chrissake."

Sam stands looking at her bike, arms crossed.

"Fuck," she says, kicking the ground.

"At least they got it here. It could still be sitting in that barn."

Sam looks over at me, her mouth pinched, but she does nod her head.

"Yeah, I guess so. But shit, Maggie, that was such a beautiful paint job. I mean, look at this." She points out runs on the tank. "Bad workmanship." She licks her finger and rubs on a spot. Her finger is all black.

"What the fuck?" she says, taking a rag and spitting on it. She rubs another spot and the rag comes up black. "Get me some water, Maggie." I run and get a bucketful. Sam starts washing the tank. The black is coming off and, under it, Marilyn is coming through. Sam's holding her face tight so she won't cry.

"Damn Indians have turned me into a sissy," she says, wiping her face with the back of her hand.

◆　　　◆　　　◆

It wasn't Mongrel's fault I didn't love him at first. He was so sure about us that he never even thought to ask me. Anyway, love wasn't a word he was comfortable with. He loved his bike. That was love to him.

"I love that bike, Mags."

"I know."

"I mean, fuck man, look at those lines. Big. Fat. Growls like some animal in the jungle. You can feel the vibration from your balls to the top of your head."

"I guess so," I say.

"Can't you see it, Mags?"

"Sure. Of course."

Mongrel walks over to me and takes my chin in his hand, bends down, and kisses me.

"You don't have to like what I like, Mags. I'm not saying that. But it's easier if you do, that's all."

"I mostly like what you like," I say.

This was where I always sold myself out. I never liked half of what Mongrel liked. He loved R & B, and I wasn't crazy about it. But he controlled the stereo. He bought the music. He was more into it.

So, I just let him take over. He was used to taking over. It worked for him. I went a long time pretending that it was all right to never have things the way I wanted them—that it was all right to always say yes.

But after a while, I got real mean inside. Then it started coming out without my even thinking about it. It caught us both off guard.

"And you can tell your buddies that they can pick up their fucking beer cans."

"Hey, what's up? The red army in town, Mags?"

"It's not always about PMS, Mongrel. I'm just sick and tired of picking up beer bottles and beer cans."

"So, I'll pay Max to do it."

"You can't always fix it with money."

"I don't get it, Mags. It seems to me that fixing it is fixing it. Then it's fixed."

"Maybe I don't want it fixed."

"Then what the fuck are we talking about it for?"

"Because I want to talk about it."

"But you don't want to fix it?"

"No."

"Christ, Mags, how many screws you got loose in that pretty little head?"

◆　　◆　　◆

We're holed up at Debra and Carey's. It's a big sprawling place with dogs and cats and kids and confusion. There's also a couple of horses in the back acre. Sam and Stella go for rides. Big Dee keeps her distance.

We mostly stick close to the house, even though there are no neighbors to speak of. It's a perfect place to plan the next step. Carey brings out the map.

"Okay," says Carey, "this here's where you are. Where you heading?"

"We're not sure."

"That not true," says Big Dee. "We all going to Key West."

"Key West?" says Debra. "That's a ways."

"We got time," says Big Dee.

"Yeah," says Sam. "Most of us got hard time, ha, ha."

"Funny," says Chan.

"So, I guess we're going to Key West," I say.

"Well, if I was you, I'd stay away from as many mountains as I could this time of the year. You get caught in one of them passes at the wrong time, you might end up camping out." says Carey.

"No thanks," says Big Dee. "I already swum in ice and I ain't campin' in no snow."

"You could head down through Nevada."

"Not Nevada. They might be looking for us there," says Sam.

"All right, then you could cut through Oregon. Go down along the bottom part of Idaho, through Boise. Then into Utah."

"Utah!" says Big Dee. "They only got one black person in all of Utah. Sings in that Mormon choir. They pays her extra to be there so it's not completely white. I don't think Utah is where I want to go."

"Well, we could swing over into Wyoming, Big Dee. Seems there's a big black population there," I say.

"We need to go to the city," says Big Dee.

"I ain't going to no cities if I can help it," says Sam. "Too many fucking cops."

"Yeah, but in the country, you're more noticeable."

"Look," says Sam, "cities just eat up your time and slow your progress. We want to get south fast. Get away from any heat up here. They probably think we're still hiding out further north somewheres. So, if we're lucky, we're still ahead of them."

"How long we staying here?"

"Long as you want," says Carey.

"We're leaving as soon as the trailer for the Harley's done, and that's the day after tomorrow," says Sam.

"So, where we going?" says Stella.

"We're going to Utah. Pick up the book of Mormon for Big Dee," says Sam.

"I'll pass," says Big Dee.

"Get you a place in the choir," I say.

"Hallelujah," sings Big Dee.

"We could watch you on TV, Sundays."

"Now that real good. Some cop watching, see me. Says, 'Hey, ain't that the big fat black woman escaped from some women's prison?' He phones his boss and next thing you know, I'm back in prison, only this time in Utah. I be the only black in the whole place. No thank you."

"You'll love Utah," says Stella. "We drove through it on the way to powwow in New Mexico."

"So, it's Utah?" says Sam.

"Sure," says Chan.

"I guess so," says Big Dee.

◆　　　◆　　　◆

One of the best things about our stay in Twisp is when Debra makes banana flambé for dessert. She pours on a whack of hundred proof that Carey's been saving up for a rainy day. When she throws in the match, *whomp*, the flames shoot up a couple of feet. She almost loses her hair. Then this blue flame licks around the pan. The kids love the light show.

## DEBRA'S FIREBOMB BANANA FLAMBÉ

This is almost as good a show as it is to eat.

Bananas
Butter (no, not marg)
White sugar (no, brown won't work)
Cognac (no, not that cheap bar brandy)
Matches
Optional: vanilla ice cream (the good stuff)

Melt a nice big gob of butter in a big flat fry pan. Bottom has to be well covered.

Cut the bananas lengthwise into two long strips. Place face down in the hot butter.

Sauté until golden. Then turn them over and do the other side. When both sides are done, the bananas will be kind of translucent, but they won't fall apart.

Now sprinkle on the white sugar. Be generous!

Here's the tricky part. Yell to someone at the table to be ready to turn off the lights in the room. The darker, the better. Now throw on a good couple of shots of cognac. Light a match. Tell whoever to kill the lights. Chuck in the match. KABOOM! BIG FIRE! This will quickly turn to a beautiful blue flame. Keep moving the blue flame around the pan.

WARNING!!! KEEP THE PAN AWAY FROM YOUR FACE OR YOU WON'T HAVE ANY

EYEBROWS, EYELASHES, OR HAIR LEFT.

You can serve the banana flambé with ice cream, but personally, I like it just by itself.

◆　　◆　　◆

We're mostly trying to put on the miles—get as far south, as fast as we can without looking like we're on the run. We make a quick stop in Boise, Idaho, because Big Dee wants to buy a fridge magnet with a potato on it. She refuses to get out of the car in Salt Lake City.

"They just waiting for dark to put on some white sheets and burn a few crosses."

"It's Utah, Big Dee, not Mississippi."

"Same diff," says Big Dee.

"Besides, it *is* dark," I say, "and I don't see no crosses burning. You see any crosses burning, Sam?"

"Not on this block, but what's that flickering down there?"

"S-a-a-am," says Stella.

"What? I'm just making a joke."

"It ain't funny," says Big Dee.

◆　　◆　　◆

Since Big Dee won't eat in Salt Lake City, we drive out of town and find a small place just off the road. A couple of gas stations, a restaurant, and a few other buildings. We're just pulling out after lunch when someone beeps their horn.

"Who's that?" says Sam.

"I don't know."

"Just ignore him," I say.

"He's pointing at something. I'm going to pull over," says Stella. She's at the wheel.

"What's your problem?" she says.

"You got a low tire," he shouts. It sounds like "tahr."

"Shit," says Stella. "Know where there's a garage?"

"Sure do," he says. "Just over yonder."

We pull in and a young guy comes over. Nice as pie. Sounds like he comes from Texas, he's got such a drawl.

"How y'all doin'?" he says.

"We're all fine. Could you check that back tire?" says Stella.

He checks it. And then he checks the other tires.

"Why, ma'am, y'all got three low tahrs. I'll put her up on the hoist. See if there's a problem."

"Lemme out first," says Sam, jumping down.

"Hmmm. Looks like you got you a little problem," says the kid. "Maybe somethin' wrong with yer shocks. I'll call Ed over, take a look. He's the expert on tahrs. Hey, Ed."

Ed saunters over. It turns out he's the same guy who told Stella in the first place that she had a low tire.

"Hey, ain't you the guy who pointed out the tire in the first place?" says Sam.

"Hell, yes. I wouldn't want you little ladies finding yourselves changing a tahr in the middle of nowheres in the middle of the night."

"Well now, that's real nice of you," says Sam. "So, what's the problem?"

"See here? See this dark scoring on the tahr?"

"Uh-huh," says Sam.

"Somethin' ain't right. Probably the one shock's not working. Yeah." He wipes his nose on the back of his hand. "See how it's rubbing here? Boy, I wouldn't go too much farther on these babies."

"You wouldn't, eh?"

"Nope, not if ah's you."

"Hmmm," says Stella.

"Hey, Mags, what you think we should do?" calls Sam.

"I don't know," I say. "He's the tahr expert."

"So, how much we talking here?" says Stella.

"Well, let's see. It's thirty-eight dollars for the shocks, but y'all will want to buy two."

"Right," says Sam.

"'Course now, labor's real cheap, maybe seven bucks."

"Oh, that's good," says Sam.

"So, lemme just haul ya down a pair?"

"Well now, let's not be too hasty. I might need a second opinion on this," says Sam.

"Next garage is at least fifty miles down the road. I don't know if I'd risk it myself," he says. "I'd hate like hell to see you little ladies stranded on the side of the road."

"Hey, that's real nice of you," says Sam, "but I got a question."

"What is it, sweetheart?" says the guy.

"Well, honeybunch, what I really want to know is, how many

women do you sucker in with this bullshit?"

"What's that?"

"See, I already checked the shocks before we left and they was just fine. And they still are. And as for this scoring, you just wiped the tahr to make it look that way."

The guy looks at us.

"You a bunch of lesbos or somethin'?"

"You don't have to be a lesbian to know when you're being properly fucked, buddy."

"Ah think we'll just let her down and y'all have a nice day."

"Well now, that's real nice of you," says Sam.

◆     ◆     ◆

Mongrel never went to a garage. Never. He was made to work on engines. If he hadn't been such a hotshot dealer, he probably would've opened his own garage. But he was making way too much money selling weed. Besides, he could always fool around with his own bike.

I think he took it apart just to see if he could put it back together again and have nothing left over. He said engines were easy. Way easier than women. If you took care of an engine, it would work for you. It was simple. But broads were mostly a pain in the ass, he used to say. They always had one or two pistons misfiring.

"Like you, Mags, you're hard to please."

"I'm not trying to be," I say.

"Nobody tries to be nothin', they just are. And that's how you are."

"So, what are you saying?"

"Nothin'. Life ain't always easy is all."

"What's the matter, Mongrel?"

"Nothin's the matter."

"You're full of crap. I know when there's something bugging you. Who do you think you're talking to?"

"Sometimes you got too much lip, Mags."

"Oh yeah?"

"Yeah."

"Maybe I like myself that way."

"I know some guys who'd punch your lights out, talking like that to your old man."

"I guess I'm lucky I didn't marry one of them."

"I guess you are, Mags," he says, heading for the door. "I got some business to take care of."

"See you later."

"Maybe."

◆　　　◆　　　◆

I can't get Tony out of my mind, partly because I can't see him and partly because he lied to me. I think the part about him lying to me weighs on me the most.

I finally take Big Dee aside and ask her why she had to tell me about Tony screwing around before he met me. She gets pretty uncomfortable before she admits that, actually, she lied to me because she wanted to keep me focused on the escape. If she wasn't so big I'd kill her.

"You mean to tell me, he never screwed around on me?"

"Well no, not really," she says.

"What do you mean, not really?"

"Well, I was worry about you. Think maybe you go all soft and not keep your mind on running."

"So, you lied to me?"

"I guess I did."

"And you probably didn't hear us either?"

"Oh, that part was true. We hear you all right."

"I don't care about that. But do you realize I accused him of doing something he never did?"

"Gee, I'm sorry, Maggie. I guess I didn't go that far in my thinking. I just didn't want you to mess up. It wasn't on purpose."

"Damn, Big Dee, how could you do that? Now I got to find some way to let him know that I was wrong."

◆　　　◆　　　◆

If it wasn't for prison I wouldn't have met any of these gals. Well, maybe Sam would've turned up at some R & B festival, but I was the kind of woman who rode behind her man. Sam rode her own bike. Different trips.

◆　　　◆　　　◆

The first big fight is in a motel about a hundred miles south of Salt Lake City. A real scuzzy dive. Cash only. No ID required. Perfect for us.

"We ain't goin' to Key West," says Sam.

"Say what?" says Big Dee.

"I said, we ain't goin' to Key West and I'll tell you why. First of all, it's too damn far. Second, it's too damn small."

"Shit, last I heard you didn't want no cities 'cause they's too big. Now it's too small. We all agree before we bust out that Key West was where we was heading."

"That's right, Sam," says Stella.

"Well, that was before I got some real maps, not that piece of worthless shit we was lookin' at in prison. I mean, it looks like fuck-all when you're looking at a small map of the whole U.S.A."

"I's goin' to Key West and fuck you, Sam," says Big Dee.

"Then you can take your black ass there on a bus."

"I ain't goin' nowheres on no fucking bus."

"Then shut the fuck up."

"Fuck you," says Big Dee.

"Look, you guys, we better keep it down."

"Who the fuck's talkin' to you, Maggie?"

"Excuse me? I'm talking because I'm in on this. I got an opinion, you know."

"Yeah, well, you know what you can do with it," says Sam.

"Fuck this," I say. "I'm going for a walk."

"Me, too," says Chan.

I unlock the door and it flies open. Snow blows into the room. You can't see ten feet in front of your face.

"Shit, man, it's a blizzard."

◆    ◆    ◆

## FOUR OF CUPS: ANGER

The card is red. Red cliffs and red flowers. And broken glass. And spiky things, like cactus. Cactus pokes you and you feel anger. Glass cuts you and you bleed red.

We're all fragile right now because our emotions are so raw. It's mostly because we're all scared. We don't know where we're going. Or if we'll get stopped. Or how long we can all be together before one of us kills another.

And that's possible. Some of the prisoners used to say that once you'd done it, it was easier to do it a second time. You'd broken the code. Anger's like a fall. Once you're in it, you're there until you crash. Too much adrenaline. Too close to crazy.

◆　　　◆　　　◆

Mongrel used to say that about me.

"You're way too close to crazy sometimes, Mags."

"Takes one to know one."

"You know what I like about you?"

"My ass."

"That, too."

"Okay, what do you like about me?"

"You piss me off."

"You *like* that about me?"

"Yeah."

"How come?"

"See, when I get pissed off, it's like I'm revved. Everything moves faster. I'm on my toes. I can see more. I'm thinkin' faster."

"And I do that for you?"

"That's right."

"So, I guess I don't have to feel guilty."

"'Bout what?"

"About pissing you off."

"How'd we get here?"

"I was talking about guilt. You seem to have got lost. Probably the weed. Must be good?"

"It's all right. Got me off track. Can't be all that bad if I can't remember what we were talking about."

"You ever think of going a day without smoking? Like straight?" I say.

"Nope," he says.

◆　　　◆　　　◆

Max didn't look me in the eye for over a week, and when he did, I wished he hadn't. It wasn't like I could explain anything to him. I was dead wrong and he knew it. And I knew it. I finally trapped him alone in front of the TV.

"We gotta talk," I say.

Stony silence.

"It won't go away till we do."

Max wheels around and spits.

"You shouldn't have done that."

"You're right, I shouldn't have."

"Dad's gonna be really pissed off."

"Don't use that word, Max. And I don't want you telling your dad."

More silence.

"You can't tell your dad, Max."

He changes channels with the remote.

"You tell him and you know what'll happen? Hmmm?"

"What?"

"Your dad will throw me out or kill me and then you'll have to eat your dad's cooking."

"I don't care. I like barbecues."

"Not every night you wouldn't."

"Manny's dad said Dad should kill you."

"That's fucked, Max."

"He said if he ever caught his old lady double stuffing, he'd kill her."

"Manny's dad said that? He's fucked. What the hell's he talking like that for around you kids, anyway? You're too young for that crap. Double stuffing. He said that in front of you?"

Max plays with the remote.

"Look, Max, I'm not trying to make it right, what I did. I can't. I was dead wrong. But I did it and that's all there is to it. If I say I'm sorry till the cows come home, it isn't ever going to change the fact that you saw what you saw."

He stares at the screen.

"I fucked up, okay? I can't make it go away. And I can't live in this house if you keep acting the way you been acting."

Max keeps channel surfing.

"Look, Max, it's not like I went and cut your dad's heart out with an axe and ate it, or something."

"No, but you fucked Tim."

"Where do you kids learn to fucking *talk* like that?"

◆　　◆　　◆

I don't know why I went to bed with Tim. I knew right from the get-go he was sniffing for money. He as much as told Mongrel that he was looking for some dame with cash. He said then he could work on his Harley whenever.

He knew Mongrel was loaded. He probably figured if anything happened to Mongrel or if we broke up, I'd get half. I was pissed off at Mongrel. Fucking Tim was my way of getting back at him. Not that I figured he'd find out. I was pretty sure Max wouldn't tell Mongrel. And he didn't—not directly, anyways. But he told his friend Manny, who told his dad, who told Mongrel.

I came home one afternoon and Mongrel's sitting in front of the TV with a beer and a joint. Only thing is, the TV isn't on.

"What you watchin', honey?"

"I'm watching myself."

"Oh yeah? What's that supposed to mean?"

"It means I'm watching myself to see whether I kill you or not."

"What'd I do this time?"

"Don't play stupid with me, Mags."

"All right, but I don't want to confess if it's something you're not even thinking about."

"How 'bout some kid comes home and finds his mom in bed with his dad's best friend? Just for example."

I feel my stomach go into a knot. Mongrel keeps staring at the empty TV screen.

"Look, it didn't mean anything. I was drunk," I say.

"Uh-huh. So, why'd you do it?" Mongrel turns around and faces me. He's still sitting down.

"I don't know. I was pissed off at you. And then I made a few margaritas. Next thing, we're drinking straight tequila and, you know, one thing led to another."

"You're pissed off at me, so you go fuck my best buddy?"

"It wasn't that simple, Mongrel."

"Well, how hard can it be?"

"Don't tell me you've never fucked around on me."

"Hey, we ain't talkin' about me right now. We're talkin' about you."

"What can I say? I fucked up. I did something stupid. I'm sorry. I really am, Mongrel."

"You're sorry? What about me? What the fuck about me, Mags?"

Now he's up and pacing.

"See, I gotta go down to the garage, buy some part for the bike—the guys behind the counter givin' each other a smile. Why? I'll tell you why, Mags. 'Cause I know that they know that my old lady fucked around on me. And not just with anybody—but with my buddy. Kind of like a double slap in the face. See, I'm the one who's sorry. Goddam, you piss me off sometimes."

"You want me to leave?"

"No, I don't want you to fuckin' leave."

"Well, what do you want?"

"I don't know what I want. I want this not to be happening."

"Me, too, but it is."

"No, maybe it ain't."

"What do you mean?"

"I mean, this time I'm fixin' it, Mags. My way. So, I don't want to know about it. Nothin'. No details. You don't talk to me about it. I don't talk to you about it. I'm goin' down to Tacoma to ride with Jake for a few days."

"When are you coming back?"

"I don't know when I'm coming back. But when I do, here's how it's gonna look. I come back, we're goin' out for dinner, then dancing, maybe some pool. We're hittin' all the spots we might run into people we know. And we're gonna have us a good time."

Mongrel walks over and takes me by the shoulders. He's squeezing.

"You're hurting me, Mongrel."

"You're lucky I ain't killin' you. So let me continue. We're going to have us a *great* time. Anyone who sees us is gonna know that everything's fine between us. And you better look real happy and have fun or I'll bust your fuckin' jaw. You understand me, Mags?"

"Yeah, I understand you."

"Good. Now, you better tell Max to tell Manny that he was just fuckin' around to piss me off. That he was bullshittin'. And you tell Max he better do a fuckin' good job because if this ain't sorted out before I get back, his ass is grass."

"All right, Mongrel."

◆　　　◆　　　◆

## VARIATION ON JIMMY BUFFET'S BEST MARGARITAS
(and he oughta know!)

Fill shaker with broken ice (not chipped).

Squeeze in 1/2 fresh lime (no substitutes).

Add 2 ounces of Cuervo Gold (no, white won't do).

Add 1-1/4 ounces of Rose's lime juice (nothing else works, so don't substitute).

Add 1/2 ounce Triple Sec.

Add a splash of Grand Marnier (secret ingredient).

Throw in an ounce or two of club soda.

Shake!

Dampen the rim of a glass with fresh lime juice and dip the rim in salt.

After two of these, you won't be able to make them any more—so make plenty while you can!

◆　　　◆　　　◆

"What about the tahrs in this snow?" I say.

"With Big Dee in the back, we shouldn't have any trouble." Stella's smiling.

"I's always glad to be appreciated," says Big Dee.

"Man, it's cold," says Sam.

"This is like real winter. I don't know if I'm ready for this," I say.

"Ready or not, it's what we got." Big Dee talking.

"I like snow," says Chan.

"Where are we going today?"

"We're heading for Navaho country. Shoe says there's a shaman down there. Guy called Joseph. Says we can camp by his place for a few days," says Stella.

"We ain't doin' none of that cold water cleansing shit again, is we?"

"Of course, Big Dee. Only down here you gotta cut a hole in the ice first. Then you jump in."

"Lord Jesus," says Big Dee.

◆　　◆　　◆

I can't remember what really happened that day. I know it sounds crazy, but the minute Mongrel walked through the door with a gun in his hand, everything froze. It was like a movie. I couldn't relate to it. But what I do remember is everything inside me wanting to live. It was like an explosion inside. Every part of my body said no. There was no way I was ready to die.

But I guess it wasn't the same for Mongrel. He must have been thinking about it for a while. Some people thought it was because of Tim. But that wasn't true. He was in trouble long before what happened between Tim and me. The accident just finished him off. He never wanted to deal with anything. He either walked away or he pretended nothing was wrong.

Sometimes I think maybe he was going to shoot me first, then himself. But for sure he was going to kill himself. Maybe at the last minute he decided to let me live. Or maybe he thought about the kids. I don't know. I don't know what happened.

◆     ◆     ◆

Joseph didn't speak English, only Navaho. His daughter had to translate for him. He had this wonderful face—wide, with lots of wrinkles around the eyes. He wore a cowboy hat with two strands of silver around the crown. There was some turquoise in it, too. He was an old man, but he had a powerful aura.

"He says you can stay as long as you want," his daughter translated.

"He did?"

"Yeah. He says you need to spend some time here because you don't know where you're going."

"I know where I's goin'," says Big Dee.

"You can't go there, Big Dee," I say.

"Why not?"

"It's your home. They'll be looking for you there. They're going to go to the most obvious places first. They're gonna check friends and family. Your ex lives there."

"Well, where the hell we goin' then? We can't just drive around forever. Where we gonna settle?"

"I don't know," I say.

"How we gonna live?"

"We're doing it one day at a time, Big Dee. Just like the program. I don't know where we'll settle, or whether we'll all stay in the same place. We just gotta take it as it comes."

"Shit, we're in the middle of nowhere," says Big Dee.

"It's better than prison," says Stella.

"Oh yeah?" says Big Dee.

"Of course it is. What the hell you thinkin'?" says Sam.

"Least in prison I knew what was gonna happen. I had my room and my stuff. Now, I just got nothin' and I don't know where I'm gonna be next. And I can't go home."

"Prison isn't home, Big Dee. You're cage sour," says Sam.

"What the hell's that supposed to mean?"

"Means you can't get out. You're like a bird that's been in a cage so long that when someone opens the door to let it out, it don't fly away because all it knows is being caged. Anything else just makes it scared. You're like that bird."

"Well, I don't know what's going to happen next."

"Me either," says Sam.

"But what about our freedom?"

"That *is* freedom."

◆        ◆        ◆

For Mongrel, freedom was riding the Harley— feeling the wind on his face, his hair flying out behind. Half the time he didn't even know where he was going or where he was going to sleep that night. That's what he liked. He said there was a part of him that was gypsy. He believed in magic.

He said you just had to learn how to step into the flow and let it take you along, and when you were supposed to stop you would. He believed that everyone you met was supposed to be. He'd talk to anyone. He said you never knew what was coming next. He had friends from all over the world—people he'd met at a café or in a bar or at the side of the road. They liked him. He always had somewhere to stay.

◆    ◆    ◆

Maybe I'm cage sour, too. I never much thought about the word freedom until I was in prison, and then it was a word that came up all the time. Freedom. It's like you're either in prison or you're free. I know that when I was inside, all I wanted to do was get out.

But now that I'm out, I want something else. It's like freedom is something I make up inside my head to keep me unhappy. It keeps moving. For the first day or so after the escape, it was an incredible feeling—nothing could keep us down. It felt like we'd gone over a waterfall.

I wake up now and I don't know where I am. I don't know where to go next or why we're here. I try to keep calm on the outside, but I don't know if I can keep it up. It's hard to sit still. I go outside for walks a lot, but there's nowhere to go. It's flat and there's no trees. I wanted to see trees when I escaped. But we're in the desert.

◆    ◆    ◆

Joseph tells his daughter that he wants to talk to me. He's sitting on the porch, smoking a cigarette. He nods at me and points at a chair. He starts to talk to me, but I can't understand what he's saying.

"I don't know what you're saying, old man," I say.

Joseph pats my shoulder and nods, but he keeps on talking. It's like he's telling me a story. I realize that he's not going to stop, so I just light up a smoke and listen. Sometimes he looks at me. Sometimes he makes gestures with his hands. Sometimes he laughs.

It's not like I can understand what he's saying, but I feel like a little kid again, listening to my grandfather. I'm just happy to be with him. Somewhere in the story, I feel myself unlock inside and I start to cry. No noise, just tears running down my face.

Joseph stops talking. He reaches over and pats my arm.

"I don't know where we're going," I say.

He nods and draws a picture in the air. He takes my hand and traces the same picture. Then he smiles at me and touches my shoulder. He lights up another cigarette.

◆　　　◆　　　◆

Somewhere in Hong Kong, some men she didn't know taped ten kilos of heroin to Chan's body. It was hard for her to breathe and the plastic around the drugs made her body sweat. She knew that if she made it, she'd never have to come back. She kept thinking about that, and how she could bring her father over later. That's what kept her going on the plane. It was like a prayer. Over and over. She couldn't eat.

When she got to the airport, she felt faint. The fear made her hands cold. She saw a man looking at her. Without thinking, she touched the packages. She had to go to the bathroom, but she didn't want the man to see her going there.

She went up an escalator to another floor. She saw a sign for the women's bathroom. She looked behind her. She didn't see anyone. She had just started to open the door to the toilet when she felt a hand on her shoulder. She didn't have to turn around. She stopped breathing and closed her eyes.

◆　　◆　　◆

When the car pulled up to the curb, I knew they were cops.

"Are you Margaret Hoffer?" they said.

◆　　◆　　◆

"The worst part is the arrest," says Sam. "After that, it's just a game. But those few seconds between when you're free, to the doubt, to when you know they got you. That's the worst."

"I think so," says Chan. "And the first day in jail. That is pretty bad, too. After that, maybe you meet someone and they smile. Feel a little better."

"You ever think you'd end up in jail, Maggie?" says Sam.

"Nope."

"Wonder why we all ended up there at the same time."

"Karma, I guess," I say.

"Maybe we were supposed to meet," says Stella.

"What for?" I say.

"I don't know. Maybe so's we could learn something. Start a group called Freedom Anonymous. Who knows?" says Sam.

"Hey, we escaped," I say. "That's pretty big learning, don't you think?"

◆　　◆　　◆

SEVEN OF CUPS: FEAR

Fear hits the stomach first and then the back of the throat. It's like a wave. It makes you close up and hide. You shut down. And inside your mind you see dark things. They come out in your dreams.

Either you sit in it and get paralyzed or you use it for energy. Stella likes to smoke out fear. That's what she uses sage for.

"You got to smoke it out, Maggie."

"Christ, Stella, my stomach's in a knot."

"You're sitting around too much. You gotta move. Gotta move the fear energy."

"I can't move. I'm stuck. I can't even think what we're going to do next. I just want to curl up in a ball. You ever feel like a little kid? You just want your mom to come and hold you and make it better."

"Waste of time thinking about it. It ain't gonna happen," says Stella.

◆　　◆　　◆

Joseph didn't know there was a place called Canada. Or California. Or that someone had landed on the moon. He didn't read newspapers. He didn't have a television. And he didn't think that news outside his community had anything to do with him.

"He don't know squat," says Big Dee.

"He don't know what's not important," says Stella.

"The moon landing? Everybody knows about that. That's important."

"Not for Joseph."

"How can he live without a TV?"

"He talks to people."

"He talk to you, Maggie?"

"Yeah, he did."

"What'd he say?"

"I don't know. I don't speak Navaho."

◆　　◆　　◆

But he must have told me something because I dreamed that night of a sacred tree. It stood alone in a field, and the branches were waving, like someone telling me to come. Come to me, it said, and its branches moved. As I walked closer, the branches separated and there was a space for me to squeeze into the tree. I got in and the branches closed behind me and I was in a darkness that was so black, I felt like I didn't have a body anymore.

I reached down to touch my chest but there was nothing there. I reached up to touch my face and it was gone. But I knew that as long as the tree lived, so would I. And I heard his voice from somewhere in the distance, speaking in a language I couldn't understand, but that made me feel good, like a song you sing to a baby when it can't fall asleep. And even though I couldn't understand the words, the meaning was so clear. You never escape, he said. Just move from one place to another and dance with whoever is in front of you. Sleep when you are tired. Eat when you are hungry. And then go home. I woke up, but I didn't know where home was.

◆　　◆　　◆

Freedom shape-shifts. It starts out looking like one thing, and then it changes later on and looks like something else. We talked a lot about freedom when we were planning the escape.

"Is this what you thought it was gonna look like when we got out?" says Sam.

"No," I say.

"Well, what did you see?"

"I guess I just saw a picture of how it used to be before I went to jail. I mean, when we were in jail, freedom sounded so good. I just wanted everything to be the way it used to be."

"Yeah, but the way it used to be was fucked."

"I know, but it looked better when I wasn't in it anymore. It's like how I feel about Mongrel. I miss him sometimes, but it's not really him I miss. It's some picture I have in my head. Like a photograph with everyone smiling in it. You don't see that everyone's got scars. All you see are the smiles. Everybody's happy in that moment, or at least pretending to be. That's what I want. I want to be back in that photograph."

◆　　◆　　◆

Big Dee is having trouble breathing.

"You gotta relax, Big Dee."

"I can't."

"You're making things worse than they already are."

"Look, it don't get worse than it already is. Not by my thinking."

"We're just trying to figure out where we're going, Big Dee. Once we get it sorted out, we'll be fine."

"Look, Maggie, don't talk to me like I's stupid, all right. You don't got a clue where we all heading. You and Sam talk like you know what's goin' down, but that's bullshit. You so busy tryin' to escape, you don't think about what's next. Where we suppose to go? How we suppose to survive? We can't stay all together like this."

"We gotta stick together, Big Dee."

"No, we can't."

"Well, what do you want to do?"

"I want to go back."

"You're joking."

"No, I ain't."

"After all we been through, you want to turn around and go back?"

"That's right."

"Jesus, now I've heard it all."

"Look, Maggie, I don't see this as any better than prison. For me, it's worse. I spend most of my life in prison. I'm use to it. Maybe for you, it's better. You got something to look forward to."

"So do you, Big Dee."

"Like what?"

"I don't know. You could get your own place. Make some friends. Be free to do what you want."

"You livin' in some dream, Maggie. I'm black. Got no education. Don't know where my family is. What I get is maybe some dump in the city and I end up on social assistance. Can't find a job so I go back to dealing to make ends meet. To hell with that. And besides, as far as I can see there ain't no blacks in this part of the country."

"What're you talking about, Big Dee?"

"How many blacks you see the past few weeks?"

"I don't know. I wasn't paying attention."

"Well, I was, and I's here to tell you, Maggie, there ain't hardly no blacks. It's like I landed on some other planet. I'm all alone out here."

◆　　◆　　◆

When my best friend, Josie, left her old man, everybody thought it was because he beat her. But she said that she didn't really mind the beatings so much. What she couldn't stand was the loneliness.

She said she got married because she thought she'd never be lonely again. But after fifteen years, all she felt was lonely. Even when he was in the same room with her. Sitting across the table from her. Making love to her. She got a little place of her own, and when I went to see her she said that now it made sense to be lonely. Now she could stand it because she really was alone.

◆　　◆　　◆

"Tony?"

"Margaret, is that you?"

"Yeah, it's me."

"Where are you?"

"I can't tell you. I just needed to hear your voice."

"Are you all right?"

"I'm okay."

"Are you sure?"

"Look, Tony, I had to phone you. I'm sorry about what I said."

"It was a crazy time. You had a lot on your mind."

"I know you didn't mess around on me, okay? Big Dee told me she'd made up that stuff. I miss you, Tony."

"Margaret, come back."

"I can't. Not yet."

"Where are you headed?"

"We're not sure yet."

"I've been thinking about you a lot. I didn't even know if you were alive."

"Oh, we're alive all right. A bit lost, maybe."

"Do you need anything?"

"No, we're fine."

"It's not what you thought it was going to be, is it?"

"No, it's not. It's pretty scary sometimes."

"You can always come back. I'll be here."

"I have to go."

"I'll be thinking about you."

"I'll be thinking about you, too.

◆　　　◆　　　◆

I always knew that Mongrel would die before I did. That's partly why I wanted the house. I didn't know where half the money was. Some of it was in diamonds. Some of it was buried, God knows where. It was one of the things we got into fights about.

"Mongrel, you got money all over the place and nobody knows where it is."

"I do."

"What about us?"

"What about you?"

"What happens if you fall off your bike and kill yourself? What about the kids? You got to get some kind of insurance."

"I don't need insurance."

"Why not?"

"Tim says you get insurance and the next thing you know your old lady pushes you off a cliff."

"That's because if Tim ever got married, whoever was stupid enough to marry him probably *would* throw him off a cliff. And she'd probably do it even if he didn't have insurance, he's such an asshole."

"Didn't stop you from jumpin' his bones."

"Low blow, Mongrel."

Mongrel reaches inside his shirt and brings out a handful of hundreds.

"You need some fuckin' money, Mags? Here!"

He throws the bills and they fly all over, landing on the floor.

"Now, after you pick them up, would you get me a goddam beer?"

◆     ◆     ◆

When Max came back with the package he'd found buried out in the bush, I made a deal with him. If he kept his mouth shut, he got a new bicycle. I counted it. There was fifty-one thousand dollars in crisp one thousand dollar bills. I knew they were Mongrel's because he really liked thousand dollar bills. He always carried one on him. He said it was for emergencies, but I knew it was because he liked to impress.

The next thing I had to figure out was what to do with the money. Suddenly, I was in the same position as Mongrel. I knew I couldn't put it in the bank or it would be traceable and there'd be passbooks or something. I couldn't spend it all or Mongrel would find out. Finally, I realized that all I could do was hide it somewhere else. But everywhere I thought about turned into a problem. What if Mongrel found it?

So, I'm sitting having a coffee with this stack of bills in front of me, thinking. I'm also trying to decide what to cook for dinner. I get down my recipe box and start looking. I don't come up with much for dinner but I do figure out the best place to hide the money. If there's one place I could be sure Mongrel would never look, it would be in my box of recipes.

◆　　　◆　　　◆

Josie said I shouldn't have married Mongrel if I wasn't in love with him. She knew I was in love with Danny. But Danny was hopeless with money. He didn't care about it. He just drifted. If he had enough, he was happy, and if he didn't, he was still happy. He was a dreamer.

Mongrel was practical. Josie told me that I was settling for the security, and I'd be sorry. But I didn't want to know.

"You're not in love with him," says Josie.

"I like him all right," I say.

"It's not the same as love."

"That's bullshit, Josie. You can't live on love. It doesn't pay the bills."

"What are you going to tell Danny?"

"I guess I'm going to have to tell him I'm marrying Mongrel."

"You're gonna break his heart."

"Look, Josie, I don't want to talk about this anymore."

"You're gonna be sorry."

◆　　　◆　　　◆

"Okay," says Sam. "This here's a special meeting of Freedom Anonymous. Now that we got our freedom, there seem to be some problems. Floor's open to whoever."

"I want to go back," says Big Dee.

"What about you, Maggie?"

"I'm still undecided, Sam. Part of me wants to keep going south, and part of me wants to go back, like Big Dee. There's all these loose ends and I can't fix any of them on the road. And I don't know if I could live with the idea of never seeing my kids, or Tony. I guess I just don't know yet."

"Chan?"

"I got no choice. I go back, I get killed somehow. But I see what Big Dee is saying. Not many Chinese out here either. Indians, maybe. Lots of Spanish. But no Chinese. Maybe go to L.A. or San Francisco. Lots of Chinese there."

"Stella?"

"I don't know. Seems okay for me, eh? I got some friends around here. Maybe stay somewhere for a while. I don't want to go back. Nothin' there for me."

"What about you, Sam?" I say.

"I can't go back. I'm the one who shot Johanna. They'll throw the fuckin' book at me. I'll never get out alive. I'm thinkin' about maybe headin' for Mexico. Me and Darlene used to talk about goin' there."

"Sounds like we all got different plans," I say.

"Sounds like it," says Sam.

◆　　　◆　　　◆

## FIVE OF WORLDS: SETBACK

I look at the tarot card, trying to figure out what it's saying. Setback. A forest fire comes raging through and wipes out everything for miles around.

A volcano erupts, the lava covering everything in its path. Storms come suddenly. Disaster.

All our plans are falling apart. We're splitting up. But in the corner of the card is a rainbow. It reminds me that even setback is only a step. Right now it feels like a disaster, but maybe it's for the best. Maybe we do have to choose our own path. We're never going to all agree on one way.

◆　　◆　　◆

We couldn't just leave like that. We'd done too much together. That's always the way it is, in every friendship and every place where you got some history behind you. Like going through high school with a bunch of kids. You never forget them. But somehow you leave. Sometimes because you want to. And sometimes because you have to.

I knew Mongrel wouldn't leave. He wasn't built that way. It wasn't his style. It didn't mean he was easy to live with. But he wasn't a runner. He stomped out quite a few times, but he always came back. He stayed away for as long as he needed to, which was usually a bit too long for me.

"Hey, babes, where you been?" I say.

"Where's my coffee?" says Mongrel.

"What, no I-missed-you-so-much-honey?"

"Don't be a smartass, Mags. Go make me one."

"I ran out."

"Don't bullshit your old man."

"I ain't bullshittin'. I stopped drinking coffee when you were gone."

"Nobody stops drinking coffee."

"I did."

"Well, I fuckin' didn't. What is this, Mags? I go away for two weeks and everything goes to shit. What do I gotta do? Stay around all the time, make sure the world don't start turning in the opposite direction?"

"Well, two weeks is long enough for me to get bored and start thinking about things. Partly because I got no television blasting my brains out, you know."

"I had some business to do."

"For two weeks?"

"Sometimes it takes that long."

"That's a load of crap, Mongrel. It never takes you that long to do a deal. Who you think you're talking to?"

"Mags, I don't want a fight."

"Who says we're having one?"

"I says. This is how it always starts. Remember?"

"You piss me off, Mongrel. It's too long. I start worrying."

"What? About me?"

"Well, who else?"

"Fuck if I know, Mags. But it seems to me that you got no problem finding things to worry about."

"It's not just me, Mongrel."

"All right, so it's not just you."

"You could at least phone."

"Mags, you gonna make me that coffee?"

"Maybe there isn't any."

"And maybe there is. You know how I like it."

"Maybe I've forgotten."

"I'll have one of my specials. You got the right kind?"

"Maybe."

"I don't want no two-week-old shit."

"It's fresh."

"When did you get it?"

"Yesterday."

"No shit. How'd you do that?"

"I figured you'd be back today."

Mongrel grabbed my hand and pulled me to him. For such a big man, he was smooth. He pulled me to him rough and fast, but he didn't hurt me. He knew how to hold me.

◆     ◆     ◆

I did love him. Even at the end when he was curled up inside himself and bitter and mean, he still had style. But he never let down his mask. Not that it mattered, I could always read him. I knew when there was something wrong. And toward the end, there was something wrong for sure. He wasn't talking to anyone, not even the kids. You could practically taste the anger in the air. Resentment and anger.

And then, I guess he must have hit some place that made him so hopeless, he just walked into the kitchen where I was baking some brownies. I was so scared of him those days that I thought if I made everything he liked and did everything he wanted, maybe we'd all be safe.

Or maybe I'd get him back. It was like he'd gone somewhere and left this other person in his place who looked just like him.

He'd had plenty of accidents, but this one was real bad. He almost lost his leg. The doctors wanted to cut it off, but he said no way. It wasn't ever going to work right and he knew it.

I guess he was trying to figure out how to play his life, but I don't think he ever came up with anything. Nothing looked real good compared to what he had before. He must have drawn a blank or he wouldn't have walked in with the gun.

"I need to tell you where the money is," he says.

"I don't want to know."

"Then do it for the kids."

"Mongrel, stop talking like this."

"I'm not talking like anything, Mags. I'm giving you some information is all."

"You're leaving and you're thinking that the money will make it all right."

"There's a lot of money, babe."

"It's not the money I want, Mongrel."

"Look, you been asking me for years to tell you where it is. So, I'm telling you now."

"You're telling me goodbye is what you're telling me."

"Mags, I can't ride. It's jinxed. The only way I could ever be on a bike again is behind someone. Or some way I don't want. And I ain't doin' that. No matter how I try to rig it, if I can't ride the way I want to, then I ain't ridin' at all. It's like anything else I look at just don't come close to it. So, if I can't ride—fuck it."

◆　　　◆　　　◆

The group's coming to an end. We all know it. It's just a matter of time now. We all sit over the map. It's not that hard to decide, considering where we are now. Sam points it out first. The Grand Canyon. It's real close.

We figure it'll be a special place that we can all remember. Like a souvenir from the big escape. Joseph tells his daughter and she tells us that it's a wise decision because the Grand Canyon is a sacred place. He says that any place that's so naturally beautiful and noble has to be sacred.

"Sometimes that Joseph talk like he read too many books on how to sound like a wise old Indian," says Big Dee.

"He's pretty smart," I say.

"He just tell it how it is."

"Well, that's pretty smart, don't you think?"

◆　　　◆　　　◆

"And there's another fifty grand in your recipe box," says Mongrel.

"What's that?"

"In your recipe box—near your mother's banana muffin recipe."

"How'd you find it?" I say.

"I got my ways."

"How?"

"I suckered Max into believing you'd already told me he found it.

So, I knew you had it somewhere. I didn't figure you'd be dumb enough to put it in a bank. That meant it was hidden. I got this game goin' with Chrissie and Max. Said I'd give the first one to find it twenty bucks. You'd be surprised how fast they found it."

◆　　◆　　◆

## MY MOM'S BANANA MUFFIN RECIPE

1-3/4 cups flour (my mom always uses Robin Hood)
2 teaspoons baking powder
1/2 teaspoon baking soda
1/2 teaspoon salt
2/3 cup sugar
1/4 cup butter (softened)
1/4 cup shortening (softened)
2 eggs
1/3 cup milk
1 cup mashed ripe bananas
1/4 cup chopped walnuts
1 teaspoon vanilla

Mix flour and dry ingredients in a bowl.

Mix chopped walnuts into dry ingredients.

Cream butter, shortening, and eggs in another larger bowl.

Mash up banana, then add milk and vanilla.

Now, alternately add parts of the dry ingredients and

the banana combo to the creamed butter-egg mixture in the large bowl. Don't beat too long or hard.

Pour final mixture into greased muffin tins. Should make 12 muffins.

Bake at 350° for about 20 minutes or as long as it takes. I go by smell. When they smell fabulous, give them another ten minutes or so. Test with a toothpick.

◆ ◆ ◆

We have to drive fast to get to the canyon before the sun sets. It's winter. The sun goes down early. We've seen some beautiful sunsets. Didn't get to see those in prison except in the late winter when the sun went down during the one hour outside.

Every time I think about some reason why I want to go back, something else happens that makes me never want to go back. Sometimes just looking at a flower, or looking at a cactus. And the big open sky. That's what you never see in jail—the sky.

"Jesus, Sam, slow down."

"Gotta get there before the sun sets," says Sam.

"We get a speeding ticket, we're fried," says Stella.

She hasn't got the words out of her mouth when this siren goes off behind us.

"Shit!" says Sam. "Okay, we're just tourists who got to get to the canyon before dark."

She rolls down the window. Big Dee's squeezed in the corner, hand over her mouth. Chan just does what she always does, which is pull her knees up to her chest, tuck herself into a ball, close her eyes, and pray. I'm praying, too.

"Yes, sir, officer?"

"Going a little fast, ma'am."

"Sorry, sir. We were trying to get to the canyon before sunset."

"Hope I'm not slowing you down."

"Not at all, sir," says Sam.

"You ladies from Canada, then?"

"That's right, officer."

"Been having a good trip so far?"

"Real good. Enjoying a real sense of freedom down here," says Sam.

"Jesus, Moses, and Mary," hisses Big Dee.

"I guess I just take it for granted," says the cop. "Land of the free. It's nice to be reminded."

He smiles at Sam. Stella stares straight ahead. He touches his hat.

"Well, ladies, I don't want to be the one to spoil your vacation. But I'd appreciate it if you would drive a little closer to the speed limit. We just don't want you having an accident, you understand."

"Absolutely, officer."

"You're only about twenty minutes away. You got plenty of time."

"That's real nice of you, sir. And thank you, eh?"

We all take a breath together.

"Shit, I never hear no one kiss ass like that," says Big Dee, when the officer's out of earshot.

"She did great," I say.

"Suckin' up to a cop?"

"Jesus, Big Dee, sometimes you're really ignorant."

"Yessir, can I kiss your ass, sir?"

"Shut the fuck up, Big Dee."

"Could I suck your . . ."

"Don't even say it," says Sam.

◆　　◆　　◆

Joseph's right about the Grand Canyon. It must be a sacred place. You can tell from the first look. It's way bigger than you can ever imagine. Way bigger than it looks on a postcard: I know because Chrissie went there once and she sent me one.

We all go quiet except for saying things like holy shit and wow. Stella finds a way down to a big ledge where we can all sit with our feet hanging over. It's such a weird feeling, looking way down like that. The more you look, the more you have to believe there really is a God.

We must have sat there for at least half an hour, watching the colors change. Once in a while our eyes connect and maybe we smile. But nobody talks. It's like talking would ruin the magic. I'm just glad we had this special time together before we all split up. This is how I want to remember us. All sitting with our arms around each other at the Grand Canyon.

◆　　◆　　◆

I think what really pissed Mongrel off about Josie was the time she did this number on him about bikers being all the same.

"Bikers are like businessmen. They're all the same."

"Bullshit," says Mongrel.

"No, it's not," says Josie. "You can always tell a businessman. Suit.

White shirt. Tie. Nice shoes. Good haircut. Clean fingernails."

"Yeah, so what's your point?"

"So, bikers are the same."

"Where the hell you been lookin'?"

"They just got a different suit," says Josie.

"Bullshit!"

"What color are your t-shirts?"

"How the fuck do I know? They're all different."

"No, they're not. They're all black."

"They got different designs on them."

"Yeah, but they're all Harley stuff. And black leather. And bandannas. And tattoos. They're all the same. It's like a uniform. Like the cops, only different."

"You know, Josie, you ever say that again, I'm gonna believe that you don't like the shape of your face."

"I like it all right."

"Well, I'd like to see the ass end of it. Maybe like headin' out the door."

◆　　◆　　◆

Josie married this really nice guy. Bought her a great house, gave her lots of money for shopping, took her out to real nice restaurants. He also beat her black and blue. At first, I thought she was crazy. Then I saw she was happy most of the time.

He just beat her up sometimes, mostly when he got too pissed. I asked her if it hurt a lot, but she said it didn't. She said she was so full of adrenaline from being pissed off that she hardly felt a thing. She said it was worse the second day.

◆　　◆　　◆

I could see Josie getting beat on, but I really couldn't picture it with Big Dee. She said it happened, though, so I guess it did.

"I always make lots of noise," says Big Dee.

"Because it hurt?"

"Of course because it hurt. What the heck you think?"

"I don't know. I never got beaten."

"Never?"

"No."

"You lying."

"Why do you say that?"

"You always put your eyes up a certain way and then you cross your arms up close to your body. That what you do when you tellin' a lie."

"What the fuck, Big Dee? You studying me or something?"

"'Course. People just like poker players. You play with them long enough, you get to read their signs. Pretty soon they have to change them. Best poker players got no body language at all or else it's an act."

"Hmmm."

"So you did get beat?"

"Only once," I say.

◆　　◆　　◆

The first one to leave is Sam. We unhook the trailer from behind the RV and leave it on the side of the road. Sam has taped up the bike's tank and spray-painted it. Everybody's pretending it isn't happening,

Sam especially.

"So, where you goin', Sam?" says Big Dee.

"Mexico, for sure," says Sam.

"How 'bout the border?"

"Say a prayer for me."

"How we all gonna know you all right?"

"You goin' back, ain't you, Big Dee?" says Sam.

"That's right," says Big Dee.

"I'll send something to you at the prison."

"All right."

"Well, I guess I better get going."

Chan runs over and throws her arms around Sam.

"Look, don't you guys get all mushy on me, all right?"

"Jesus, Sam, let it down for a minute."

"Fuck you, Maggie."

"Fuck you, too, Sam. When you're drinking tequila, think of us."

"See you, Stella."

"Drive careful, Sam."

"Hey, I'm the wild horse," says Sam. She walks over to the bike. Then she turns around with this big smile on her face.

"We did something pretty amazing, eh? Busting out. Wow. It still makes me laugh to think about it. Whatever happens, I ain't ever gonna forget what we done."

The four of us stand on the road as she pulls out. She doesn't turn around, but her right hand goes up. Two fingers. The peace sign. Big Dee's shaking her head.

"I hope she makes it."

◆　　◆　　◆

## SEVEN OF WANDS: COURAGE

Just that sign she made. Two fingers. And how she held her body. She was going off by herself. She didn't need anybody. The card has all kinds of symbols on it, mostly totems of some kind. They look solid and ageless and fierce. I don't feel courageous. I feel like my stomach is never going to unwind. And I forget to breathe sometimes.

In the center of the card is a dragon and a stained glass window. The dragon is afraid of nothing. The person in the stained glass window looks like he's afraid of everything. A hand holds a talisman. Something to hang on to.

The card talks of inner demons or fears and how we have to be courageous enough to come face to face with these fears and then go through them. I just want to be on the other side of them. See them behind me.

◆　　◆　　◆

One of the things I liked about Mongrel was that he never let on that he was afraid. He wouldn't allow it. He couldn't understand why I'd wake up in the middle of the night and hang onto him. He used to wrap himself around me.

"It's okay, Mags."

"I'm afraid."

"Nothin' to be afraid of. You just scaring yourself."

"Don't leave me."

"I ain't leavin' you, babe."

"It's dark."

"Okay, I'll turn the light on. There. See? You're fine. I'm here."

"Why am I so afraid, Mongrel?"

"I don't know, Mags. I ain't got a clue."

"Tell me a story."

"Which one?"

"I don't know—a funny one."

"How 'bout the one where I sold the nettles to that asshole Bert?"

"You told me that one just a while back."

"How 'bout one about Icepick?"

"Yeah, you haven't talked about Icepick for a long time."

"Icepick was the coolest guy I ever met."

"Cooler than you?"

"Close."

◆　　◆　　◆

Without Sam, there's no competition between her and Stella. They both wanted to be the leader. Stella was the eagle and Sam was the wild horse—and neither one of them liked to be second in line. Now, because Stella's definitely the leader, I figure we can relax a bit. Of course, Big Dee has other ideas.

"Why should you be the leader?" says Stella.

"Because it's my turn," says Big Dee.

"Not this time."

Big Dee doesn't seem too upset about it. She's going back anyway.

Her mind isn't on what to do next and then after that. She wouldn't be much of a leader.

"So, you're definitely going back?"

"Uh-huh," says Big Dee.

"Then you don't mind if we keep heading south for a while? You don't need to be back on some particular date or nothin'?" says Stella.

"I thought maybe I show up for Valentine's Day."

"Now, the guards would like that. You could be their Valentine present. Tie a big red ribbon around you and show up at the front gate."

"Ha, ha," says Big Dee. "I can see me there."

"Well, try not to see me with you, all right?" says Stella.

◆　　　◆　　　◆

When Mongrel's mother died, he didn't say anything. I just happened to read the letter saying that she'd died in her sleep, and if he wanted any of her belongings to write to this address. He never wrote.

◆　　　◆　　　◆

Stella says you got to be real careful with hate because it's like a boomerang.

"We're like CB radios—sending signals all the time, eh?" She said that whatever we send out, even if it takes a long time, will come back. It makes you careful. It makes you start to watch your own mind like it was a television. Different channels. Different moods.

It was like your mind was the last frontier. You could still make it the way you wanted it to be. You could go to your place by the ocean. You could make up anything. And it was free.

The more I thought about it, the more I realized that I let everything screw up my thinking.

◆　　　◆　　　◆

Stella said it might be good to spend some time off the road. She said people on the run had to find a place to hole up and get their head straight.

"I know this place down in New Mexico."

"Not another Indian reserve?" says Big Dee.

"Indians been pretty nice to us," says Chan.

"No, Big Dee, it ain't a reserve. It's this sneak spot I found one time. Off the highway. Kind of a magic place, eh? Big rocks, sort of a red color, if I remember right."

"No Indians?" says Big Dee.

"Hell, there ain't nobody there except maybe a few snakes."

"Shit, I hates snakes," says Big Dee.

"There won't be none this time of year. Too cold."

"How you know there ain't nobody there?"

"Because nobody goes there. It's fenced off and signs say you can't come in. But I found a way. Perfect place. We can spend a few days there, figure out what we gonna do. Pretty cold at night, though, this time of year.

◆　　　◆　　　◆

It was freezing at night.

"Shit, I never been so cold in my whole life," says Big Dee.

"You bitch a lot, eh?" says Stella.

"Look, Stella, you grow up in the snow. You use to it. Where I grow up, it's warm—palm tree warm, palmetto bug warm. You know what I's talking about?"

"No, I don't," says Stella.

"Well, what I'm trying to say is that this is too damn cold for me. I hardly sleep at all last night."

"Why don't you sleep out by the fire then?" says Stella. "That ironwood burns all night long. Keeps you warm."

"Oh sure, and I wake up with some snake in my pants."

"Probably not the first time," I say.

"Hell, Big Dee, I already told you there ain't no snakes this time of year. They're sleeping."

"What if they wake up?"

◆　　　◆　　　◆

Big Dee's going back. Chan says she wants to go to L.A. or San Francisco. Stella's not sure where she's going, but she'll probably stay with some Indians in the area, somewhere. And Sam's already gone. I'm going to end up alone. I've never really been alone. And it's not like I can just turn up in some town and start all over. People are suspicious. They want to know where you come from.

I know I could work at some diner. But what if one of Mongrel's friends rides in? They probably all know by now that he's dead. And most of them probably think I did it. They could turn me in. Or I might end up on one of those "most wanted" shows on TV—my face plastered all over. Always looking over my shoulder. Always wondering if someone's looking at me strangely.

I've already changed my hair—cut it all off. I used my scissors to cut it in one of the motels. I never liked short hair, but it makes me look different, and looking different is more important right now than looking the way I like to look. We all look a bit different, except Big Dee. It's pretty hard to change her.

◆　　◆　　◆

Mongrel didn't like short hair on women.

"They're dykes," he says.

"How do you know?" I say.

"Look at their hair, for chrissake, Mags. No broad would do that to herself unless she's a dyke."

"It's the style, Mongrel."

"You tell me what guys are gonna want to fuck some dame with her hair like that."

"God, Mongrel, it's not always about fucking."

"Yeah, it is, Mags. That's what guys think about, whether you like it or not. It's about when you're going to get laid next. You see some dame on the street who's a fox, you think about getting laid. I watch your ass when you bend down to pick something up, I think about getting laid. It's the second thing I think about—right after my bike."

◆　　◆　　◆

Josie said that being married to a biker was like sharing the place with your old man's lover. You got to feel second-rate most of the time. I guess she was right. I don't think you can ever get it exactly the way you want it. There's always a snag.

◆　　◆　　◆

There was money buried all over the place. Mongrel drew me a map.

"Mongrel, you're scaring me."

◆　　◆　　◆

The first thing I did when I woke up this morning was walk over to a rocky area away from our camp and throw up. Maybe it's the food. Maybe it's the tension. When I turn around, Stella's there.

"Feeling sick, eh?"

"Yeah, maybe something I ate," I say.

"Nobody else sick," she says.

"Not so far, anyway."

"When was the last time you were in your moon?"

"I haven't had a period in months."

"Not pregnant, eh?"

"No way," I say.

"Better find out, just in case."

"Look, Stella, I'm *not* pregnant."

"Probably not, or at least you don't want to be. I'm going into town to get food this afternoon. I'll pick up one of them tests at the drugstore. I done it lots of times."

◆　　◆　　◆

When Chrissie got pregnant, I was real quick to tell her what to do. I thought giving the baby up was the only answer. When I got pregnant with Chrissie and Max, it wasn't exactly planned, but it wasn't a bad surprise either. Mongrel made it a lot easier. He wanted a couple of kids.

◆    ◆    ◆

"I's too old for this," says Big Dee. "My ass is froze solid. I can't sleep. There's nothin' to do here. And I's sick of all of you."

"Thanks, Big Dee," says Stella.

"It's the truth."

"Well, start lying then, 'cause I'm gettin' sick of your attitude."

"How come everyone's so bitchy?" I say.

"Feeling stuck together," says Chan.

"We are stuck together."

"We're all going different ways. Why not enjoy this time, eh? You won't see it again. This is a sacred place."

"Don't start with that Indian shit," says Big Dee.

"It's not shit," says Stella, flicking the ashes from her smoke at Big Dee.

"Well, I ain't up for it right now."

"You don't have to be up for it, Big Dee."

"You know what I mean."

"No, I don't."

◆    ◆    ◆

Max never got over it. Not that he was ever that close to his dad, but he stopped being close to me. When the ambulance arrived, he came riding up on his bike.

"What happened?" he says.

"It's your dad," I say.

"What about him?"

"He had an accident."

"What'd he do?"

"He shot himself, honey."

"Is he okay?"

"No, Max. He's not okay. He's dead."

Max stopped in his tracks. He didn't know how to take in the news.

"It's your fault," he said.

"No, it isn't, honey. He killed himself."

"Dad wouldn't do that."

"Well, I would've thought that, too. But he did. I was standing there when he did it."

"He did it because of what you did."

"That's not true, Max. He did it because of the accident. Because he couldn't ride anymore."

The cop is looking hard at me. I'm too rattled to know what to do. I just sit down and light up a smoke. It hasn't really sunk in yet. Max heads for the kitchen.

"Don't let him go in there," I say.

"I want to see my dad."

Max tried to run past the officer, but the cop catches him and holds him tight.

"I hate you," he says.

◆       ◆       ◆

I didn't do it. Not that I wasn't thinking about it. I was. I thought he was like some wounded animal that needed to be put out of its misery. I even stood over him one night when he'd passed out in his chair. It would have been so easy.

I could have shot him up with something. No one would have known any different. An overdose. Everyone would've understood. Why would I be so stupid as to shoot him in broad daylight and then put my fingerprints all over the gun? Shit, I'm not that dumb.

"But why did you pick up the gun?" my lawyer said.

"I don't know. It just didn't look right there."

"But you wiped it off."

"Yeah."

"Why?"

"I don't know. I guess it seemed like the right thing to do at the time. That's what they do on TV. Someone wipes off the gun, don't they?"

"If they're guilty."

"Yeah, but I'm not."

"I'm sure that's true, Margaret, but the circumstantial evidence is not in your favor."

"Evidence can be wrong."

"Of course it can."

"You think I'm guilty, don't you?"

"I didn't say that, Margaret."

"But that's what you're thinking."

◆　　　◆　　　◆

We spend three days in the Texas Canyon, which isn't in Texas at all—it's in New Mexico. It's a strange place, full of big boulders and magical rocks. The ground is practically bare. No grass. Just a few ironwood trees. The wood is real heavy. We drag hunks of it back to the campfire. Stella knows how to make the best fires. Once you get it going, that ironwood burns forever.

On one of my walks, I find this cactus. It's a big one—the first one I've ever seen. Stella tells me it's a barrel cactus. The plants in this area are all stiff and prickly. It's not like there's any grass that you can lie on. Everything you touch hurts.

But the weather is warm during the day. I've been sitting in the sun, trying to get some color. I got real white sitting in prison.

"How can you do that?" says Big Dee.

"What?"

"Cook yourself."

"I'm too white."

"That's pretty funny. I never understand it. Seeing white people lyin' down on the beach, turning over and over, trying to get black. But none of them really wants to be black."

"Don't start, Big Dee."

"Chill, Maggie. Hey, I ever tell you I used to think that maybe, when I grown up, I be white?"

"No, you never did."

"Well, I did. I thought that. Far as I could tell, all the good stuff went to the girls with blonde hair and blue eyes. So, I figure that maybe I don't want to be this color no more. So, I said to my momma,

"Hey, Billie." That's what she call herself—after Billie Holiday. "Hey, Billie," I say, "I don't want to be this color no more." She laugh and laugh. Say I might as well get use to it. Boy, I was mad."

"Hmmm. Where's your momma now?"

"I don't know," says Big Dee.

"She's not in Key West?"

"No, she left a long time ago."

"You don't ever see her?"

"Last time I see her, she's getting on a bus, says she's going to New York. I never hear from her again."

"You never tried to find her?"

"How I suppose to do that?"

"I don't know, call the police or something."

"Oh sure. What am I gonna say? Hey, you find my momma? She probably a hooker. How many dead nigger hookers you find this year?"

◆　　◆　　◆

I wonder if Sam made it.

I wonder what Max is doing right now.

I wonder if Mongrel is still around out there, like a spirit or something.

I wonder if I'll see Tony again.

I wonder if I'm pregnant.

I wonder if I can carry on.

I wonder if we'll get caught.

I wonder maybe if I'd been different, he wouldn't have killed himself.

◆　　◆　　◆

Maybe if I'd read the signs better. I knew there was something real wrong. Maybe I could've got him some help? I don't know what I was thinking. I just kept hoping he'd get over it—snap out of it. Every day, hoping. Hoping and getting more scared. He was losing it right in front of me and I didn't know what to do. He was shutting down. And he was shutting me out. He never came to bed with me anymore.

"Mongrel, it's not good for your back, sleeping in that chair all the time."

"I'm all right."

"You sure you don't want to stretch out? I could give you a back rub or something."

"I said I was all right."

"Honey . . ."

"Don't start, Mags."

"What do you want me to do?"

"Go to bed and leave me alone."

◆　　◆　　◆

Freedom is a lot of different things. Different things to different people. For Mongrel, it was riding. Being on the road. Not paying any taxes. I don't think I really liked being free all that much. And that doesn't mean I liked being in jail. I didn't.

But too much freedom isn't good either. It's confusing. There are too many choices. I liked it when I had someone to build my life around, who made most of the big decisions. I like to know where I'm going to sleep and what I'm going to eat.

◆　　　◆　　　◆

Stella and Big Dee go to the Safeway in Demming, which is just a ways down the highway from where we're camped. I look on the map and see that we're near a place called Truth or Consequences. I like the name. It makes you think. Tell the truth or live with the consequences. Tell the truth *and* live with the consequences. Tricky either way.

Stella does the shopping. She buys chicken and potatoes and cream corn. She gets a bag of marshmallows for after the meal. She hands me the pregnancy test. She cooks this incredible-tasting chicken and potatoes, wrapped in foil, with butter and rosemary. I can't believe how good it tastes.

◆　　　◆　　　◆

## STELLA'S CAMP-STYLE ROSEMARY CHICKEN AND TATERS
(for five or so)

10 medium-sized chicken thighs (bone in)
5 medium-sized potatoes
Butter
Salt
Pepper
Rosemary (fresh is best)
Tinfoil

Take a couple of thighs and a chopped up potato (otherwise, it takes longer to cook than the chicken).

Lay them on a good-sized piece of tinfoil.

Slather on the butter.

Add salt and pepper to taste.

Chop up the rosemary and sprinkle lots of it on the top.

Now, when you seal up the tinfoil, have the seam on top so it's easy to open. You might have to check inside a few times.

Place in the coals of a great campfire.

Cook until done!

◆　　◆　　◆

We're all sitting around the campfire, eating good food. Someone cracks a joke. Everyone laughs. I think it's the closest we've ever been. When we finish eating, the sun's already down and it's cold. Stella mixes coffee and hot chocolate.

The only noise you can hear is the fire cracking and trucks over on the highway.

"Jeez, Stella, where'd you learn to cook like this?"

"Old Indian method," says Stella.

"I guess tinfoil is an old Indian secret," I say.

"That's right," says Stella. Big smile.

◆　　◆　　◆

When I was a kid, I wanted to be an Indian. I liked how they dressed in the books I read. Moccasins with all that fancy beadwork. Men with long hair and strong noses and shiny eyes. They looked powerful and wild. They wore feathers. They rode horses. They were different.

I never thought about what had happened to the old Indians who got photographed a long time ago. Proud-looking people. Elegant. Then they got beaten.

Max learned different stuff in school. He wasn't getting told the same lies I was told when I was his age. I was glad about that.

Stella told me that a lot of the history we learned in school was a crock of shit to cover up whatever really went down—which was plain and simple wrong.

I've learned a lot from this escape. I feel like it's changed us. Different things are important now, and all we have to listen to is us. The only radio we have is the one in the front of the camper. It's got so much static, it's hardly worth listening to. We just listen to the news once a day. Nobody's talking about us, anyway, except maybe at the prison. I'll bet they're still talking. Some of the ones who knew Stella—the natives. And, of course, everyone knew Big Dee.

Big Dee was a force in the prison. She had a way about her, especially with women who lacked confidence. She wouldn't let them stay down. She was like a mother bear with her cubs. She taught them how to be proud of themselves again. She didn't care what color they were.

Now that we're on the road, we talk a lot. Tell each other stories about our lives.

"I never had no clear picture of where I's heading," says Big Dee. "Just kinda went along with things. Jail just come along. Hey, after that first time, it wasn't so bad. I looks around. All right, I got a bed. Three meals. Not always good, but filling. Ha, ha. That's how I got so big. Most of this here"— she grabs a handful of fat on her stomach— "I get in jail. Wow," She shakes her head. "I done a lot of time."

"I see a very clear picture," says Chan. "Every step I take, I watch and I go more and more in that way. I just never want to do how everyone else do. Always looking for my own way. Maybe stupid, but I had some good time, too. I can't go back. I never see anyone again, my friends, my sister, my father."

"I knew it was coming," says Stella. "I knew I had way too much anger inside me. Couldn't stop it. And when I'm real mad, I'm not afraid of no one. So, the first time I punched out a cop, man, it felt so good. Except I bust my hand. That hurt like a sonofabitch. That was the beginning. I liked it too much. Standing there in front of a bunch of cops, not afraid of them, and so drunk I didn't give a shit. I knocked out two cops one time. I did some time for that one, eh?"

"I didn't see this at all. It came right out of the blue. I knew he was going to die before me, but I thought he was going to wreck up the bike and crack his skull open. He hated helmets. Said they were for limp dicks. Boom. One bullet. My whole life shot to shit. Nope. I didn't see this one coming at all. Uh-uh."

◆　　◆　　◆

The pregnancy test is simple. Squat down, pee on the stick, and if it shows one blue line, you're not, and if it shows two blue lines, you are.

I wait until everyone's roasting marshmallows. Then I go behind some trees. It's freezing cold. Cold enough for steam to rise when I'm peeing. I have to wait three minutes in the dark, counting the seconds in my head. I'm just about to flick on my lighter.

"Need some light, Maggie?"

"Jesus, Stella, quit sneaking up on me, would you?"

"Thought you might be doing that test."

"Well, what if I was?"

"Might need a flashlight."

"I got a lighter," I say.

"Might need to talk about it after."

Stella shines the light on the stick. No matter how much I don't want to see them, there are two blue lines.

◆　　◆　　◆

## WOMAN OF WORLDS: PRESERVER

A woman stands, pregnant. And a bird flies, carrying something in its mouth, probably for building a nest. Some native woman is weaving something. All the stuff that women do. I remember being pregnant with Chrissie. I loved looking at myself in the mirror. I couldn't wait until my belly was really noticeable.

"Look, Mongrel, you can really see it now."

"You look gross."

"I do not. It's beautiful. You really think it looks gross?"

"Babe, I never seen you look so good."

"You mean it?"

"Come here, I'll show you."

Woman of Worlds is about taking care of the young and moving them along so they get to be adults. And you hope they don't end up too hurt or broken. We have to look after the world, too. We can't let it get too damaged either. It's about always having to be the nurturer. It makes me tired sometimes.

◆　　　◆　　　◆

I guess the big meal was for a reason. Stella tells us she's leaving. The food was her way of saying goodbye. I figured as much. There's been something about how she's been acting. Quiet. Thinking a lot. It's better for her down here. She's got connections. She won't say exactly where she's going.

"Less you guys know, the better, eh?"

"We wouldn't tell."

"Hell, I know that. Just better you don't know. Then, if you ever get asked, you tell the truth."

"How you gonna get there?"

"They're comin' here."

"When?"

"Probably get here tonight. They know this place. They come with me a couple a years ago."

"How'd you contact them?"

"Phoned them from the Safeway. Why? You think I send smoke signals?"

"Maybe."

"Things've changed. Some of us Indians even know how to send a fax."

◆     ◆     ◆

They arrive around midnight. Slide in with just their parking lights on. Park a ways from the fire. They're driving this beater. Actually, we heard them a long time before we saw them. Mongrel would have been under the hood in a New York second. Two of them walk over to the fire. Stella says something I don't understand and they all laugh.

"This here's Maggie. And Chan. And Big Dee."

"I'm George. He's my brother Billy." Everybody shakes hands, nods.

"Nice fire."

"Stella made it."

"Oh yeah?"

"Coffee?"

"Okay."

"You want something to eat?"

"No. We just ate in Demming."

"Where'd you go?"

"McDonald's."

"Hmmm."

"So, Big Dee, you'll get the camper back to Shoe?"

"I sure will, Stella."

"Chan, I hope you'll be all right in L.A. or wherever you end up."

"I miss you already, Stella," says Chan. The firelight shows a path of tears down her face.

"What about you, Maggie?"

"I don't know yet, Stella. Jury's still out, what with the new information and all."

"Well, whatever. You're the one who thought this whole thing up."

"I hope it goes good for you, Stella."

"I hope so, too."

We can hear the car for a long time. We sit listening, as though as long as we can hear it, she's still with us. Then we can't hear it anymore.

◆　　◆　　◆

Stella taught us how to use dried cow shit to burn in the fire. At first, I thought it was gross, but after seeing how well it burned and finding out it didn't smell bad at all, I got into it. It gave off a blue flame. I used it to heat the coffee after she was gone.

◆　　◆　　◆

It must have been hard for him to walk into the kitchen like that. With his mind made up. There was probably nothing I could've said. He just didn't want to go by himself. He never liked being alone. He always rode with someone. He was always real social. Except near the end. Then he spent all his time alone in the basement. Working on the bike. Not that he was ever going to ride it again.

It's hard to imagine what he was thinking, coming up those stairs, with a gun in his hand. I thought for sure he was going to shoot me. I held onto the counter just to steady myself. I'd been afraid for weeks, but now I was shit scared. My hands had gone all blue and my knuckles were white. I kept saying to myself, it's gonna be all right, it's gonna be all right, it's gonna be all right. But something in the pit of my stomach told me that wasn't true.

When I heard the shot, I screamed. I screamed and turned around. There was red all over the front of his shirt. All I remember was crying, no, Mongrel, no, Mongrel, no!

◆     ◆     ◆

The funny thing about someone dying is you think you see them all over the place. I'd see some biker about his size and I'd think it was him. Or I'd hear his voice behind me and turn around fast.

I even had a dream one time where I was in an elevator and I looked over and he was standing right beside me. I told him I thought he was dead, but he just smiled and said no, he wasn't. I started crying in the dream and he put his arms around me and I could smell him. I knew it was him by his smell.

◆     ◆     ◆

Stella's going off leaves a big hole. It's not the same now. Chan's gone real quiet. Not that she ever said that much. But now she's even worse. The silence is heavy. Big Dee's quiet, too. She builds a fire for breakfast. It's not as good as Stella's.

"I guess we leavin' here," says Big Dee.

"I guess so," I say.

"Know where we headed?"

"I was looking at the map. We could cut right through Arizona, along the bottom, to San Diego. Then up to L.A. Drop off Chan. Then take it from there."

"Sounds like a plan."

"How about you, Chan? Go to L.A.?"

"Okay," says Chan.

"Well then, let's get packing. Anyone want to take some cow shit along for a souvenir?"

◆     ◆     ◆

Mongrel was the worst for souvenirs. He had to buy a T-shirt everywhere we went, or a fridge magnet, or something. I hated it. It was just a bunch of junk as far as I was concerned. Most of it was made in Taiwan anyways. A fridge magnet of Texas, made in Taiwan. The fridge was covered with them. He had drawers full of T-shirts he'd never wear. Mostly Harley-Davidson stuff. He must have bought one in every town he visited.

"Look at this one, Mags."

"Uh-huh."

"This is a cool design."

"Uh-huh."

"You don't like it?"

"It's all right."

"All right? It's fuckin' great!"

"I'm not into T-shirts, Mongrel. You know that."

"It's not just a T-shirt. It's a fuckin' work of art. Look at it."

"It's a Harley."

"Of course it's a Harley."

◆     ◆     ◆

I'm not sure we ever really talked to each other. We traded words. Or smartass remarks. We were best together when we weren't talking.

Sometimes we'd be sitting on the couch watching something together. He'd reach over and tell me to get my ass over closer. And I'd sit snuggled into him. We liked watching funny things together. We liked to laugh together. We laughed at the same things.

◆　　　◆　　　◆

"What are you laughing at?" Me talking.

"At you," she says.

"Why? What did I do?"

"It's not what you do, it's how you is."

"And how is I?"

"You don't have to make fun of me, Maggie."

"I'm not really."

I like the way Big Dee talks. It's like a different kind of dance. She's dancing some Latin dance, all kind of loose. I'm dancing, too, but some other kind of dance. It's different, anyways. More held in. I guess it's stiffer.

"You is holdin' onto a secret," she says. "You thinking a lot. Tryin' to make some decision. I read you like I read the cards."

"I'm the one who reads the cards, Big Dee."

"That's so, Maggie. But I reads people, and you full to busting about something."

"Good choice of words."

"So, what you up to?"

"I'm trying to figure out which is worse—having a baby in prison or having it on the run."

"You pregnant?"

"Seem to be."

"You serious?"

"Uh-huh."

"Well now, that certainly put a new spin on things, don't it?"

"Uh-huh."

"So, you looking for the right answer."

"That'd be nice."

"It's the one that rings true and pure. It's the one that make you feel the best. The one that don't hurt nobody. Sometimes takes time to figure that one out."

"I don't have a lot of time, Big Dee."

"Can't run out of time, Maggie."

"For chrissake, Big Dee, you're starting to sound like Stella."

Big Dee sits quiet for a while. Then she speaks.

"Chan's up to something. She used a pay phone at one of the shops."

◆　　　◆　　　◆

Arizona's dry as a bone. The rivers are all dried up. The plants are dry. There are these big, tall cactuses—some of them three times taller than me or more.

I don't want to live here. It's nice to visit, especially now that it's winter everywhere else. I mean, this is better than rain and cold any day of the week. Hell, it's January and I'm in shorts and I've been wearing sunglasses ever since we hit Utah.

Sometimes it seems like we're just another group of tourists traveling in the RV. We're not alone. Lots of others are doing the same thing. I wonder if they're running away from something, too.

We stop to get gas. We try to find the most interesting beef jerky. Chan likes Dr. Pepper. I like Classic Coke. Big Dee won't drink anything but Diet Coke. We stop at the side of the road to take a piss. We pass some time looking at dopey tourist junk. We laugh at some of the postcards. We eat ice cream. We argue about which restaurant to eat at. We fight over where we're going to sleep at night.

Sometimes I'm sitting in the back of the camper wishing they'd both just disappear or get caught. And then out of the blue we see a couple of deer right there on the side of the road. We pull over just to watch them, nobody making a sound. Times like that are real incredible.

Chan's scared about something. I mean, before, she hardly said anything, but she was right there, watching everything, listening, taking it all in. She was curious, like a cat. She wanted to understand. She didn't care if she talked. She liked to listen.

But now she's gone quiet in a different way. She still talks about the same amount, but the rest of the time she's nowhere in sight. Lost inside her head.

I still don't know what to do. I think, after we drop Chan off, maybe we'll head over to Sonora. Mongrel's friend Icepick lives there, or at least he used to. Of course, he probably thinks I killed Mongrel.

Sometimes I wake up and look over at Big Dee, sleeping on the floor, a blanket on top of her and her jacket on top of that. And Chan curled up in the corner. We're sleeping in some rest stop and I'm asking myself, How did this all happen? And how come it happened to me? But the one that really gets me is, How could he have shot himself? I still can't get my head around that one.

◆　　　◆　　　◆

## THREE OF WANDS: COMPASSION

The hand in the center of the card is a hand from a Chinese statue—one of the big ones. Fat little hands with graceful fingers. Those statues always have a nice smile on their face. Nice and relaxed, saying, It's okay, it's okay, everything's going to be okay.

Everything in the card is soft. A rose. A flock of birds. A butterfly and a big red sun setting somewhere near the equator in the east, where the sun gets huge. We saw that kind of sunset when we went to India one winter. You sure learn about compassion there. You have to turn it off or you'd never stop crying.

◆　　　◆　　　◆

We know something's up as soon as we hit Tucson. Chan says she has to be at a particular mall—something about a connection. I don't like it. Neither does Big Dee. It means someone from the outside knows about us, and that we're arriving at a certain time. We tell Chan this but she says her connection doesn't know anything about the escape. That it's about other business—about setting up in Los Angeles.

It's mid-afternoon when we pull in. It's hot, the air all wavy from the heat coming off the pavement. Chan says she has to go to the pharmacy. We park the RV back quite a ways, but we can still see the entrance to the store. Chan tells us that she'll be back by four o'clock. It's three now.

Big Dee and I sit with the doors open, playing blackjack, trying to keep cool in more ways than one.

"I don't know what you feelin', Maggie. But me, I feel nervous."

"Me, too. She's been way too secretive about this. Why didn't she tell us about the phone calls?"

"Beats me. I'll take another card."

I put one down. Big Dee looks at her hand.

"Hit me, again," she says. "I'll stay."

"How'd she know to connect with someone here? I mean, this is the middle of nowhere."

"I don't know. But what I do know is we're going to have a serious talk with her. She can't do this kind of mystery stuff. It makes us all feel weird. I mean, she's part of the group."

Big Dee's dealing when we hear a screech of tires and a horn blowing. Next thing, we see Chan run out from between the moving cars, heading in our direction. Then we hear some loud cracks and she goes down.

"Jesus," says Big Dee, "close the doors."

"Don't do anything, Big Dee. Just try to act normal."

"I think she got shot, Maggie."

Then we hear people shouting. We sit there paralyzed until we hear sirens coming. Two cop cars come screaming into the parking lot

"What do we do now?" says Big Dee

"We do what everyone else does. We get out of our vehicle and go over to see what happened."

"I don't want to know."

"Me neither, but if we pull out now, it's going to look suspicious. Besides, we gotta know how she is. You stay here. I'll be back."

"Don't leave me alone," says Big Dee.

"I'll be back right away," I say.

I jump out and walk toward the store. There's already a crowd of people gawking. I push my way to the front. There's a guy on his knees, holding onto Chan's wrist, checking for a pulse, I guess. She looks bad. She's been shot. Blood all over the place.

"She's gone," he says to nobody in particular.

The police are pushing everyone back. I take a last look at her, try to find something in her face. Some sign. But there's nothing. All the way back to the RV, my knees are shaking. I open the door and sit down.

"You better drive, Big Dee."

"She dead, isn't she?"

"Yeah, she is."

"I knew she wasn't gonna make it. I could feel it in my bones. Just like Darlene."

"Let's get out of here," I say.

◆　　◆　　◆

It's a quiet drive, heading for California over the mountains. There's a snowstorm. It makes the driving harder.

"At least she got to see snow," says Big Dee.

"Uh-huh. Remember how she looked when she sunk in?"

"I sure do. She look so surprise. She was all right, wasn't she? Kind of quiet, but never cause no harm. It's a shame."

"We gotta do something for her, Big Dee."

"Maybe we can bury her stuff and put up a cross or something."

"What if she wasn't a Christian?"

"Hell, I don't know. Ain't it the thought that counts?"

◆　　◆　　◆

Turns out there's only one thing Big Dee has to see and then she'll be all right about going back to jail. I'm thinking it's some mountain, or some sacred special place, but it turns out all she really wants to see is that big Hollywood sign that you always see in pictures. It's way up on a hill.

"That's *it*?" I say.

"That's all I want to see," she says.

"How come you want to see that?"

"I don't know, just do."

◆　　◆　　◆

It's really something, coming into L.A. From miles out we know where we are because of the smog. The closer we get, the worse it gets.

"I don't know how people can live in this," I say.

"People can get use to most anything," says Big Dee.

"I guess so. You keeping your eye on the map?"

"Yes, ma'am."

"It should be coming up soon."

"I don't see nothin'."

"Well, stop looking at the map."

"Hey, there it is! There it is! Look, Maggie, there it is!

"Well, I'll be damned, Big Dee."

"Ain't that somethin'?"

"It sure is."

"I always want to see that Hollywood sign. Now I have. Too

bad we don't have no camera."

"Yeah. Too bad we didn't take some pictures of all of us. Now it's too late."

"I got some nice pictures in my head," says Big Dee.

"Me, too," I say.

"Us all in the snow, makin' them angels for Chan."

"Yeah, and now she's a real one."

I don't know why I said that or why it set us off, but next thing we're falling apart laughing. I mean, it's not funny—it's tragic, really. But I can't stop and neither can Big Dee. By the time we finish, we're both crying from laughing so hard.

◆　　◆　　◆

Sometimes I remember things about prison that make me think I just plain can't go back. I hated all the noise. Doors crashing shut. Right in the middle of a conversation, some announcement coming over the speaker. All day, those announcements. And the food. It's what happens when you have to cook for too many people and you don't have enough money. So, you cut corners.

Mongrel and I always ate the best. I think he was always trying to make up for the big wedding he never gave me.

"That's what the money's for, babe."

"But it's really expensive."

"I don't care. We got the cash."

"But it's too much."

"There is no such thing as too much, Mags. When you gonna understand that about me?"

"I don't know, Mongrel. Sometimes it looks like you're just paying the price to show off."

"So?"

"So, you're showing off."

"So what, Mags? I like to show off."

◆　　◆　　◆

## 0: FOOL-CHILD

See, Mongrel knew he was taken care of. He had that kind of belief. He was sure of himself, so he could act like a fool. He liked to play a lot. He was like a big kid. He had so much energy when he needed it. It made him reckless. That's why he had a lot of accidents. He was having too much of a good time and not paying attention.

The number of the Fool-Child card is zero. It's about spirit—being everywhere and nowhere. You follow the spirit instead of being practical. It's about a leap of faith and new beginnings.

I guess that's what we're doing. Taking some kind of leap of faith. Big Dee knows for sure she's going back, but even so, when she's looking at a waterfall or a rainbow, I can see her wondering sometimes if she's doing the right thing.

◆　　◆　　◆

We decide the best thing we can do for Chan is bury her belongings in the sand on Big Sur and let the Pacific take them home for her. We're avoiding the freeways. We've done most of this trip on secondary roads. That's why it's been so pretty.

I did this road on the back of the bike, once, with Mongrel. It was really something. This time, we're going to catch it as the sun's going down. That could be pretty special.

In Santa Barbara, we go down a pier and eat fish and chips. Every meal's starting to feel like the last supper. It must be real busy in the summertime here. It's pretty busy right now and it's only February. I can't imagine what it's like in the summer. Wall-to-wall people. And the whole place smells like suntan lotion. Mongrel would never go to a beach.

"You think I'm gonna sit on some beach with a bunch of fags? I don't go to the beach. I don't wanna change the color of my skin. I'm white and I like it that way."

◆　　　◆　　　◆

I have a dream. I'm walking down a big wooden wharf. There are lots of people, but somewhere in the crowd of faces I see Tony. I wave at him and he smiles, but then he turns around and starts to walk away. I try to run after him but people keep getting in my way. I feel like I'm losing him.

I stop to catch my breath. I look over at a man in a wheelchair. He's bent over double, but as I look at him, he lifts his head and I can see his face. He raises his hand and shakes a finger at me. It's Mongrel.

◆　　　◆　　　◆

Max was born when Mongrel was doing time. Mongrel never got to touch him and he only saw him through a thick piece of Plexiglas.

There was something about never being able to touch Max that kept Mongrel at a distance from him. He didn't get to know Max the way he did Chrissie. And Max never quite got used to Mongrel either.

◆　　◆　　◆

Mongrel's funeral was big. Lots of people. Lots of bikes. Lots of food. Lots of booze. I think we partied for three days straight. I don't remember big chunks of it. People would come up to me saying how sorry they were about Mongrel. I was so drunk, I thought they were sorry about the accident—his leg. I told them he'd pull through. They'd get this weird look on their face.

The third day, I woke up dry heaving. It finally hit home. He was dead and I was alone. I might even be a murder suspect. The house of cards fell down.

◆　　◆　　◆

Chan's funeral is real small. Just Big Dee and me. But the higher power, whoever she is, has sent us one hell of a sunset. There are people parked all along the road, taking pictures.

Big Dee puts all Chan's stuff, which isn't much, into a cookie tin. I dig out my sacred object—the Corona beer cap—and drop it in. Then Big Dee seals the tin shut with some duct tape. We crawl down from the side of the road to the beach. We dig a hole and carefully place the cookie tin in it.

Big Dee sings "Amazing Grace" so pretty that I can't help crying. We sit quiet until the tide comes in so high that it covers where we've been sitting. Then we climb back up to the RV.

"I's never gonna forget this trip, Maggie."

"Me neither."

"Sometimes I don't want to go back."

"I know."

"But I just don't know how to take care of myself anymore, least not on the outside. I guess I'm gettin' too old."

"Yeah. It's harder when you get older. If I was twenty right now, I think I'd head to Mexico, like Sam did."

"I'd go back to Key West. But even I say that I know it ain't what it use to be. I probably hate it now. Too many tourists. That always the way, you notice that? Some place real nice. Everybody pretty much happy. Then money comes in and it bring trouble with it."

"Yeah."

"Wasn't that an amazing sunset, Maggie? Hard not to believe there a God when you see somethin' that pretty. Make you forget about everything, don't it?"

"Uh-huh."

"Where we headed tonight?"

"I don't know, Big Dee. But if this road goes on much longer like this and we got no light, we might just be pulling over and sleeping on the side of the road. Hope you don't mind."

"Fine by me," she says.

"Just the two of us left, now. Funny, huh?"

"What you gonna do, Maggie?"

"I don't know yet. Being pregnant kind of complicates things. I hate the thought of having a kid in prison, you know, having to give it up."

"Maybe you get off—maybe some new evidence show up. You don't know."

"I won't be getting off, Big Dee."

"What about that thing for women who been abuse by their old man?"

"He didn't abuse me."

"You said one time he did."

"That was a payback."

"What for?"

"For fucking around on him."

◆　　　◆　　　◆

We went everywhere that night. To Lou's for dinner. Lou brought out this real expensive bottle of champagne for us. We played pool. We danced close and laughed so that everyone could see.

Mongrel bought drinks for the whole bar. We were having a great time. We both got pretty loaded. I wasn't sure about Mongrel riding in that condition, but he got us home all right. The kids were over at Josie's.

We were still laughing when we got into the house. I turned around to say something and got caught with a punch that spun me around a couple of times before I smashed into the wall. I slid to the floor. I saw this blood running down the front of my dress.

"Get up, you whore."

I just sat there in shock. Mongrel walked over and yanked me up real hard. Then he pushed me up against the wall.

"You look like shit."

"Fuck you," I say. I spit a bunch of blood in his face, and he back-hands me. It's kind of true what Josie said about not feeling it. I'm so drunk and scared and pissed off that I don't feel much of anything. But my thinking gets real clear. Like glass. I do this quick spin out of his reach, and get to the fireplace. I grab the poker and swing it like a baseball bat, barely missing his head. He stops right in his tracks.

"You could've fucking killed me, Mags."

"You come one step closer and I will." I'm way out of control.

"Put it down, Mags."

"Don't come any closer."

He steps in, I take a swing. He catches it across the arm. I know it had to hurt because I swung really hard. Mongrel's face goes white. He grabs the poker and heaves it right through the stained glass window. Then he grabs me by the hair and hauls me into the bedroom. I feel my dress being ripped off. He takes me hard, from behind. I keep telling myself it'll be all right, it'll be all right, it'll be all right.

◆    ◆    ◆

Josie was right about Danny. When I told him I was getting married to Mongrel, he said, "I thought you said you wanted to marry me."

"I did, but . . ."

"You're marrying that biker."

"I need someone to take care of me."

"I can take care of you."

"With what?"

"I don't know—whatever."

"See?"

"See what?"

"It wouldn't work."

"How do you know it wouldn't work? You won't even give it a chance. You're going to marry that ape with the Harley."

"He's not an ape."

"You're making a mistake, Mags. You don't love him. I know that and you know that."

"How do you know?"

"Because I know you love me."

"How do you know, for sure?"

"It's a feeling, Mags. You can't make it up. It's either there or it's not. It's like energy. We have that energy. It's electric. Shoots between our eyes. You can almost taste it sometimes."

"Maybe for you."

"Uh-uh. You feel it too. You're transparent, I can see right through you."

"No way."

"You're stupid if you do this. And at some point, you're going to realize that you made a mistake. I don't care if it happens in a year or way down the road. Then you come and see me."

"I gotta go, Danny."

"You don't have to."

"Yeah, I do."

"Vaya con Dios, then."

"Wish me well."

"I just did."

◆   ◆   ◆

I'm not sure exactly why I want to see him, maybe just that he was connected to Mongrel. But we go see Icepick anyway.

By the time we get to Big Hill, where he lives, the sun is going down. The hills are covered with ponderosa pines. I came here one time before with Mongrel. Icepick was scary. I couldn't take my eyes off him.

He moved so fast you almost didn't see him. Smooth and fast. He seemed to be all over the place all the time. Mongrel said he was like Daffy Duck on speed. He'd be talking here, and then all of a sudden he was there, and you hadn't seen him make the move.

He had this funky, beat-up old cabin near the top of Big Hill. We came up on the bike at night. Mongrel almost lost it a couple of times. The road had some bad potholes and washouts.

Icepick came down the road to say hi with two pit bulls on a thick chain. It was pretty impressive, I have to say. He was full on, right from the get-go.

◆　　◆　　◆

"So, did you do it?"

"Jesus, Icepick, I haven't even got out of the RV. This here's Big Dee."

He looks over at Big Dee, then back at me.

"She stayin' here?" he says.

"For chrissake, Icepick."

Big Dee looks over at me. I can see she's pissed off. I don't know what to say. I just shrug my shoulders. You never know with Icepick.

"You guys eaten?" He's in the kitchen already, doors opening, pulling out stuff. He's working on the recipe as he goes along. We get beers, cold. There's a joint. He whips up this amazing stuff with mushrooms he gets shipped in. An appetizer. Sautéed in butter. Lots of cilantro. He can cook. And he doesn't stop moving the whole time. Big Dee's watching him.

"Whoa," she says.

"What's up, momma?"

"Whoa, slow down, take a pill. I's gettin' wired up just watchin' you."

"Yeah, it's how I am."

"Don't it make you crazy?"

"Uh-uh. It makes everybody else crazy. Me, I like it. So, Mags, did you off Mongrel?"

"Icepick, don't you think I'm getting sick of answering that question?"

"It's easy. Yes or no?"

"No."

"That's it?"

"That's it."

◆　　　◆　　　◆

That's when I took the night school course—after I got beaten. I didn't feel like being around the house. Mongrel pretended he didn't care, but I knew he felt shitty about what he'd done. My face was black and blue and I had bruises all over my body. I wore sleeveless tops and shorts just to rub it in.

Mongrel got the window fixed and did some stuff I'd been nagging him about for a long time. He didn't even blink when I told him I was thinking of going back to school. He usually never wanted me going anywhere at night without him.

I probably could have had an affair with Doug, the guy who taught the course. I knew he was up for it. But I wasn't into getting knocked around again. Josie was right about that, too. It hurt a hell of a lot more the day after.

◆　　　◆　　　◆

"I hear he fucked up his leg real bad."

"Yeah, it was bad."

"But he could still ride?"

"He could of. But that wasn't all."

"What do you mean?"

"Mongrel wasn't alone when he went down."

"Oh yeah?"

"He was with this young chick. I guess he was looking over his shoulder, going to pass this semi, but the semi hits his brakes all of a sudden. He doesn't see Mongrel in his mirror. Everybody'd been drinking. Who knows how it all went down. It happened too fast.

"Anyway, Mongrel goes into a skid, slides under the semi, and the tank gets punctured—at least, that's what they figure, 'cause there's gas all over the engine, which is hot. There's sparks. Boom. The chick doesn't even make it to the hospital alive. Lucky for her. She was burned all over.

"Mongrel wakes up in hospital. He's got horseshoes up his ass. He got thrown clear. Nobody can figure out how. He didn't even get burned—not at all. And he's got something to fight for, you know what I mean? They want to cut off his leg."

"No shit?"

"Yeah, so he gets through that part all right. He keeps the leg. But he can't do anything with it. He can't bend it at all. It's like a dead weight. Plus he's got this dead chick on his mind. Which is really how come he can't get back on the bike."

"How come you never tell that part to me, Maggie?" says Big Dee.

"I don't know. Just tryin' to keep it simple."

"So, it sounds like you got a motive. You shoot him?" says Icepick.

"No, he shot himself."

"That's what you say?"

"That's what I know."

◆　　◆　　◆

I don't know what I was thinking all those years. He never liked to ride alone. And he'd never ride with a guy. So, when I wasn't there, he was riding with some other chick. And I knew it. And he knew I knew. He never talked about it and I never asked. But after he fell, I couldn't let it go.

"Who was she?"

"I don't know. Just some chick I picked up."

"Where?"

"In a bar. Where do you think?"

"I don't know. I didn't spend all my free time thinking about you fucking around on me."

"You know where this is heading, Mags?"

"No, where is it heading, Mongrel?"

"It's heading for trouble."

"Maybe that's what I'm lookin' for."

"Mags, she wasn't important. All right? She was some dumb little chick who wanted to fuck a biker. Tell all her friends. It's too bad. She wasn't a bad kid. Now she's dead."

"Thanks to you."

"Let's not go there, Mags."

◆　　　◆　　　◆

"It ain't just the law's after you," says Icepick.

"What do you mean?" I say.

"Some of the guys figure you should be with Mongrel. Especially since you put him there."

"That's bullshit."

"Maybe. I'm just telling you how it is."

"So, you telling me I should stay away from the law *and* the bikers?"

"Mags, I ain't telling you what to do. Like I say, I'm just telling you how it is."

"I might as well go back in."

"Like I said . . ."

"Yeah, I know. I have to figure it out myself. It's just that I see shit no matter which one I pick—inside or out."

"That's how it is sometimes."

"I hate it."

"Big rock. Hard place."

"What would you do?"

"Me, I'd go in. Take a couple of years to let things go real cool on the outside. Then I'd resurface."

"But I might get twenty-five. End up being a lifer. Get out after a minimum of, what, ten years? And then I won't be able to look the wrong way or I end up back in for a couple more. I don't want to get life."

"Like I said, hard place."

◆　　　◆　　　◆

One thing that bugged me about Tony was how he was a bit too into that drug and alcohol thing. Sometimes he got too righteous. He seemed to think that everyone had a problem, even if they just drank social.

I never got drunk that often, but I liked getting a buzz on. I don't think I could stand the idea of being straight all the time. I need a break from the real world sometimes.

Tony said he was a lot happier now that he was sober, but then I don't know what he was like before he quit drinking. Maybe he was an asshole—except, as far as I could tell, whoever was an asshole when they were a drunk pretty much stayed an asshole after they quit—only now they were a sober asshole. I'm not sure which is worse.

◆　　　◆　　　◆

"I think I'm going back."

"Uh-huh?"

"I mean, if I have to stay away from bikers, that means I can't get a job."

"I guess so."

"If I can't work, where am I gonna get the cash? I'll have a baby to take care of."

"I thought Mongrel left you a whole lot a cash."

"Well, he did, but what about when that runs out?

"Maggie, you worryin' way too far ahead."

"You got to think ahead, Big Dee."

"What for? It don't change nothin'."

"How do you know?"

"I know."

◆     ◆     ◆

Over dinner, Icepick tells us this story about working construction with this guy. The guy's always borrowing his truck. Only problem is, when the guy brings it back, it's always out of gas.

So, one day Icepick fires the truck up, gets it out of the driveway, and it dies. Out of gas. So he gets a gas can and starts walking to the gas station. Only, it turns out they're renovating, so he has to go another mile or so to another one. Anyway, he finally gets there and gets some gas.

He's walking back, about halfway home, and who goes by but this guy who's always using the truck. I guess the guy just looks over quick, looks back, and drives on. He doesn't even stop.

"He don't even stop, the prick!" says Icepick.

So, a couple of months later, Icepick's driving down this same street and there's the same guy, pulled over with the hood up. Icepick turns right around. Goes up to the guy, nice as pie, asks him what the problem is.

"No shit. You're out of gas. Well, no, problem," he says. "I got a gas can right in the back of the truck."

Inside his head, he's thinking, "Yeah, the same fuckin' gas can I hoofed two fuckin' miles with when this fucker passed me by."

So anyway, he's over-nice to this guy. He's telling jokes. They get back to the guy's jeep. Icepick waits to make sure it starts. And all the time this guy keeps looking at Icepick. He's fucked up because he knows that Icepick knows. And Icepick knows that he knows.

"So, what's the point?" I say.

"The point is, you take the high road."

"C'mon, Icepick, you were fucking with him. How's that the high road?"

"I was only fucking with him a little."

"He probably thought you were going to cut his throat."

"Don't worry, I thought about it."

"How long did it take you to cool down?"

"About a month."

"That's pretty fast."

"For me it was."

"How come you didn't *do* the guy?"

"I did him."

"How?"

"I fucked with his head."

◆      ◆      ◆

Max could hold a grudge forever. Chrissie couldn't hold one if you paid her. It's funny how kids can be so different. They were totally different from square one. Chrissie was always happier. Not so many ups and downs. Max was all over the map—one second he's totally happy, and then, boom, he's in a bad mood. It was hard to keep up with him. Finally, I just gave up—tried to live with him the best I could. He wasn't always a lot of fun.

I wonder about the one I'm carrying now. What's she going to be like? I know it's a girl, don't ask me how. As crazy as it sounds, when I first found out I was pregnant, in the desert, I told Stella a part of me wished it was Mongrel's—that I had a little bit of him growing inside me. Not that I don't want it to be Tony's. It's hard to explain.

◆　　　◆　　　◆

Maybe he's doing it so we'll leave faster—who knows? It's hard to tell with Icepick. Seems like he's trying to pick a fight or something.

"What's the matter with him?" says Big Dee.

"Who knows?"

"We didn't do nothin'."

"I know, Big Dee. It's my fault. We shouldn't have come. It's just the way he is. Even Mongrel thought he was a bit of a wing nut."

"Must of come from dysfunctioning family, I guess," says Big Dee.

"Sometimes you're pretty funny."

"Thought you like it. Look, sugar, this guy is way weird, okay? He already kill a few people. There's probably some ugly stories we don't even want to know."

"Probably."

"What say we hit the road?"

"Sounds good to me."

◆　　　◆　　　◆

We pass through Sacramento. There's a sign saying Folsom Prison. Big Dee says we should go for a visit—pay our respects to Johnny Cash. Mongrel said Johnny Cash never set foot in Folsom except to sing.

Part of me wants to see it again, but I've got these bad memories from visiting Mongrel there. The problem with visiting someone you love in prison is that you can't always know if you're going to be in the mood for a visit when you get there.

Sometimes you go and you're not in the mood, or he's not, and it's not like you can see each other again right away if it doesn't work out. For us, there were sometimes weeks between visits. It was harder, too, because of the kids. Plus sometimes, just talking to him or looking at him, I'd want to make love to him. But we couldn't even touch hands.

◆　　　◆　　　◆

I know something's up when I see him come into the kitchen wearing this shirt that I like. It isn't something he wears outside. It's not biker gear. It's white. Like one of those shirts you see pirates wear. It looks great on him.

He sits down. I'm making hash brownies.

"We gotta talk, Mags," he says.

I don't notice until I sit down that there's a gun on the table. It's just sitting there. He doesn't have it in his hand. And he's looking at me.

"What are you doing with the gun, Mongrel?"

He looks at it like he just realized it's there. Then he picks it up and looks at it as though he's studying it. And then I see that his face is wet. He's been crying or he's crying now.

"It's all fucked up, Mags."

"You're just having a bad day, Mongrel."

"No, Mags, I'm having a bad life."

"Mongrel . . ."

"I got to talk to you about the money."

"I don't care about the money."

"You will."

"Mongrel, stop . . ."

"Look, Mags, I done all the thinking I can do about this. No matter how you slice it, I killed that girl. She was younger than Chrissie—just a kid."

"She was old enough to fuck."

"Let's not go there, Mags. I don't want to think about it no more. And I can't ride no more either."

"You could if you wanted to."

"Not the way I like to. I can't even walk right." He bangs his fist on the table. I could see it coming but I still jump.

"You remember that dog we had, the one when we were living in the cabin?" he says.

"Rusty."

"That's right—Rusty. You remember what happened to him?"

"Yeah, he got killed by a car."

"That's what I told you at the time. But he didn't get killed by the car—I shot him."

"I didn't know that."

"He did get hit by a car. It fucked him up real bad. So, I shot him. I had to—you know—put him out of his misery."

"What are you getting at, Mongrel?"

"I want you to do it for me."

"What?"

"Put me out of my misery."

"I can't do that, Mongrel."

"Well, Mags, you got a choice. Either you shoot me or I'm gonna shoot you first, and then me."

◆　　◆　　◆

## SEVEN OF CUPS: FEAR

Fear is like this giant wave. And you're under it, knowing it's going to crash down on you and not knowing how it will end. Fear is what you feel when you still think there's hope. Maybe you'll survive the wave. Maybe you'll live.

I don't have any choice. He isn't kidding about killing me. I can see it in his eyes. He's real tired. He's finished. He's looking right at me when he starts reaching for the gun. Just for a second I think about running, but I know he's a good shot. He'd get me. My hand reaches the gun just before his. He smiles.

"Good for you, Mags."

◆　　◆　　◆

"You shoot him, didn't you?" Big Dee is talking.

"What do you think?"

"I told you. I think you done it."

◆     ◆     ◆

Big Dee has a dream. She sees us both in a tunnel, running away from a light that's getting closer and closer until it comes right up to us. And then it passes. She says we're all dirty because the tunnel is wet and muddy.

We walk out the other end and her father's standing there. Big as life, she says, and he has this smile on his face. She says she can't breathe. And she's got her hands up so he can't hit her face. He still manages to land a few good ones before she wakes up.

"Maggie?"

"Yeah, Big Dee?" It's pitch dark. We're sleeping in the back of the RV.

"I had me a bad dream."

"It's just a dream, Big Dee. You're all right. Go back to sleep."

"But it was scary."

"You'll be all right."

"Maggie. . ."

"You want me to come hold you for a while?"

"Uh-huh."

I slide over onto her mattress and put my arms around her.

"That better?" I say.

"Uh-huh."

"You're like a little kid sometimes, you know?"

"Uh-huh."

"Nobody's gonna hit you, Big Dee."

"I know."

"I won't let them."

"I know."

◆　　　◆　　　◆

There's a blizzard in Oregon. It's way too cold to sleep in the RV. Big Dee wants to stay in a Motel 6 because she's never done it before. It's clean. There's a nice big TV. The bed's comfortable. I take a long bath. Then I phone Tony.

◆　　　◆　　　◆

There was an investigation after the accident. The girl was underage. The mother wanted Mongrel dead. We were in town one time, just parking the truck. This woman comes over and starts yelling at Mongrel. It's the mother. She comes right up to him. He's on the passenger side. She calls him an animal and slaps his face. He doesn't even turn his head. I'm looking at her, and all of a sudden she looks at me. I've never seen that much hate come out of anyone's eyes.

◆　　　◆　　　◆

"How come you never tell me about the girl when you talk about that accident?" says Big Dee.

"I don't like talking about it."

"How come?"

"Because it makes me jealous."

"He dead, honey."

"I know he's dead, Big Dee. But I'm still jealous. As long as I didn't know for sure, it didn't hurt me. But after it got shoved in my nose, it really made me crazy. I couldn't leave it alone."

"Jealous is real bad."

"She was fourteen."

"Pretty young."

"Younger than Chrissie, for chrissake. I mean, what was he thinking?"

"Generally, when it come to sex, not a whole lot of thinkin' goin' on."

◆ ◆ ◆

"Where are you, Margaret?"

"We're in Oregon. We drove twelve hours straight today. We had to beat a snowstorm that was heading for the pass."

"Are you coming back?"

"I think so, maybe. I don't know. Big Dee is, for sure."

"Margaret, I have to see you."

"Tony, there's been some changes. I mean, things aren't quite the same."

"What do you mean?"

"We lost Chan. She got shot in Tucson. It was awful. She was running towards the RV and then, bang, she got it from behind. We were freaked. We don't even know what it was about. Probably some drug thing. Anyway, we had to leave her. There was nothing we could do. We just sat there."

"Is she alive?"

"No, she's dead."

"Jesus, Margaret. What about you? Are you all right? How's Big Dee?"

"We're both fine. Look, Tony, this is a bit tricky. I don't know how it happened, I thought I was in the menopause, but I guess I wasn't."

"Don't tell me you're pregnant."

"Well yeah, I am."

"That's it. You have to come back. No. No, I'll go down there. Look, how many hours are you from Bellingham?"

"Let me check the map. Okay. We could make it in about four hours, depending on the roads. There's a lot of black ice. That might slow us down."

"I'm booking off. I've got a friend, Janet, a writer. I think I told you about her. The one who kayaks. She's got a place in Washington. She lives on the Lummi reservation."

"On a rez?"

"We ain't goin' to no damn reserve," shouts Big Dee.

"Chill out, Big Dee. All right, Tony. She won't mind us crashing in on her like this?"

"She'll love it. It'll give her something to write about."

◆　　　◆　　　◆

I did go back to visit Danny once, after I'd been married to Mongrel for a long time. He was happy. He had a music store that was doing great. He was making good money. Who would have guessed? He had a wife he really liked. A little girl about seven. He showed me a picture.

He looked good, too. Older, of course, but he still had nice energy. He was just as easy to talk to, only he had less to say. It was like a time warp. I told him I'd probably made a mistake. He said he figured I'd show up to tell him that at some point.

He said he didn't really love his wife in that romantic way, but he liked her a lot. And there was his little girl, who he thought was wonderful. It was family. It does keep you together sometimes. Even if you're not in love. I told him I still remembered how much I loved him. He got this little smile on his face. He just shook his head, smiling. I told him I'd come back and see him again sometime. But I didn't.

◆　　◆　　◆

## VI: LOVERS

In the corner, there's a boy sitting on a rock and somebody's talking to him. The moon makes this outline around them. It makes them glow. And there's water behind them. All that stuff around love.

I can't understand why love is always tied up with the dark. Like moonlight. And making love in the dark. Mongrel wanted to make love just about any time. Danny liked it best in the middle of the night when I was half asleep. I'd try not to wake up—not completely. It was like making love in a cloud.

But the other thing about the card is all the opposites. Man and woman. Black and white. Sun and moon. That's the thing when you're in love. It's about opposites—like love and hate. And choosing one or the other. Mongrel and Danny were so completely different. There are no guarantees.

◆　　◆　　◆

Freedom's just a word. It means different things to different people. Big Dee doesn't see it the way I do.

"Nobody get to be free, Maggie," she says.

"I don't know."

"Look at Johanna."

"Oh Christ—now there's one good reason not to go back."

"She probably dead, anyhow."

"I can't say that would break my heart."

"She still got a hook in you."

"She was cruel."

"Yes, she was. But as long as you hold onto it, you never be free."

◆　　◆　　◆

Icepick came up for Mongrel's funeral. God only knows how he got across the border. I wouldn't have let him through.

There were bikes from one end of the cemetery to the other. There was enough black leather to cover a football field. A friend of Mongrel's made the coffin. It was a beauty—all carved wood. Traditional Harley art, of course, but it was real well done—lots of detail. And black leather and studs on the inside. It was a piece of work.

The boys made sure it was an open coffin. They were probably waiting to see if he was going to tell them whether I did it or not. I could feel the vibe.

I was glad he wasn't shot in the head. It looked a lot like him, but it wasn't quite right. Something about the make-up. But I guess they have to put something on the skin or the face looks too gray or something. So, he looked a bit, I don't know, too pink. Maybe too perfect. And empty. It was just his shell on display. It gave me the creeps.

One of the only things I remember about Mongrel's wake was Lou cooking up this big pot of chili. Enough to feed an army. And beer bread. Two of her specialties. She said she liked the beer bread because it was tasty, but super simple.

◆　　◆　　◆

## LOU'S SUPER-SIMPLE BEER BREAD

> 3 cups self-rising flour
> 2 tablespoons sugar
> 1 can beer (room temperature)

Mix ingredients and throw into a bread pan.

Bake at 350° for 1 hour.

You have to eat this the day you bake it or it's hard as a rock by the next day.

You can also add all kinds of things for variations:

chopped onion (a couple of tablespoons)

caraway

thyme

dill

cheese

cinnamon and raisins

or whatever

The day Mongrel saw me making this bread, he said, "What! You wasted a whole can of my fucking beer to make bread?" (He loved the bread.)

## LOU'S FIRE-EATER FUNERAL CHILI

1 large can kidney beans (drained)

1 large can pinto beans (drained)

1-1/2 pounds lean ground beef

1/2 pound ground pork

1 small can tomato paste

2 large Spanish onions (cut into small chunks)

10 cloves garlic (chopped)

3 red bell peppers (diced)

3 large chili peppers (chopped)

3 large jalapeño peppers (chopped fine)

3 teaspoons ground cumin

2 tablespoons ground cayenne pepper

2 teaspoons ground white pepper

3 ounces chili sauce

1 teaspoon brown sugar

1 lime

1/4 cup grated Parmesan cheese

Salt (to taste)

Tabasco sauce (add if not hot enough)

A glob of ketchup if you feel like it

1/2 cup good pot (yes, you read that correctly)

In a large pan, brown the beef and pork. As the meat's starting to brown, add in the chopped onion and garlic. Sprinkle in cayenne pepper and white pepper. Sauté all this together with a bit of salt.

Transfer this mixture to a big pot and turn down the heat. Add cumin. Stir. Now take that small can of tomato paste and mix it up with a half cup of water or so. Add this to the mixture. Stir. Add the chili sauce. Stir. Add the peppers.

Throw in the darn beans. Stir. Squeeze in the lime. "Yumbo." Add the cheese.

The brown sugar is a taste thing. Don't overdo. Same with the ketchup. Put in a bit—taste. A bit more—taste. Anything left? Throw it in!

As for the pot, you can add it toward the end. If it's real good weed, just smoke it and the chili will taste better anyway. That's what Lou says and she oughta know.

◆　　◆　　◆

Somewhere in the fog of the wake, I'm close to passed out in a bedroom, and Tim comes over to talk to me. He's telling me how

Mongrel was such a good friend and everything. He's really drunk.

"He was a bro!" As he slurs it out, his hand squeezes this can of beer he's holding and it spills all over him.

"Fuck," he says, rubbing it into his T-shirt. "Fuck him," he says. He turns his head and tries to focus his eyes on me. "Fuck you, too," he says.

◆　　◆　　◆

We had to drive through the reservation to get to Janet's place. Parts of it looked like some third world country.

"This shouldn't be," I say. "Look at that."

"Uh-huh," says Big Dee, "looks like Blacktown to me."

"Even the roads are worse. You notice that? Every rez we've been on, the roads are terrible."

"Uh-huh," says Big Dee.

"It's wrong."

"You got that right," she says.

◆　　◆　　◆

Tony is standing on the doorstep when we pull up. I suddenly feel awkward. Part of me wants to run and throw my arms around him. Another part wants to turn around and head for the hills. I don't know what to do.

"What am I going to do, Big Dee?"

"Park the RV," she says, "*before* you jump out.

"I feel like I'm going to be sick."

"Might spoil the moment."

"Jesus, Big Dee."

"Go see the man. He's waitin' for you."

Next thing, I'm holding onto him as tight as I can. I can feel his heart pounding. He holds me away from him and looks at me.

"Where's your hair?"

"Oh, I left it in a motel somewhere in Utah."

"You look good."

"You, too."

I see a woman standing over by the door. She's got one of those smiles that lights up everything around her.

"Hi," she says, "I'm Janet. Hope you're hungry. I just made a big pot of soup. Bring in your gear. Who's this?"

"This is Big Dee," I say.

"Welcome, Big Dee," she says, throwing her hand straight out. "I guess you guys have had quite the adventure."

"That one way of lookin' at it," says Big Dee.

◆　　◆　　◆

It seems Johanna didn't die, but she came real close. Tony said he went to visit her. He was expecting the usual—how pissed off she was about the escape and how she was going to get us, and all that. But it didn't go like that at all.

He said she'd really changed. That she'd had a near-death experience and it had turned her around. She even talked about how she was sorry for how she'd treated some of the prisoners. She decided not to come back as a guard. She was going to go back to school for a few years. Maybe become a counselor.

"You're not serious," I say.

"It's the truth," says Tony.

"Shee-it, don't that beat all," says Big Dee.

◆　　◆　　◆

So, this is how it's going to look, more or less. Tony is going to take us to the border where we get put in holding cells until the police arrive. Then the police take us to the closest station, and then the sheriff comes to the station with a van or something. Probably, us being fugitives, we'll get the whole ball of wax—cages, shackles, and cuffs. Well, been there, done that. Then we go back to maximum to face the music.

Tony says that back at the prison, we've got star status now. All the gals are rooting for us. That makes us laugh. I tell him I don't guess we'll be starting any more twelve-step groups on our own again, and he laughs at that.

He also tells us that he got this postcard. Someone in Mexico, judging by the stamps. Just his name and the prison address on it. Picture of a Harley beside one of those big cactuses. Big Dee and I smile at each other. Tony says he's not asking any questions. I say good, because I don't want to have to tell him any lies.

◆　　◆　　◆

We make love like we never did before. I can't sleep at all. I want to feel every time he moves.

"You awake?" I say.

"Uh-huh," says Tony.

"I wouldn't mind if I died right now, I feel so good."

"Don't say things like that, Margaret."

"I'm not going to die on you, Tony. You couldn't get rid of me if you tried."

"I love you, Maggie."

"That's the first time you've called me that."

◆　　◆　　◆

## JANET'S LUMMI RESERVATION LAMB STEW

2 pounds lamb stew meat

2 large onions, chopped in nice healthy chunks

5 shallots

2 cloves chopped garlic

6 big carrots, cut in threes

6 potatoes, cut in fours

Dozen brown mushrooms, medium-sized

1 can tomato paste

Olive oil

Salt

Pepper

2 Bay leaves

Crushed chili peppers (dried)

Ketchup

In a big stew pot, pour in some olive oil. Sauté garlic, then add shallots, and then add the onion. Now throw in the lamb and brown it. Add salt, pepper, and about a teaspoon of crushed chili peppers. Let simmer for a while at low heat.

Take that can of tomato paste and mix it up in a cup of water. Add to meat mixture. Stir.

Now throw in the big chunks of potatoes and carrots. Add bay leaves.

Now everything should be in a nice thick sauce. If it's too dry, add water. But don't let it get too soupy. Bring everything to a boil and let the stew simmer for 20 minutes or so. Then I turn it off or leave it on really low for an hour. Then I bring to a boil again.

When the potatoes and carrots are soft, I add the mushrooms. They are only in the stew cooking for about 20 minutes. I guess you could cook the stew all in one go, but I like to bring it to a boil for a while, then turn it off for a while, then bring it to a boil again.

So, this is something to cook on a cold day when you're at home anyway. A tablespoon of ketchup added toward the end gives the stew a smooth taste. I add water from time to time if it gets dry. You got to experiment.

Janet makes lamb stew on our last night. I don't know if it's really that good or if I just know it's going to be the last good food I'm going to eat for a while.

Mostly it's quiet around the table, everybody lost in their own thoughts. Tony and I smile at each other from time to time. Big Dee doesn't eat much and her smile isn't right in the middle of her face.

"Tony says there may be some new legislation coming up that could affect your trial," says Janet.

"That's what he says," I say, looking at Tony.

"Abuse changes the situation," says Janet.

"I wasn't abused," I say.

"But Tony told me the story," she says.

"Which one?"

"About your husband killing himself."

"He didn't kill himself."

The room goes real quiet. They're all looking at me. I reach over and slide a smoke out of the pack on the table. The first hit's always the best. Makes me feel a little woozy, like I'm in a dream.

"See, I was in the kitchen making brownies. Hash brownies, actually. Mongrel liked them. He'd been acting strange for a while—kind of scary.

"He walks into the kitchen. He's limping real bad. The truth is, he's dragging himself around. It's hard to watch him when he's walking. It doesn't look good on him. You see, he used to have this kind of swagger when he walked. Maybe he was arrogant, but it suited him. Now he's all crippled up. He sits down hard in his chair.

"I'm kind of surprised because he's wearing this white shirt. My favorite. And his hair's still wet, like he just took a shower or something. I don't know how to describe it, but he looks really beautiful. All the lines have gone out of his face.

"'We have to talk, Mags,' he says.

"There's something about the way he says it that makes my stomach turn. Right about then, I see that he's got one of his guns lying on the table in front of him.

"'What're you doing with the gun, Mongrel?'

"I don't want to go into all the details about the accident but, bottom line, when he went down he took this young girl down with him and she didn't make it. She got burned to death. Gas from the tank. Sparks from the slide. Boom. She went up like a torch.

"'She was just a baby,' he says.

"'Yeah, well, she was old enough to fuck.'

"I don't even know why I said it. I mean, it wasn't like I hadn't done it to him. And with his best friend. Fucking around's always the last straw. No one gets over that one, I don't care what they say.

"'I want you to know where the money is,' he says.

"'I don't care about the money.'

"'You will,' he says.

"There was money all over the place. And diamonds. Thank God, Chrissie was on the outside. She had to dig most of it up because I was already in jail. Lucky for us, it was mostly in thousands. They take up less space. You can put them in safety deposit boxes. She buried some, too. It was like in the old westerns.

"'I can't ride anymore,' he says.

"'You could if you really wanted to.'

"'Not the way I want to.'

"I don't know how come some people can handle change and others just can't seem to adust. It's like what Big Dee said about the women in prison—some are built to endure, some don't make it. Like

Darlene—she wasn't strong enough. And Chan had bad luck. And Mongrel had too much pride. You never know until the crunch how someone's going to play it.

"'Either you pick up that gun and shoot me, or I pick it up and shoot you first and then me.'

"'I can't do it, Mongrel.'

"So I get up from the table and I walk to the sink. I look out the window and there's this red-winged blackbird on the feeder outside the window. I'm thinking, Well, if this is the last thing I get to see, it could be worse. I really like red-winged blackbirds. They always seem magical to me with those bright red feathers, so perfect, on each wing.

"I hear this sound behind me, so I turn around. He's got the gun pointed at his head.

"'Help me, Mags,' he says.

"I walk over to him and I take the gun out of his hand. My hands are shaking so hard, I have to rest them on the table. I point the gun at his heart. He's looking right at me.

"'I love you, Mongrel,' I say.

"'I love you, too, babe,' he says.

"And then I shoot him.

"It seems like a long way off, somewhere in my head, when the shot rings out. All I know is I can't let go of the gun. My knuckles are white.

"I turn around to see the blackbird fly away. I turn back and I swear he's looking right at me and he's smiling. All I can think is he still has a lot of class. Funny how your mind works.